ALSO BY ANDREA LEE

Russian Journal

Sarah Phillips

Interesting Women

LOST HEARTS IN ITALY

LOST HEARTS IN ITALY

A NOVEL

ANDREA LEE

RANDOM HOUSE

NEW YORK

Published in the United States by Random House, an imprint of The Random House Publishing Group, a division of Random House, Inc., New York.

RANDOM HOUSE and colophon are registered trademarks of Random House, Inc.

Grateful acknowledgment is made to Farrar, Straus and Giroux, LLC, for permission to reprint an excerpt from "A Map of Europe" from *Collected Poems 1948–1984* by Derek Walcott, copyright © 1986 by Derek Walcott. Reprinted by permission of Farrar, Straus and Giroux, LLC.

LIBRARY OF CONGRESS CATALOGING-IN-PUBLICATION DATA
Lee, Andrea
Lost hearts in Italy: a novel / Andrea Lee.
p. cm.
ISBN 1-4000-6169-5
1. Women authors—Fiction.   2. Americans—Italy—Fiction.
3. Triangles (Interpersonal relations)—Fiction.   I. Title.
PS3562.E324L67 2006
813'.54—dc22   2006040805

Printed in the United States of America on acid-free paper
www.atrandom.com
2 4 6 8 9 7 5 3 1
FIRST EDITION
Book design by Pei Loi Koay

To those I love, and loved

In it is no lacrimae rerum,
No art. Only the gift
To see things as they are, halved by a darkness
From which they cannot shift.

—DEREK WALCOTT,
FROM "A MAP OF EUROPE"

LOST HEARTS IN ITALY

1

MIRA

The call comes three or four times a year. Always in the morning, when Mira's husband and children have left the house, and she is at work in her study, in the dangerous company of words—words that are sometimes docile companions and at other times bolt off like schizophrenic lovers and leave you stranded on a street corner somewhere. There are moments when Mira, abandoned in the middle of a paragraph, sits glaring furiously out past the computer at the chestnut trees in her hillside garden and the industrial smudge of Turin below in the distance and the Alps beyond. Then the phone rings, and she breaks her own rule to grab it like a lifeline. And eerily enough, as if from hundreds of miles away he has sensed her bafflement, her moment of weakness, it is often Zenin, a man who once wrecked part of her life.

Oh, not Zenin himself, not at first. His billionaire's paranoia is too strong for that. He never calls her on a cellphone, always from his office, never from one of his houses, from his yacht, from his jet. The call is placed by any one of a bevy of young Italian secretaries, the kind who announce their names in bright telemarketers' voices. *Pronto,* it's Sabrina. Marilena. Or Veronica. It's different each time, but always the kind of aspirational Hollywood-style moniker that in Italian sounds slightly whorish.

È la dottoressa Ward? È proprio lei? The secretaries insist on asking twice if it is Mira. And they love her title, which is Italian grandiosity for a simple college degree. Zenin, the parvenu, loves it too, loves having a cultured woman to disturb. If anyone else answers, husband or children or maid, the girls have instructions to hang up. And after that, Sabrina or Marilena or Veronica always inquires, with arch emphasis, whether it is convenient for her to talk. Convenient as interpreted by a drug dealer or a stool pigeon, or of course a philandering wife.

Sometime during that familiar question, Mira's body undergoes a swift unwelcome transformation: melting between the legs, throat suddenly garotted by an ancient knot of tears. Outdated reactions of the body, whose memory is longer than that of the heart.

Feelings left over from a time years earlier, when she was very young and lived in Rome. When she was still married to her first husband, an American as young and new to Europe as she was. Married and deep in adultery with Zenin, the Venetian tycoon whose cold sensuality and provincial vulgarity represented, to the girl she was back then, everything mysterious and desirable about Italy. A robber's cave of wonders she was desperate to explore. It was a time when the dye of secrecy darkened every part of her life, and with a mixture of shame and longing she used to pray for calls like these. Because every call meant an assignation, and Zenin, at that point, was her religion.

Nowadays she hasn't seen Zenin for nearly ten years. And when she realizes who is calling, the older Mira simply says to herself: bastard. Sometimes in English, sometimes in Italian. *Bastardo.* A toothless insult, but one that translates exactly.

But she doesn't hang up. She always talks to Zenin.

This time, as usual, he asks what she is doing.

Working.

Working? Writing? Writing what—love poems? His familiar voice, with its Veneto accent, is teasing, that of an uncle talking to a beloved but difficult niece. And as always, it is surprisingly small, as the voice of the conscience is said to be. Not high, but faint and dry, as if lacking an essential fluid.

No, I'm writing an article about a cheese festival.

A cheese festival! Oh yes, laughs Zenin. I had almost forgotten how greedy you are. I'm sure you're fat now, living in Turin with all the *fonduta* and truffles. Fat and badly dressed. A plump little provincial *madamin*. That's what happens with a Piedmontese husband, *neh?* By the way, is he faithful?

Faithful enough for me.

A good wifely answer. And what about you, darling?

Don't you wish you knew, says Mira evenly.

She can picture him clearly in his vast company headquarters in the industrial hinterland of Rovigo, a few hundred miles east across Piedmont and Lombardy. Veneto lowland country, where the great floodplain of the Brenta and the Po spreads from Petrarch's green hills to the Adriatic in an expanse of cornfields, brick villages, grim rural factories, and the occasional lunar beauty of a Palladian facade. There, in his element, sits Zenin, tall, morose, and badly dressed, exuding his heavy aura of power over an acre of desk where he directs an empire that for children around the world is a byword for fun, a constantly evolving civilization of miniature toys and plastic gadgets, free gifts that lure them further into the sweet Cockaigne land of cereals and snacks. Mira winces sometimes at breakfast, watching her sons squabble over Zenin's prizes.

I'd give everything I own to know, says Zenin. I'd love to fuck you again, Dottoressa Ward. Let's meet next week. In Paris. Or New York. If you can get away for four days, come to Mauritius. There's a new hotel there you'll like. Just choose—I'll arrange everything.

What is interesting is that Zenin's voice doesn't change when he says the word *scopare—fuck*. His voice takes on an erotic tremor only when he says *arrange everything*.

Mira agrees, as she always does. *Va bene*—all right—has a ceremonial sound. Like the close of a church service, a sign of acceptance and submission. She even adds a hint of comradely amusement, because after all this time she understands that Zenin has no power over her. She listens to him promise to call on Monday with plans and then puts down the phone. Knowing she won't hear from him for months.

And as usual she sits turning the mystery over in her mind. Why Zenin bothers to go through this threadbare ritual. Why she lets him.

Her eyes run over the ranks of photographs crowded on the shelf near her desk. Mira and her present husband, Vanni, hamming it up in front of the Taj Mahal. School shots of her eight-year-old and six-year-old sons, Stefano and Zoo. Her daughter, Maddie, in a white commencement dress, brandishing a bouquet. The jacket photo for her first travel book, a dozen years earlier, where she peers rather belligerently out of a grotto in Matera. Boisterous family groups with scuba gear, on skis. Their Turin villa in the throes of restoration, the garden full of rubble, medieval brick doorways open to the weather. Her parents and sister, yellowed by seventies celluloid, waving from the steps of her childhood house in Philadelphia.

A defensive wall of memories, a gallery of life on two continents. The life she rebuilt in northern Italy after she left Rome and the ruins of that first marriage, that love affair. Yet nothing is a complete defense against Zenin. She thinks of an early story by Moravia called "Madness," in which a rich Roman housewife amuses herself by pretending to an old flame, who lives far away, that she is an insane recluse. They have long telephone conversations in which she describes her ordinary family days as a series of hallucinations.

In the same way, when Zenin phones, the rest of the world recedes. They alone are real, two points of brightness connected by sound waves and the past. But as the connection is established, like lights on an electronic map, she imagines a third point lighting up somewhere else. *Mai due senza tre,* as the Italian saying goes, never two without three. The essential third point is her first husband, Nick, Zenin's former rival. Hidden somewhere in the glass and steel corporate wilderness of Canary Wharf or Wall Street or the Bund in Shanghai. Mira never hears from him but she gets regular news from their daughter, Maddie, of his life in London, his family, his career in international finance. Nick is somehow always present at these encounters in space, where all times are one time.

It was always less like a triangle than a game, she thinks. One of those annoying electronic games her boys play, where computer-generated civilizations battle each other, or the kind of ancient board combat that people claim dates back to the Olmecs or Hittites or sunken Atlantis. A game with a dozen shifting alliances. Young married couple against the old libertine. Lovers against husband. Rich against not rich. Europe against America. A game of skill that at its hottest and hardest should have concluded, according to a military code of honor, or to the rules of storytelling, with an execution. At least a suicide. Except that the three of them obstinately remained alive. All three of them, Zenin, Nick, and Mira, have one thing in common besides a susceptibility to passion. And that is a stubborn, rather bourgeois attachment to life and its consolations.

So now, nearly two decades later, they're all alive, widely separated, no longer hagridden by lust and jealousy, grown older and lazier, less exacting about their pleasures. Zenin, Mira reminds herself, is actually a grandfather. Nick has a beautiful second wife and two girls besides their own daughter, Maddie.

She herself is so immersed in the controlled chaos of family and work that she barely notices she is happy. The only thing that revives their game, their three-sided connection, is the empty liturgy of these phone calls from Zenin, which recall a moment in time when raw excess made them a casual aristocracy, apart from the rest of the world.

It's nostalgia, thinks Mira, returning to her work. Not for love, of course. For being young.

But later she thinks that the calls are a way of saying, You still belong to me. And she knows that some part of her does belong to Zenin. And a part to Nick as well. As we always belong forever to people who have hurt us badly, or been badly hurt by us.

1985 · IN THE AIR

The story of Nick and Mira and Zenin begins with an act of generosity. Anonymous and spontaneous, the noblest kind. A graceful impulse on the part of a woman Mira never met. That's the reason, one July afternoon, that she is sitting in a first-class lounge at Kennedy Airport.

Because a secretary or administrative assistant in the bank that has sent Nick Reiver, her husband, from Manhattan to its Rome office, has done him a friendly turn. Devised an illegal treat for his wife. For her transfer to Europe, a first-class ticket, where company policy barely stretches to business class. Afterward, Mira always pictures this generous secretary as a Billy Wilder character, a Fran Kubelik grown older, full of wisecracks but with a kind of virtue that goes deeper than a heart of gold. A sort of elemental sweetness that only Americans have. And this well-meaning woman stretches the rules for Nick not just because he is fair-haired and handsome in a way that always tempts secretaries to make exceptions for him, but because he has the same sweetness. It shines in him. It inspires the favor, and what eventually comes out of the favor blows it all away.

The immediate result, though, is that Mira, twenty-five years old and very pleased, is sitting in the first-class lounge. Having kissed her mother at the gate and disposed of the shamingly huge old suitcase from the attic of her parents' house in Mount Airy, Philadelphia. The kind of strapped mastodon of a cracked-leather case that is meant to be dragged over borders in the wake of famine or pogrom, and appears in old pictures of Ellis Island.

Except that the Ward family is black, a clan of teachers and lawyers rooted in Philadelphia for generations, set in their ways and their neighborhoods as only middle-class mulattos can be. Still, the suitcase has always been upstairs under the eaves, legacy of some flighty distant cousin or great-aunt, and when Mira's mother came to help pack up Mira's West Side apartment, she bullied Mira into accepting it, arguing its practicality with a vigor that suggested the bag was stuffed with maternal wisdom. Its presence looms over Mira as her mother's car inches through La Guardia traffic on a simmering August afternoon, her mother calculating dollar-lira exchange rates and reminiscing about a trip she took to Rome in 1966, where near the Campidoglio, she and her sister Marjorie were asked directions in broken Italian by a group of tourists from Alabama.

Poor ignorant things, they thought we were natives.

And you *were* natives, says Mira smartly. Only not Italian. You were the kind of natives who wear grass skirts and carry bananas on their heads. The kind of natives they used to string up back home in Alabama. Oh, hush. Mrs. Ward, a widow belonging to the frugal, wary Depression-bred generation of African Americans who call themselves "colored," is always easy prey for her two quick-witted daughters, Mira and Faith, with their Ivy League diplomas and scathing tongues. She is crushed at losing Mira to Europe, but also troubled in her private sense of justice, this because Mira, the impertinent younger child, the one who never listened, the one who against all good advice married a white boy and rejected law school to take up the precarious trade of writing, Mira now is blithely setting off for a new life of adventure and entirely unearned luxury.

That first-class ticket, for example. Neither of them understands what it really means until they wrestle the barn-size suitcase onto a cart and propel it wobblingly toward Alitalia check-in. And, with the display of the magic ticket, the bag and all complications are wafted away. It's a slow afternoon at the airport, and suddenly Mira is surrounded by the attentions of men and women who seem to live for deference. Lackeys, she thinks with delight. Minions.

A tanned Italian in a green jacket flashes a brilliant smile at her and relieves her of the suitcase. Which, instead of a humiliating encumbrance, suddenly becomes a charming piece of eccentricity. And Mira thinks, This is what it means to be rich. This sudden grand simplicity, this rescue from petty embarrassment. A revelation so absorbing that it makes her kiss her mother goodbye with the same pitying impatience that she felt when she left on her honeymoon. An embrace at the gate, a promise to call, a wave, and Mira is gone, confusing a departure for Europe for a departure into the world of money.

A weekday in late August. Except for Mira and an attendant, the first-class lounge is empty.

Though in the future Mira will try many times to recall the details of where she first met Zenin—two places, the lounge and the first-class section on the Rome flight—she can't, of course, because they are nowhere. They are part of those outposts of anonymous functional opulence where languages and nationalities crisscross promiscuously. Enclosures of nonstyle upholstered in weird uncolors of blue-gray, green-brown, and apricot, garnished with laminated briarwood or funereal fresh flowers. Places that, like expensive hotels, represent the bland apartheid of wealth. The kind of places where they will meet when they are having their affair.

To Mira it is new, so she acts bored. Is anyone in the airport trying and failing so emphatically? She leans back on a couch and sips a glass of white wine and picks at a little square of salted pastry, and has no idea that her face is tense and glowing with excitement, like that of a child on Christmas morning.

And as she sits there, a man enters. Zenin. He nods to the attendant, circles the room, and then leaves. He moves so fast that Mira, seated with her back to the door, has the impression of only a shadow flickering along her peripheral vision, and yet she feels the disturbance left by the movement, the swift reconnoitering of a predator or a thief.

In a hotel bed one afternoon, a few years later, she asks Zenin why he did that, and he tells her that he heard two male attendants talking about *una ficona*. A good-looking piece of ass. A colored girl, maybe Cuban or Brazilian or North African, traveling first class. He wanted to take a look, but didn't want to be stuck waiting in the room. Zenin never sits and waits.

And what did you think I was? demands Mira. A prostitute?

No, *un'avventuriera*. An adventuress, Zenin says, with uncharacteristic panache. A type who could interest me.

What Zenin sees is a young woman with one of the mixed-race faces common on the streets of New York and Los Angeles and Miami. Faces of a mongrel beauty that is about to become fashionable in advertising. Off-color girls, Nick Reiver calls them, his mockery barely masking the bedazzlement of a New England boy enamoured of Asian and Cape Verdean beauties since prep school. He thinks his wife is the prettiest off-color girl in the world. But the only thing that is remarkable about Mira's face is how its planes are angled forward. Eagerness and curiosity are built into her bones.

She has a head of frizzy curls that spill over her shoulders and a slight, almost childish figure. Long legs and small breasts. No makeup on her sand-colored skin. And for her trip she is wearing a black knit dress, bought at Saks but still cheap, and bagging noticeably along the seams. It's a dress that saw Mira through her first job as an intern at a fashion magazine and made frequent appearance at the Lower East Side and Williamsburg dives where she and Nick used to eat and dance and get high. The kind of dress a very young woman buys when she hopes to make an investment in grown-up glamour. Around her waist she has tied a striped Indian cotton scarf, and she carries a Panama hat stolen from her husband.

And of course she has a wedding ring, a dark band of rose diamonds that belonged to Nick's grandmother. Four years have passed since their wedding in the Harvard chapel, and she is very married, having arrived, like Nick, at the complacent proselytizing point that holds that all evil springs from conjugal drought. That all the world should be married.

She also carries a book, because she always has a book, joined like a permanent growth to her hands. Mira lives in books and intends to write them. This book is certainly Tolstoy, either *War and Peace* or *Anna Karenina,* because those are what she reads and rereads in those days. Mira and Nick even read *Anna Karenina* aloud to each other as they backpacked through Greece on their honeymoon, beguiling the hours, like so many other incautious lovers, with an old tale of ruin.

So Zenin sees Mira and her book, but she doesn't see him. Not until they are on the plane together, just the two of them up in the first-class loft. Even then she hardly notices him because he is already settled when she arrives, stretched out in the far corner of the last row, wearing a sleep mask and swathed in blankets like an invalid. She doesn't recognize the man who circled the waiting room. But she does notice how the staff rein in their movements near him, as if, she laughs to herself, the pope were sleeping in that seat.

Mira doesn't read a word during her flight. She's too busy reveling in the unexpected luck that allows her to sit isolated as an empress, with thick white linen spread before her and a glass of champagne in her hand. While below her, packed in steerage, as she was on her two previous student trips to Europe, teem the lumpen tourists. Rattling newspapers, breathing a thick proletarian miasma, flirting, snoring, farting, waiting for their meals in little plastic troughs.

A white-haired steward who looks like an ambassador and a beautiful stewardess with a coiled braid seem to be there to wait on her exclusively. Speaking to her in French and English and complimenting her extravagantly on the few Italian phrases she has learned. Telling her she will love Rome, all Americans do. They are formal and respectfully cosseting, as if she were a royal baby, but there is also a hint of benign amusement in their manner, as if they know it is all a delicious joke, that in another life it could be Mira, the young off-color girl, waiting on them. Indulgently, as if her excitement were infectious, as if it were refreshing to come upon a passenger for whom flying in that expensive aerie is not a bore, they regale her with tastes of every dish on the menu. An epicurian hodgepodge of foie gras and spaghetti *all'astice* and white truffles and *maltagliati alla selvaggina* and *budino* and *semifreddo* and chocolates and a shot of espresso that doesn't keep her head from whirling from the red and white wines they keep bringing out and introducing as if they were characters in a play—Brunello and Sauvignon Piere and Malvasia, not to mention the grappa and Calvados they press on her as digestives.

Mira accepts it all, and hardly notices that they have left far behind the frowsy East Coast sunset, through which her mother, no doubt wailing and gnashing her teeth, is driving back to Philadelphia. Drunk and happy, giddy with release from the strain of packing and goodbyes, she forgets completely where she is going. She toasts herself as Dire Straits break into their mock hymn to summer, "Twisting by the Pool."

An hour or two later, she wakes up sober in the rushing twilit limbo before dawn, between continents, realizing that she is exactly nowhere, high in the air, between worlds. Between lives. Alone, except for a man wrapped up like a mummy, who might actually be a corpse for all she knows. And all at once, as if she is looking down on a map, she sees the life she is leaving: the bosky fieldstone streets of her Mount Airy childhood, the dormitory bricks of Boston where she studied and married, the skyscrapers of New York piercing the glittering sky with bellicose ambition like a bundle of spears. All of it tossed behind her like discarded bedcovers.

And where is she going? To Rome, a city that she has never seen, and to Italy, a country that she has avoided as much as any Harvard English major can, after the obligatory breakneck tours through Shakespeare and the Romantic poets. At senior common-room gatherings she has seen how great academicians worship Florence and Rome; has heard the *Ciao, come stai?* of Nobel laureates, and their swaggering talk of villas. Has seen it all barely moved. Her foreign language is

French, her thesis dissected Marvell's "Upon Appleton House," and she has been in Italy exactly one night, sleeping in a cornfield near Trieste when she and Nick hitchhiked back from her honeymoon.

Longing to live abroad, they had hoped to be sent to Paris. Because that is where you live when you are just married and crazy in love.

Rome is almost as good, an adventure, certainly; a great thing for a young man with an eye toward an international future, for an ambitious young couple. But Mira's thoughts grow dark and jumbled when she thinks of Rome, even when Nick flies off to start work there and calls her twice a day to tell her how marvelous it is; how glowing the summer, how splendid the food, the beaches; how he has found them an apartment with coffered ceilings.

What comes to mind when she thinks of Rome is an old coin her father brings her from a tour of Italy he made with other high school principals. Mira, five or six, mad for tales of treasure, expects a Roman coin to be a disk of gold. Instead, she sees a battered piece of greenish bronze, not even round, with remains of a leering face that her father explains is the Emperor Tiberius. And ever afterward she envisions Rome as a place smudged with age and disappointment. In her student trips, she visits London, Paris, Athens, but never Rome.

Now she sits in the dark plane and resists fear.

Miranda Ward is good at going into new worlds, at being a foreigner. She is one of the generation of black children pushed out of the bourgeois ghetto of their parents to become pioneers in private schools and camps that before the seventies had never admitted a black or a Jew. She's used to the feeling of being inside, yet not, watching. It suits her inquisitive nature, though at times it can be heartbreaking. When, at Harvard, she falls in love with Nick Reiver, of Little Compton, Rhode Island, and Camden, Maine, and marries him, to the bemusement of both families, she enters yet another new country. And then there is New York, and the magazine world, where she has her first success, ironically enough, with an article describing the restlessness and trials of her early school years.

Now she's leaving again; but this time with Nick waiting for her. Her husband, who feels sometimes like the brother she never had, who with his blue eyes and old New England family tree is less expert at being an outsider than she is. In fact—except in her family—he has never been an outsider at all, a fact that Mira in disgruntled moments sees as a failing in Nick, a basic lack in his education. But he is as curious as she is, her best friend, and the love of her life. They took on New York together and they will take on Rome. With that thought, Mira relaxes and falls asleep again.

And in the morning, as she's finishing her breakfast, before they begin their descent to Fiumicino airport, the man in the back walks up to the front of the compartment and sits down across the aisle from her, and in heavily accented English says good morning.

It's that simple, their meeting. It happens when and how Zenin decides it will.

First the ritual exchange of pleasantries between wayfarers. The same here as it would be sitting on backpacks waiting for a train in Goa. How long will she stay in Rome? Mira explains that she will be living there, that she is joining her husband, who has been transferred.

Mira is a flirt and likes to annoy Nick with tales of men who pursue her. Yet this man doesn't look like the gorgeous stranger one meets on the voyage out. He doesn't even look like her idea of an Italian. He is tall and thin and stiff-moving in a way that gives a curious feeling of theatrical rusticity, like a dancing scarecrow in a musical. Odd, but not funny. Later, Mira will play with this idea, imagining a fetish stuck into the ground in a village of Hollywood savages.

His cheekbones are high, carving his lean face into crude angles that look almost Slavic, and his eyes are narrow, dark, and flat, absorbing light. He is deeply tanned and wears his lank ash-brown hair long, like an out-of-date rock star. Old. He looks old to her, somewhere in the range of parents and professors and in-laws. He has on a pair of pale linen trousers, a light sweater, and a pair of slip-on shoes without socks. And a big watch with three faces. His bony hands are large and freckled, and as he sits talking to her, they dance restlessly on his knees like the hands of someone ill at ease. Except that he doesn't seem to be the slightest bit nervous. Instead, a kind of impatience surrounds him like a force field. She wonders how rich he is.

She understands that he must be important because of the genuinely servile way the cabin steward brings him coffee.

You are American, he says. From where?

Philadelphia, she says. And I've lived in Boston and New York.

But your parents. What country are they from?

Mira is so used to this pushy question that she doesn't get annoyed.

My parents and grandparents and great-grandparents are all American, she says evenly, speaking in a clear didactic voice. It would be hard to find a family more American than we are. We are African Americans with other blood mixed in. Irish and American Indian. One of my great-great-grandfathers was a Dane who came first to the Virgin Islands, and then to Virginia. Others were West African slaves.

She waits for the exaggerated astonishment this little soliloquy usually inspires in the United States, where race is always an emotional issue. But Zenin simply nods. Italy is also a mixed country, he says. Arabs, Greeks, Africans, Slavs, they have all arrived and stayed. For hundreds of years. It happened in my province. The Veneto.

He introduces himself. Zenin. Ezio Zenin, from Rovigo, a city near Padua. He says it as if she ought to know who he is. She hears the first name, but she discounts it, is never to use it. For her, he will always be Zenin. That strange, stateless name. When she asks about it, he tells her it's Venetian, from an old noble clan.

But we are not noble, he adds after a pause. Not so fortunate. My father was a peasant from Istria. From a family of peasants, poor as beasts. Maybe they got the name because they were at one time the property of an aristocrat. He smiles mirthlessly, and his flat eyes meet hers. Slaves, too, perhaps.

All this time the light through the plane windows is growing paler, then redder, then warming into daylight as they pass over Dover and veer toward the coast of France.

Zenin asks her whether she works, what she does, and Miranda announces that she is a journalist, that she writes articles for magazines, that she plans to write a book.

This seems to interest him. An American writer, *una scrittrice americana,* he says softly to himself, his hands dancing on his knees. I am an industrialist, he tells her.

Oh, I see, says Mira, who has no idea what this means, except that it involves assembly lines. Satanic mills. What do you make? seems to be the required question.

I make all the toys in the world, he says in a tone that sounds to Mira both conceited and rather depressed. Grabbing an airline magazine out of the rack, he shows her an ad featuring a famous brand of chocolates and a parade of garishly colored plastic animals attached to miniature vehicles: cars, bicycles, motorcycles, pickup trucks. Mira, nonplussed, can think of nothing to say.

They make awkward conversation until the plane tilts, revealing far below a panorama of blue waves and a coastline that in the sunlight shines a barbaric brown-gold. Italy. She presses her face against the window, and suddenly a wild excitement seizes her, the excitement of her first student glimpses of the Old World, where myths took on flesh. The Tyrrhenian sea. Islands strewn like gold guineas marking the trail of Ulysses' love affairs and slippery escapes.

That is where I am going now, says Zenin, gesturing out the window. An island called Ponza. I have a boat docked there. A big boat.

Later, Mira will repeat this childish boast for her husband's delectation, and they will both laugh. An Italian toy king, with a yacht. A beeg Eurotrashy boat. Only you, you wench, would pick up somebody like that. The young husband and wife laughing gleefully, confidently. One of the strongest bonds between them is their insatiable taste for the ridiculous. Still, Mira, even as she giggles, has a small doubt in the back of her mind, sensing that it is harder than it seems to make fun of Zenin.

As the plane follows the Lazio coastline and begins the descent toward Fiumicino, Zenin hands Mira his card.

Give me your number in Rome and I will call you, he says in a tone that admits no refusal. He is already calling for a pen, and though they are landing, the steward unbuckles his seat belt and, staggering slightly, brings it.

A few years on, when large cracks are running through all the certainties in her life as a result of this moment, Mira is never able to explain to herself why she now digs obediently into her bag, opens her address book, and reads off her new telephone number. With all the familiar expedients open to a pretty girl—changing a digit, coyly refusing—she simply lets Zenin into her life. And studying the moment later, she finds nothing more than a flicker of impulse. No animal attraction, no tempting scent of danger, no discontent with what she already has. Just a flash of idle curiosity, the kind that leads a child to poke a stick into an anthill or lift the lid of a forbidden box. An action that, like the unknown secretary's gift of a ticket, cannot be undone.

After Zenin takes the number, he finds no further need for conversation. He sits there like a statue, like an accomplished fact.

And Mira looks out at the dunes of Ostia below them: the port, the grass-choked ruins, the tawny red roofs, the marshaled beach umbrellas of the bathing establishments. Until Zenin abruptly asks how old she is.

Twenty-five.

That is very young, is all he says.

Feeling vaguely insulted, she wants to retort that twenty-five isn't young at all. But the landing announcement is playing and Italy is roaring up to meet them.

So Mira smooths her black dress, takes up her book, and sits quietly, too. Until the plane jolts, comes to a halt, and there she is. Living abroad.

THE FLIGHT ATTENDANT

When I first heard Turi and Sandro going on about the American girl, the colored one, I thought she must be an actress or a model. Or maybe a footballer's wife—we get all the *bella gente* up there in the bubble, and you should see my autograph book. Last week it was Christian De Sica, then Ruggero Deodato, and before that, Maradona. But when the girl came upstairs, I thought, This one never paid full fare. She looked too young, like a teenager from the provinces. Not bad-looking, if you like that *mulatta* type, but badly done up in a black dress with the hem falling down and run-over sandals. Of course you can't tell with Americans; we've had famous models in here and they looked terrible, with flip-flops and dirty jeans. Always throwing up in the toilets. At least this girl had an appetite.

Back in the galley we made a bet that Zenin would try to pick her up, but Zenin the pharaoh just kept on sleeping, wrapped up like a baby. That tears it, said Turi in dialect—he's Pugliese, too, a village twenty kilometers from mine. If old Zenin had been alone with a nice blonde like you, Manuela darling, he'd wake up and not lie there like a dried codfish. We all know Zenin, rich as a sheikh from Giochi Favolosi. I collect his toys myself, all the cute little animals on a special shelf in my apartment. But Zenin is a peculiar customer, always restless, jumping around on the flight or else flat-out asleep. And there is something about those eyes of his that give me the creeps. He has his own jet, but sometimes we see him on the New York run. Like all these rich men, he's a womanizer, but not as much of a pig as some I could name.

Anyway, as we're coming into Fiumicino, Turi whispers, Goal! And I see Zenin, the fast worker, sitting beside the girl, calling for a pen. We hardly get the hatches open when Zenin hops up and runs downstairs to where a transport is waiting to take him over to the private field. And the American girl just sits there looking dazed until I bring her jacket and nudge her out of first class. I notice she has on a wedding ring, and I think, You little tart. Later, Turi sees her at Arrivals. She's with the husband, he says, a good-looking blond boy in jeans who could have been Zenin's grandson, and he and the girl are kissing and carrying on beside the baggage cart like village kids do along the town walls. That's what they look like. *Solo ragazzi.* Just kids.

Well, best of luck to them, I say to Turi. They need it.

2

NICK

2004 · A CHINESE CROWD

He hasn't called that bitch in years. Not since their daughter, Maddie, got old enough to do it for him, to play the classic role of children of divorce, that of an electrical transformer, where two alien currents briefly meet and communicate with hidden sparks. Through Maddie he sends messages to Mira about tuition and airline tickets. And when Maddie comes to spend weekends and school vacations with him in London, he talks to her sometimes about her mother. Nick does not think he rants. He simply talks away his recognition of the constellation of features emerging with such damnable consistency in his eldest daughter's teenage face, talks reasonably in a measured, good-humored, paternal way about trust and fairness and the necessity of having moral points of reference, whether or not one chooses to believe in God. Though it makes his second wife, Dhel—a Swiss-Vietnamese art consultant far more beautiful and elegant than Mira ever was—roll her eyes with exasperation and take Maddie's part, he then goes on to highlight, diplomatically, the many flaws his ex-wife has displayed over the years. Her flightiness and disorganization, even in paying school fees, her immaturity and general disregard for the feelings of others. It's an advantage to Maddie in the long run to hear these observations, of course. A simple and logical way of putting things in the clear.

He never dreamed he could bore anyone like that.

The surprising thing is just how long it can take for pain to show up. Pain and bitterness. And how complete and tangible an artifact it is when it comes into the light of a completely new existence. Like those statues unearthed in Rome from time to time during the excavations for the new subway lines. The Christian Democratic government's final burst of glorious public works, during the time he and Mira lived there. He remembers photographs in *L'Espresso* of earthmoving machinery and crowds of Roman workmen encircling a goddess in a pit. Rubble all around, a clay-smeared shoulder, a bare breast, a broken arm. And a face—vacant, flawless, staring at the Mediterranean sky.

Just that way, memories, fragments from Italy, from that demolished first marriage, turn up from time to time in his days. In this new age, this complete, successful, and engrossing life lived between his happy home in London and the international boardrooms of finance in different corners of the world, where he flies to tend money like a skillful—a very skillful—market gardener raising a series of crops. A golden age without the perils; the built-in evanescence of a real golden age; a precious alloy, strong enough to last.

Still, the fragments crop up, as they say stones rise to be harvested in New England fields, as shrapnel swims to the surface in already closed wounds. He might be in his office on Canary Wharf, twenty-seven floors up, staring out toward the Thames over the bleak council-house grid of the Isle of Dogs. He might be eating noodles in an airport lounge in Singapore or on the fast train from Hong Kong to Guangzhou, drinking tea, hammering on the computer. He might be riding the DLR, or the Tube from Notting Hill Gate. He might be in bed with Dhel drawing her tea-colored hair over his eyes in one of the morning trysts they snatch when he flies in from a trip on a schoolday and she can run home from the office to Chepstow Villas. He might be watching overpriced Saturday afternoon cartoons with his younger daughters, Eliza and Julia, at the Electric Cinema. In all these scenes, from time to time a shard.

Often just a nonsense phrase, the kind he and Mira used to toss back and forth in the car or in the bathroom, catchwords between two kids who, though they belonged to different races, had grown up middle class in the same generation of seventies television shows and AM rock, the same textbooks, camp songs, and urban legends. Over shoulder boulder holder. Saright? Saright. I'm Popeye the sailor man, I live in the garbage can . . . and she's cli-hi-mingg a stair-hair way to heavann.

Or a line from Pound or Auden, engraved in his mind in the poetry seminar where they met as Harvard undergraduates. Where cross-legged on the rug in the instructor's living room, Mira, lone brown face, queen bee of the ferociously ambitious little group of sophomores and juniors, would camouflage her lack of preparation by waxing emotional over single obscure lines. She used this bullshit technique, Nick recalls, with *"The River-Merchant's Wife, A Letter."* "Two small people, without dislike or suspicion," she gushed. Only a great poet like Pound could find such perfectly simple words to translate a description of true love. Two people who are made for each other.

A few times, Nick has wondered why he didn't strangle her. Just a few times over the years this comes to mind, usually when he is in the packed street crowds of Asia, where everyone manages somehow to be alone. Crowds that it is the good fortune of a rich foreign visitor to avoid if he wishes, traveling instead in expensive cars that slice through jammed intersections like hot knives through butter. Nick is a powerful man nowadays, one of the tall blond expatriate masters of the world, the *gweilo's gweilo*, his adoring second wife tells him teasingly. And he has paid his dues, and knows the worth of these petty satisfactions. But there are times when, at the end of a long day of meetings, before cocktails, he plunges deliberately into the rush-hour congestion on the sidewalks of Causeway Bay or the Bund. Plunges out of his air-conditioned executive fishbowl into the heat and crush and fumes— for refreshment, the way you jump into a swimming pool.

And there in the slow mob of pedestrians, he might see a pair of sauntering sweethearts, window-shopping Cantonese or Singaporean kids marked by the special thinness that one has only once, the transparent thinness of early maturity, when, without knowing it, you are immortal. And completely permeable. When you can walk indifferently down the street with a lover because you have become that lover. Two small people without dislike or suspicion.

Or he might see a couple of young tourists. American or European or Australian. Students, backpackers, roaming Asia. Riding the Star Ferry, shuffling in line for the plane to Koh Samui, the girls with their tits wobbling free in those cheap silk tops they buy in the street markets. Perhaps quarreling or kissing or even drunk and puking in the gutters, but always wearing that air of charmed ignorance that means "foreigner." Not just foreign to the place, but foreign to age and care, caught in the bubble of shimmering egoism that makes distant countries, once gained, become theaters. Stage sets for private dramas that in the end are always about jealousy and boredom and the injustices of desire.

It happens, then, that he can imagine his hands tightening around Mira's throat. On his knees over her in a parody of a sexual position, as she lies like a toppled statue in their old bed. The marital bed she defiled, the shameless whore, the slut, the hussy, the harlot, the strumpet, the adultress. The sad tabloid insults come scuttling out like roaches during this flicker of a vision, which gives him a feeling of luxury, like the thought of a sexual adventure. The luxury of rewriting his demeaning part in a story. And at the same time he feels a sense of ingrained error, as if, like a dull schoolboy, he is being called to examination, over and over again, and fails every time.

It's different, he thinks, when someone dies. When someone dies, there's that patch of blankness that makes it possible to accept. A certain satisfaction in encountering the finite. But when someone is lost to you and still lives, it's an absurdity. Rags and motley tatters of sensation hang on the flutter as if on a fool. And who is the fool? Is it always the cuckold? Is it King Arthur, King Mark, Charles Bovary, Karenin?

These thoughts have come to him not at home in London but in Asia, in the anonymous pedestrian heart of the street. And Nick keeps walking, and gradually he is calmed by the fumes, the choking stink of gasoline, spices, frying food, and sewage that after a dozen years of visits is both alien and famiiar. And the hot crush, the colossal indifference of the crowd. It's magnificent, that indifference, unlike anything in Europe or America. It reminds him of a phrase seized from his late-night reading. In a letter from Yeats to a friend who sent him a Chinese statue, the poet wrote, "The East has its solutions always and therefore knows nothing of tragedy."

1985 · ETRUSCAN PLACES

There's a place I have to take you, Nick tells Mira. All those years ago, on that first blazing August morning in Rome.

From the moment he first saw her pushing that ridiculous suitcase, looking disheveled and grubby, peering around in the airport crowd like a mail-order bride—he's felt like a conjurer with the power to pull wonders out of thin air. Since they grabbed each other and kissed, and he smelled her perfume and her tired body. It's time to show her marvel after marvel, facets of their new life. So he rushes his wife and her suitcase back from the airport in the first surprise, the little open Fiat that is somehow part of his expatriate package, and laughs when she asks if they are now in a movie. Repeating, with greedy anticipation, like a parent whose children have just started to open a mountain of Christmas presents, that this is just the beginning. Whisking her through the thinning morning traffic through the periphery of Rome to the Centro Storico, skimming by the Colosseum and the other sunlit monuments with the casual arrogance of possession, which Mira, quick to read his mind, understands; she doesn't even ask him to slow down.

Next comes their new home on Via Panisperna, a narrow village of a street that runs from Santa Maria Maggiore down toward Piazza Venezia in the stony urban valley between the Esquilino and the Viminale hills. Here in a motley stretch of irregular buildings, tiny dark shops, a small disheveled street market, and herds of cars parked on sidewalks is the palazzo, a smog-stained sixteenth-century building with blackened oriel windows set under the eaves.

It belongs to the grandmother of a friend of his at the bank, an old princess, who always rents to foreigners. With the help of a wall-eyed *portiere* who calls Mira Signora, they wrestle her giant bag across a shallow courtyard full of battered stone vases of oleanders and the smell of cats. Up a dim slippery flight of stone steps and in through a pair of mahogany doors. To stand in a long marble hallway waxed to a yellowish glow. Opening onto an enfilade of enormous rooms, each with tall draped windows and a crowd of gleaming dark antiques. For a minute Mira stands frozen with the impression that she has strayed into someone else's apartment. Then Nick grabs her and races her through living room, dining room, kitchen, and study.

This is—this is *princely,* says Mira, craning her neck. How can we afford this?

A deal. Nick gives a casual, magisterial wave of his hand. There may be a problem later on with heating—I can't figure out if there is any—but we don't have to worry about that now.

The owner, he adds, will make space for their own furniture when it comes in from New York. Mira is speechless, unable to imagine her wedding presents, her carefully chosen sofa and bed as looking anything but paltry and cheap among this rich jumble of ages and worn opulence. Coffered ceiling, as Nick promised, parquet that wavers up and down like melted and refrozen ice; a long table and a Venetian chandelier; rubbed velvet armchairs and settees; dim gold stucco curls around mirrors that reflect their ghostly faces, laughing helplessly like children when the adults are out.

When they reach a bedroom, Mira, mistaking Nick's haste for a rush to make love, slides her arms around him and whispers in his ear. After two weeks not touching her, it's like drowning. He almost caves in, but then with difficulty pulls away.

Whoa, steady. A little self-control, girl. We can christen the bed and the kitchen table and the rest of the place later. There's a place I have to take you. Go take a piss and get a glass of water, and then we get back in the car.

Are you crazy, darling? It's hot. I'm asleep, Mira whines, but Nick notices she doesn't refuse. He knows his girl—she could be half dead, she could have six deadlines or four exams, but if you suggest something new, a mystery excursion, a new Williamsburg club, an uninvestigated drink, or a new drug, she's up and out.

You can take a nap when we get there, under a pine.

A pine? Where are you taking me, you nasty boy? Some kind of alfresco Roman orgy?

Without waiting for an answer she is already in the big gloomy bathroom, splashing water on her face, shoving back her hair, humming an old camp song, "In the pines, in the pines, where the sun never shines . . ."

Then they are back in the little car heading toward the sea on the expressway called Cristoforo Colombo. Christopher Colombus. Their seat belts unbuckled, Mira leaning uncomfortably over the gearbox to rest her head on his shoulder and slide her hand inside his shirt to where she can feel his heart beating. Gravely, without haste, reestablishing physical possession. The roof is up, and they are listening to music. *Hex Enduction Hour.* Burning Spear's *Marcus Garvey. London Calling.*

Italian drivers around them try hard to pass them, and Mira, exhaustion forgotten, stares with delight out the window at the motley array of traffic barreling along in carefree anarchy: midget trucks, delivery vans, all ages and sizes of Fiats, sports cars, Vespas, motorcycles. She giggles at the sight of a young family crammed onto a single Vespa, the mother casually giving her baby a bottle as she clutches her husband with her knees. Italy, Mira thinks. Europe. And as she studies the shoddy apartment buildings and roadside shops of the Roman suburbs, and the bleached grass slopes of the *campagna* beyond them, she observes as always how close the horizons seem compared to America. *Piccolo mondo antico*—that's a famous Italian movie, isn't it? The small antique world that is now hers.

At the coast, Nick turns north toward Civitavecchia. Beyond the small beach towns' stucco apartments and forests of TV antennae, the sea reflects a platinum glare on the bare midday sky, and on the right the scorched hills roll up through a network of Etruscan names, toward Orvieto and the extinct mines of Tolfa.

You're still not telling me where we're going?

No. We're almost there. The tape is playing Madness, "One Step Beyond."

They turn off at Cerveteri, the Etruscan city of the dead. Nick discovers it after a cheerful tipsy Sunday at the beach in Fregene with some of the young Roman bloods he works with at the bank. Even stuffed with spaghetti *alle vongole* and Frascati, he's enchanted and determines to bring Mira here as a surprise on their first day together in Italy.

Now, pulling into the parking lot, he feels ceremonial. He has unveiled the chief marvel of the day. A phenomenal landscape. Acres of tumuli, big domed tombs shaped out of tufa, like huge bubbles in the earth, running up the grass hills toward Tarquinia and the other city-states. Lion-colored hills, dotted with poppies and live oaks. Far in the distance, a packed flock of sheep moves slowly across a slope like a single dirty sheepskin. Radiating from the cypresses and pines that shade the entrance to the archaeological park is a chorus of cicadas so continuous and loud that it sounds like heavy machinery. It is the lunch hour, the parking lot empty of cars and tourist buses, the ticket office shuttered.

Mira climbs slowly out of the car. My God, Nick. What an incredible place. You knew I'd love it.

I knew.

You always know everything.

Without waiting for the park to open, they sneak in, climbing over the low entrance gate. Nick with a flashlight and a tin box of carefully rolled joints tucked into his pocket, carrying a bottle of champagne. Not chilled, he says. In fact, more like boiled.

Well, champagne soup makes the picnic, says Mira, darting ahead. I can't believe there's nobody. Come on. We own this place for the next hour.

An image added to the collection in Nick's memory: the sight of Mira in her crumpled black dress against the domed tumuli, huge and thick as bunkers, scurrying along with an urgency that for a second looks tragic, like a widow in a war movie.

Nick, she calls. You know, this is where Lawrence got hooked on Etruscans. And what's his name, the guy who wrote *The Garden of the Finzi-Continis*? That starts out right here at Cerveteri.

Mira, Nick recalls, loves the first chapters of novels, and knows her favorites practically by heart.

Just then from behind them come shouts and a burst of barking, and they turn to see a thickset old man with a feathery crest of white hair, with two small yellow dogs by his side. Shouting something. *È vietato entrare durante il periodo di riposo!* he repeats, stumping up to them. Repeating in parroted English and German as the dogs sniff their legs. Forbidden. Verboten.

Shit, whispers Mira. Prison on my first day.

No—quiet. Let me talk. Nick says something quickly to the old man, a burst of words among which Mira's elementary Italian can catch only *americani* and *chiedo scusa*. His stern sun-blackened face relaxes and suddenly breaks into a smile of a thousand fractal wrinkles as he replies to Nick.

What is it? What's he saying?

I told him that we're Americans on our honeymoon, and he's telling us how much he loves us. It's half in dialect. He's telling me how the partisans used to hide out in the tombs. Until the Americans came and ended the war.

Look at him, says Mira, smiling up at the man as she kneels to stroke one of the little dogs. He's a peasant out of Horace. No, he's an ancient Etruscan.

The old man is studying Mira in turn. *Bella, sua moglie. Una bella ragazza di colore. Andate pure. Andate a vedere tutto. E ricordate*—he quickly stuffs away the ten thousand lire that Nick puts into his hand—*ricordate che si possono fare dei bei figli anche nelle tombe.*

He said you're beautiful, say Nick, as they walk away. A beautiful colored girl, he snickers, giving her a dig in the ribs. Or was it off-color? Anyway, it's a compliment in Italian. He said we can go in, but we should watch out for vipers. And he said—

Well?

He said it's possible to make beautiful children even in tombs.

That afternoon at Cerveteri becomes part of their gallery of private jokes. You took me to a cemetery and ravished me. You ghoul. Necrophile.

But what both hoard in their memories is the sensation of complete freedom. By some miracle, or perhaps by the agency of the ancient Etruscan caretaker, no one shows up for an hour. The whole necropolis remains eerily deserted as if there were some holiday or catastrophe that they hadn't heard about. And Nick and Mira duck into and out of the long rows of tombs like children playing in the ocean. In from the battering midday sun, the boiling dust of the rocky paths lined with thistles and wild fennel, where armies of lizards and grasshoppers flee at their approach. Into the sudden darkness of the tumuli, which they discover are actually oddly cozy and domestic feeling. Stripped, in order to supply museums, of their sarcophagi and the quotidian ornaments that once surrounded the dead, the tombs are dry and solid feeling, with their low entryways and lintels and their small alcove-lined rooms. They have fun moving from light to darkness, eyes dazzled, back and forth from the underworld to daylight.

They find the crude light switches that illuminate the tomb of the aristocratic Matuta family and stare at the niches for twenty bodies and the red and black traces of painting on the walls. They light up other tombs with the flashlight, straying further into the field on paths increasingly overgrown with nettles. And finally, at one of the smallest, farthest places, a tumulus not even fully excavated, they move swiftly inside after a brief sweep with the flashlight. The moving beam illuminates a few bottles and condoms strewn about the ground. And this ugly debris gives them a feeling of affectionate communion with all the village kids who come here to drink and fuck under the indulgent eyes of their ancestors, a first glimpse of the palimpsest of generations that is Italy.

Here they sit down cross-legged to smoke a joint. After a few minutes, they strip off their clothes and make love clumsily, half against the gritty tufa wall, half in a small alcove made to hold a short sarcophagus. Even in the darkness, the noonday heat is so intense that their sweat evaporates as soon as it forms and their lips on each other's skin feel cracked and feverish and dry.

Later in their lives, each of them will think of this episode as a supreme romantic milestone. Equal to the first few times they made love or confessed their love or when they impulsively decided to marry.

But what they actually feel before they mythologize it is more modest: a benign taste of darkness granted to them like a family secret by whatever shades still lingered in that ancient place. A truth so unadorned that they feel obliged to dress it up with grand emotions. An acceptance, as if they'd come home. An Etruscan truth, the kind Lawrence writes about, one that they won't appreciate for years to come. In fact, Nick will never appreciate it. After their marriage is over and he has a few long nights to unstitch remembered incidents, he wonders why the hell he brought her to Cerveteri. Why not a place with water—Hadrian's Villa or the gardens of Ninfa? Lilies, stone garlands, the sound of fountains, and fluid green light. Would things have been different if he hadn't brought her to a city of the dead?

Years afterwards, Mira will reread *Etruscan Places* and feel a shiver of recognition at Lawrence's words describing Cerveteri: ". . . and the land beyond feels as mysterious and fresh as if it were still the morning of time."

THE ANCIENT ETRUSCAN

I've been the caretaker at Cerveteri since 1959, when they cleared out the last land mine, and my problem since then has been keeping the living out of the tombs. *Tombaroli,* grave robbers, gypsies, and even a gang of Tunisian squatters. Drug addicts up from the port at Civitavecchia. And of course, courting kids. You should see the filth I have to rake up: bottles, rubbers, syringes. So I send trespassers packing, but this pair were Americans, and that's my weak point. It's not fashionable to like them these days, but I still see them charging up the coast from Gaeta in the fall of 1944, when Badoglio was at his last gasp and we partisans were living on chestnut soup and chopping bullets out of corpses. Grinning black and white GIs tearing into the village in jeeps and dumping a mountain of cans in front of the church. Campbell's soup, Armour beef—for me they can do no wrong. And this couple were decent kids, and good to look at, the boy blond like a movie actor and the girl like one of those Brazilian dancers on TV. *Una bella coppia*—a beautiful couple. Let them have a honeymoon present, the way their fathers poured out tin cans of food.

3

ZENIN

2004 · THE TARTAR OF THE LOWLANDS

A sound of girls laughing. That is Zenin's lifelong private flash point, which can send him into a dull rage, continuous and diffuse as a migraine. Laughter rising like a flood that needs to be channeled and controlled. Girls' gabble and laughter through walls, silvery, chaotic, unstoppable like the seething adolescent uproar of his four sisters, packed into the tiny room they shared in the destitute years after the war, when Zenin's family lived with—lived on top of, more like it—Zio Dario at Stra Pa in a freezing village house in Boara, just outside Rovigo, a shitty place whose plumbing was the Adige River out back.

Teasing laughter like that of the girls at school who called him *il tartaro*—the Tartar—because of his foreign-looking lankiness and narrow eyes and one memorable year, when he'd suddenly outgrown his single pair of long trousers, made up a mortifying chant: *il tartaro in pantaloni cinesi*—the Tartar in Chinese pants. Unseemly rowdy laughter like that of the factory girls at his company headquarters when they go out and get drunk, presumptuous sluts that they are, on International Women's Day. Terrified giggles from his two daughters, now adults, to whom he has been a distant, guilty father since his much-publicized divorce shook the Catholic stronghold that was the Veneto in the sixties. Haughty laughter, like that of his ex-wife, Cecilia, before they got married, when she was still the notary Bertin's beautiful daughter and the prize catch of his small provincial city.

Was it Cecilia and her sneering bitches of girlfriends—the rich bourgeois girls who played tennis at the Circolo—who laughed at his mother's misspelled letters? It was forty years ago, and it's hard for Zenin to recall the circumstances, but he remembers the letters, written in characters like chicken scratches on every kind of paper, from the coarse blue-lined stuff schoolchildren used after the war to wrapping paper, even newspaper.

Letters she sent him from Rovigo to the big echoing barracks in the Dolomites where he was doing military service. Cecilia certainly laughed at the letters, but he remembers other laughter at the barracks, having to beat it into the head of Diberti, a pimpled oaf from Mestre, that it was a miracle his mother—who had grown up barefoot, working like a man in the fishing fleet of Chioggia—could read and write at all. This was 1955. Not so unusual for the desert that was postwar Veneto, but Zenin was and is still shamed by those loving chicken scratches.

These things come to mind whenever he calls Mira. He knows that his *signorine,* that gaggle of birdbrained secretaries on the other side of the office walls, burst into giggles whenever he gets an office call or visit from any woman. From his ex-wife; to his present girlfriend, a good-humored, extremely pragmatic blond antique dealer from Verona; to the wily Tere, mother of his only son; to any of the diminishing number of casual lovers who sometimes pursue him at work. The *signorine*—homely to a girl, since Zenin doesn't want screwups at work—giggle harder when he has them call Mira with those instructions about not mentioning his name. The amorous life of the boss—with his bags of money, his sad hungry smile, his tall chilling figure, his expensive yet somehow badly fitting suits—is a staple of company folklore.

Zenin is famous. In his own country, his name is synonymous with the postwar explosion of prosperity and also with a kind of enlightened yet patriarchal way of handling big business that some call regionalism. He is best known for an ever-expanding army of plastic cartoon miniatures that invades millions of children's houses every day, camouflaged in boxes of breakfast cereals and snacks or marching straightforwardly across television screens. Nowadays he produces in China but keeps his headquarters in Rovigo. Not two kilometers from the route he used to trace out on foot and bicycle, and later by Vespa, with his father, an itinerant vendor of knives and kitchenware. Zenin has never gone public, never wanted or needed to. Vain and cautious, he keeps a medium-low profile, neither hiding like Cuccia and other sacred monsters, or flaunting himself like Benetton and Agnelli. Like other self-made men, he has remained at the most elementary semaphores of success: cars, yachts, a jet, houses, a villa on the Brenta once owned by a prince. And women—a trail of beauties, some famous. Fewer, though, nowadays. And never another wife.

His best friend, a journalist everyone calls Macaco—Monkey—a faithful sycophant and small-town eccentric who drives around in a battered Cadillac, said to him recently, At our age, a love affair, or even just plain fucking, is too much trouble. Even with Viagra. But the great thing would be to have a mouth—no girl, just a girl's mouth—there in the bed to give you a blow job every morning. A different mouth every day.

That's one way of looking at it. And Zenin has enough money so that he's got mouths when he wants them. Usually Russian or Chinese mouths these days, attached to bodies whose youthful perfection is so consistent that he's stopped noticing. And he has his pragmatic girlfriend, a cheerful sporty aristocrat who knows everyone, who shares his tastes, and is even a sincere Juventus fan. He has his loyal family and his son, Daniele, a university student who is genuinely a good boy and the only person in the world Zenin loves with a trembling, self-effacing, sentimental love.

So why does he still call Mira? He hasn't seen her for years. He's sixty years old, with more money than anyone knows about, and has hanging around his neck like a stone garland his own personal wreath of troublesome women from the past. Most would be overjoyed to hear from Zenin.

But only Mira sounds annoyed when he calls. Annoyed, yet strangely acquiescent. She never hangs up on him, as he half expects, when he is acting like a buffoon and a provocateur, making crude jokes and blunt propositions. Her wary voice on the line revives for him, for an instant, the excitement he always felt with her of intruding, of breaking into somewhere he doesn't belong, with her half consent. A strange play of remoteness yet accessibility that makes him remember the thrill of being a sharp provincial boy on the way up, making his first trips abroad. Of all the foreign girls he has had, Mira is the one who made him feel foreignness most. It's what made fucking her so good.

What are you doing?

Working.

All his life, perhaps because of his mother's chicken scratches, Zenin, who never reads books, has cherished the vision of a woman writing, dressed in some kind of fluid light-colored clothing, surrounded somehow by a dark wood frame. A woman of culture. It is a charged erotic image that has little to do with Mira, yet he drapes it around her. It was what made him pursue her when they first met.

So. Next week. Milan. Paris. New York.

Zenin makes his proposal, his fictitious plans, hears Mira's assent, and then puts down the phone. Feeling curiously enlivened by the ritual. One of the small idiosyncratic luxuries a rich man has to procure for himself. Because once Zenin owns something, he doesn't let it go easily.

1985 · LUNCH ON THE WATER

Che cazzo faccio qua? What the fuck am I doing here? Zenin wonders the first time he flies down to Rome to see Mira. Running after a little American girl, as if I didn't have enough pains in the ass.

It's a slow time of the year for Zenin, and so he's been amusing himself by calling Mira a few times a week during the month and a half since they met on the plane. Without any particular plan in mind, he has attached himself to her life as she begins to learn his country. Her complete indifference as to who he is, to what his name means in Italy, is tantalizing, as is the insulting friendliness, the lack of flirtatious reserve, with which she greets his first calls. From the start, peppering him, Zenin, with questions about places and customs, even requesting actual translations, as if he were some sort of glorified tourist guide.

In his predator's way, Zenin senses that beneath her breezy American self-assurance, Mira is disoriented, fumbling in a new language, feeling her way blindly in the maze of Rome. That what makes her vulnerable is her greed to see and know everything at once. The fact that she is married and clearly happy only adds a certain zest—a familiar one for Zenin, but not to be disdained. It took weeks, longer than he had thought, for him to convince her to meet him for lunch.

The airport taxi jolts him—asshole of a Roman driver—as they swerve off the *raccordo anulare,* and Zenin is as surprised as usual by the greenness of the city. It's the end of October. Getting chilly up north, but here in the irresponsible Mezzogiorno, people are still in sandals. Sunlight molds the dreamy boskiness around the crumbling stones of parks and avenues. Pines, palms, sun; it relaxes Zenin, makes him feel like he's on vacation. There is nothing like it in the Veneto, where green means utilitarian expanses of cornfields or vineyards, or the sparse jewels that are the gardens of Venice. Each time he visits Rome, he thinks, *cazzo,* a building here in the historic center would be a good deal. He has a friend in the Beni Culturali office who owes him a favor and who'd find him a cinquecento palazzo from some ragged aristocratic clan. But then he'd have to come up with something to do with it. And to tell the truth, a certain heaviness of spirit has settled over him lately. He's tired of buying things and then having to do something with them. Tired of his routine in general. That's why he flew to Rome today.

Nobody at home, not even his secretary, knows he's here.

And when Mira walks into the bar near the Pantheon, he thinks, Not bad at all. Even the *barista,* an insolent young Roman with a greasy ponytail, jaded with a surfeit of blond Germans in shorts and Californians in halter tops, takes an eyeful, announcing, *Ammappete, che figacciona.* What a dish. She's horribly dressed, of course, in jeans like a student and a shapeless cotton sweater that disguises her breasts. But there are the long legs and round ass Zenin noticed in the cheap black dress she wore on the plane, and under the mass of frizzy hair pinned up in the heat is a tawny-skinned face that suggests not one but many faraway places. And she's carrying a book.

You thought you would be bored? he teases her, when they are sitting at the table having drinks. In front of them, merging currents of tour groups surge around the massive pillars of the Pantheon, and the piazza resounds with a continuous low hubbub like the roar of distant seas. It's noon, and they are going to lunch, yet Mira orders a cappuccino in the ridiculous way Americans do. Zenin has seen them drinking cappuccino all day in Venice. She says she always carries a book, that it's good luck, that she has a theory that when you don't carry a book, the car breaks down, a train or planes gets delayed, and you're stuck for six hours somewhere with nothing to do.

She shows him the book, a novel in English by a writer called Edith Wharton, information that Zenin instantly deletes like all things useless to him. The fact of the book is important, not the book itself. What interests him now is the pulse he can see beating at the base of her throat like the heart of a small animal. The unbelievable tenderness and youth of the flesh over beating blood that suggests the secret of her entire body, hidden like the smooth wood of a sapling under the awful clothes. Zenin has often sat contemplating a number of pretty young girls and always glances down deliberately to notice how coarse his own hands seem by contrast. Peasant paws, huge and blunt, strangely restless, irreparably marked by middle age and tropical suns. When he was younger, before he got rich, he was ashamed of them. His wife and other girlfriends criticized them. But now he takes pleasure in the sight of these ugly hands that have the power to touch the most exquisite skin in the world.

Does your husband know you're meeting me for lunch? he asks, with the sudden blunt tone and aggressive look he uses—in business or with women—to move negotiations along. But Mira doesn't giggle or look flustered. With a smile that is at once good-humored and slightly disdainful, she says that of course her husband knows, that she tells him everything, that it's normal for a couple to have separate friends. That's the way things are done in America, in their circle from work and university. A perfect brush-off.

But at the same time, the curiosity that he has noticed as one of her elemental qualities continues to shimmer from her face and her eyes. Reaching toward him. It's as if two parts of her are speaking separate languages. Zenin rarely wonders about personalities, but now, without realizing it, he asks himself whether it is the mixed blood visible in her face that makes her able to send this double message. And he wonders whether she has actually let her husband know.

In any case, he has plans for this afternoon that she certainly won't want to tell him about.

He calls abruptly for the check and tells the waiter to call a taxi. Gratified by a flustered look from Mira, not quite so sure of herself now. We won't have lunch in the center, he tells her. We'll go outside the city. I have a surprise.

Like Nick, he has a childish desire to impress her.

At this point in his life, Zenin is at the first stage of weariness after the prolonged priapic revel that occurs when a man makes a huge fortune in a short time. Divorced for years, he had run through the usual list of models and actresses and husband hunters from impoverished noble families. When he took the plane with Mira, he was at a momentary loose end, having just broken up with a serious girlfriend, an Australian of Italian background whose parents made it clear they expected marriage. Mira, less beautiful than many of Zenin's girls, attracted him in spite of the gauche eagerness of her face, which was exotic, he thought, and needed to be impassive to convey real beauty. Listening idly as he dozed in his sleep mask, he'd been amused by what a little pig she was, how she gobbled every course on the menu, much to the mirth of the cabin crew, who were used to rich women starving themselves. It was almost with a feeling of obligation that he came and flirted with her as they had approached Rome. But when he found out she was both married and a writer, a sudden change came over the way she appeared to him. She, the little adventuress, acquired a certain rank. While Zenin felt smaller and humbler.

So he took her number and began calling, late in the morning, when she was sure to be alone. And from the beginning he made extravagant proposals. Just to let her know what was possible with him. Come with me to Sardinia, to the Seychelles, to Istanbul for the day.

Proposals she turned down with such incredulous laughter that he suspects she sees him as an entertaining part of her new life abroad: an
Italian lunatic on the phone. Worse, he suspects that he might be the
subject of jokes between her and her husband.

But today he's changing the pace.

He tells the taxi driver, a small bald man with batlike ears, to take
the old Ostiense road down to the coast. You've been this way before?
he asks Mira. She says yes. That's all she says. The cab is hot, and Mira
sits in a corner as far from him as possible, with a look on her face that
tells Zenin she's wondering if she's being abducted. Don't worry, I'm
not Barbablù, he tells her. You know, Bluebeard.

I'm not worried.

Silence, as they pass through fields where harvested wheat is already
bound in plastic-covered bales, and enter the shadow of the *pineta,* the
thick coastal wood of umbrella pines, here contained in the five-mile
wall of the Savoy royal hunting preserve. At the end of the wall, Zenin directs the driver down a back road near the sea, first paved, then unpaved,
past sand dunes and cane fields, illegal apartment blocks, and a gypsy
trailer camp. Peasant women walk by with bundles of cane on their
backs. Zenin feels what for him is agitation, the wary feeling he gets
when he is not sure his plans will work.

A sandy stretch of road, complaints from that son of a bitch of a cab
driver, and they turn out of the cane fields into the sudden blinding
dazzle of the sea. A dark blue expanse beyond a small rocky cove
strewn with plastic refuse, and dried seaweed.

The driver stops the cab and gives a low whistle of amazement. For
there, three hundred yards out, is the great white boat that, most of all
these days, makes Zenin feel that he is Zenin. The *Regina Confusa.* A
confirmation. Built by the Soria brothers of Viareggio, bought as a bargain from De Luca the Genovese when De Luca went bust. Lower than
most, not like the other giant motor yachts shaped like steam irons you
see lined up in the marinas in Monte Carlo or Porto Rotondo. A boat
whose size invites satire, her decks designed to be carpeted with starlets. Now sitting in front of the small ugly cove like a swan in a puddle.
White as a temple, an apparition from a romance novel or a gossip magazine, solid as an island out there in the Tyrrhenian in the midday sun.

I brought it here for you, Zenin tells Mira, who has gone very still beside him.

Not strictly true, since Zenin had ordered the *Confusa* transferred from Ischia to Civitavecchia, and they had to pass here anyway. But true enough. And he sees, with a stab of pure pleasure, that he has dazzled her.

A Zodiac is already buzzing toward them, manned by one of the crew, a curly-headed young Pugliese. She takes off her shoes and gets into the launch like a sleepwalker, shading her eyes with her book.

Lunch on the upper deck. Spaghetti with *tartufi di mare,* a white Frascati, thin but potent, a poached sea bass, fresh orange ice, coffee. The curly-headed deckhand moving back and forth with the dishes, observing Mira from all angles, judging her by the suntanned ghosts of other decorative women who haunt the boat. The white awning flapping in the breeze, the boat moving subtly like a breathing creature, the nondescript strip of Tyrrhenian coastline looking as all coastlines do under a heat haze from the water, like the promised land.

Mira has two helpings of pasta. The girl is remarkably adaptive, Zenin notes. Already, the inquisitive look is brightening her eyes.

Regina Confusa, she says. The confused queen. What does that mean?

Every boat is named after a woman. But I have never been able to decide which one.

You have a lot of girls.

Not so many, Zenin says with a deprecating grin, thinking of how many, the troublesome weight of them all, the sisters, the daughters, the others.

Are you married? she asks suddenly. In all their telephone conversations, she has never asked this before.

I am divorced.

Oh. An American tone of understanding. Divorce, thinks Zenin, is an everyday solution for them, like getting glasses for shortsightedness. But this girl can't possibly understand what divorce meant in a provincial Italian town in the seventies. The first years it was legal in Italy. Somber family councils, a medieval air of excommunication, threatening notes on his car windshield, the priest suddenly thundering anathema through the varnished walls of the confessional. He doesn't enlighten her.

After the coffee, the well-trained crew vanishes so completely that the ship feels abandoned.

What happens now astonishes Zenin. Printed indelibly in his mind long afterward is how Mira turns to him when they are belowdecks making the obligatory tour. He is eying her lazily, unsure as to whether he wants her or not. He feels indolent, at peace: it is almost enough that he amazed her with the sudden vision of who he is.

They have passed through the big salon with its teak-framed Morandi and are standing inside the doorway of his cabin when Mira abruptly shuts the door behind them. And turns to him with her eyes blazing in a face suddenly grown pale.

I guess this is where it happens, she says, speaking distinctly in a hard voice that surprises him. Would you like me to undress now?

Zenin thinks she probably had too much wine at lunch. And the last thing he needs is a drunken woman making a scene on board. He makes a movement toward her that is both irritated and protective, as he might to one of his sisters who is making a fool of herself. But Mira shakes him off.

No, she says fiercely. I chose to come here, didn't I? I'm not stupid, or a child. I knew what climbing aboard this boat meant. Now let's finish the deal the way you do it.

As Mira speaks, she drags off her jeans and knit top. Afterward Zenin recalls the action as instantaneous, as if she had burst out of her clothes with sheer vehemence. Actually, she struggles impatiently, and finally kicks her way out of the jeans and underpants. But to Zenin, caught in a trance of surprise, she is one second dressed and the next naked, like a sword magically unsheathed.

Like so many aggressive people, Zenin can't bear bluntness in others. He is so shocked by the bizarre speed of her stripping and by her ridiculous ferocity that he just sits down on the end of his bed. With a flabbergasted expression that would be comical if anyone else were there to see it.

And in the bland luxury of the stateroom, with its pale carpet and inlaid wood paneling, he looks at her body without the slightest trace of desire. A body whose contours are still nearly adolescent, like a bundle of slim branches, almost pathetic in its symmetry. He sees with no enjoyment the dark smudge of hair between her legs, the hair on her head spilling over her shoulders like wild foliage. He sees that she is shaking slightly, and that the brightness in her eyes is tears. He doesn't understand that she is struggling not against him but against something in herself.

All at once Zenin feels old and tired and disgusted with life in general. What has he been thinking of? All this trouble for a melodramatic American girl. Married. And completely insane. *Matta da legare.* It becomes urgent to get rid of her as soon as possible, ashore and out of his sight without complications.

Dai, vieni, he says. Come on. Put your clothes on. Don't worry. I will get a taxi from Ostia. And he is surprised by the ragged tenderness of his own voice, as if, without knowing it, he has been moved. Moved by the ridiculous theatrics she is pouring on as if she were a virgin about to be ravished.

Later, when Mira comes up on deck with her face washed and clothes put to rights, she does not apologize. She just remarks in a reflective voice, as if to herself, that she doesn't know what came over her, that she has been acting crazy, she feels crazy these days, that it must be something in the air, all the changes in her life. That she's just realized she's completely out of place in Rome.

Zenin, furious, is silent. He has already ordered a pair of taxis, one to take her back to town, one to the airport for him. Has given the captain orders to continue on to Civitavecchia. He is impatient to get home, back to the office, can't wait to see the last of this little bitch. Never again, he thinks venomously. Better a prostitute than this kind of ball-busting complication.

But then, just after she climbs into the Zodiac with him, before the engine starts, she looks him in the eye and says in her gauche way; The two of us won't see each other anymore. But thank you. Thank you for lunch.

Zenin mutters something, still more angered that she should take the liberty of making a pronouncement that should be his. In fact he feels his anger growing into something like a decision. Perhaps, he thinks, he will let a certain amount of time pass and then call this troublesome girl again. Next time, he'll be the one who decides how things turn out.

The Zodiac speeds away toward the shore where the two taxis stand, the drivers goggling at the big white yacht that stands out in the afternoon like a dream and the man and the girl speeding toward them like pictures from a magazine. And the young deckhand with his curly hair and sun-blackened face catches Zenin's eye with a subdued look of admiration at Zenin's presumed swift conquest, and Zenin wants to slap him.

THE DECKHAND

My boss, Zenin, is old, *ma è pieno di fica*—but he gets lots of pussy. That's how it is when you're that rich. My cousin got me this job as deckhand, working from May to October when the *Confusa* goes to Antigua and there's a whole new crew. When I started last year, I was seventeen and had never left my village in Brindisi. I was no virgin, but the only live girl I'd seen naked was parts of my *fidanzata,* my girlfriend. But since I came on board the *Confusa,* I've got a close look at high-class pieces of ass like you see on television. Not just Italian—foreign, too. Actresses, models, once a princess. This last girl was American, a colored girl, cute, but not his usual standard, and in fact he didn't even spend the night with her. Just a quick screw.

Of course the girls want to marry him, but the boss isn't having any. He had a wife already and that's enough. So they come and they go. The rules for us are strict: always formal, no chitchat, no staring, even when they're stretched out in the sun with their tits out for God and the angels to see. Or rubbing up against you when you help them into the dinghy. And some of those tarts really rub up against you. My girlfriend tells me that if she finds out I've been fooling around, she'll slip aboard in some port one night and quietly, quietly cut off my balls. But there's no harm in thinking. Lucky boss. *Uomo fortunato.*

He makes a mountain of money selling those toys that come with the candy, but they say he was poor once. You can tell by the way he breaks into Veneto dialect. And by the way, when he's alone, he eats white beans and onions, shovels them down just like my uncle the fisherman does. But Zenin's like a different kind of uncle. To my mind he's like what the old people call *lo zio d'America.* That means a man who left his family, left Italy, went off across the ocean to someplace like America and made a bundle. The uncle with his millions from America, that's Zenin. He has what we all used to dream about back in the village.

4

MIRA

So they are walking through Harvard Yard, mother and daughter. Mira, like a thousand freshman parents, is delivering a child to a new geography and life. Boston, in the unseasonably hot September, has a different tint of pollution from northern Italy, a texture of sunlight that makes the red-brick city seem vibrant and unreal, and both Mira and Maddie, groggy from jet lag, tired from a week of packing and combing the shops on Via Mazzini, dance along in the unconscious giddy feeling of vacation they always have on their first morning in America.

Maddie, a chestnut-haired beauty who like the other freshmen girls towers over her mother—as we did over our mothers, thinks Mira. Where did it start, with Lilliputians?—is sick of questions about what it's like to be an American girl coming to live in America for the first time. And questions about how she chose her parents' college. She wrote about both on her college apps, and now wants everyone to shut up.

Basta, she says to her mother. Enough. Mira and her children speak Italian to one another in the States, the way they speak English in Italy. As a secret language. And to show off a little, just a little, at fraught moments like this.

Because, of course, the Yard is awash with emotion, as well as with cars, boxes, and bewildered freshman families.

Above all, thinks Mira, there is the tide of young flesh, the stunning beauty of these immature faces now seeking one another, seeking out destiny, a key, in the features of strangers of their own age. And the parents—one of them me—blowing around them like dried husks. Wandering through the green lawns, the eternal bricks, like lost souls. Bemused by this one-sided tragedy of loss that their child feels with so much joy. A liberation for our children—what agony to understand this. And how much pain it takes to conceal it. And she recalls her own ecstatic relief when she saw her parents' car disappear. And when she left her mother to fly to Rome.

Many fathers are there, fathers jovial and paunchy in khaki shorts, hauling boxes, moving big shiny four-wheel-drive cars. Nick, of course, is not. He will come in from London after Maddie is settled and Mira has left.

In a line for registering boxes or receiving keys, Mira flirts and plays one-upmanship with one father, who may just have been her year in college. Muscular, handsome, with small glasses, young face under gray hair. With the look of pink, steamed cleanliness that some rich Americans have.

Beverly Hills, actually, he says. And you?

Italy. Turin, says Mira, trumping him. You know, in the north. Barolo country.

With mothers, Mira competes in the good old feminine tradition, with her Italian haircut, her expensive casual clothes, just right for ruefully lugging boxes, her chummy demeanor toward her daughter.

You are the most gorgeous mom, says Maddie.

Oh, go on—you know you're the gorgeous one.

Maddie has a cramped suite looking out onto billows of elms. A blond Chicago roommate with pipe-stem wrists and a squeaky voice, and a serious Mexican roommate with a high forehead and a mature air. Unpacking, they squeal over jeans, computers, leopard-skin pumps. They are ready to drag Maddie off, to become part of a frieze: the Three Graces. Their mythology, their world.

But it's not! Mira wants to scream. It's my world. Nick's and mine. The Yard is foggy with our ghosts. How many times did we kiss on these paths? Look, over there is the university church where we got married. That shimmer in the air—it's our expectations, our day-dreams, our future that didn't happen!

When they go to lunch, Harvard Square is full of dusty wind and street musicians. Black panhandlers with matted braids call Mira sister, and she hands them change along with a big grin.

I'll get in touch with my roots, Ma, I promise, Maddie tells her sarcastically in Italian.

Near Starbucks they run into a Reiver cousin. A senior, a hockey player, six foot three, muscles, a round unawakened face. And blue eyes like Nick's, now skating over Mira with embarrassment.

Hey Maddie, you made it. You should come over for dinner. I'm off campus in Central Square. This is my girlfriend, Nessa. Nessa, this is my cousin Maddie. She grew up in Italy. And this is . . . this is . . . her mother . . . his voice trails off.

Mira feels annoyed, then tolerant of his lack of manners. He's a kid after all.

I'm Miranda Ward. Maddie's mother, she says with a warm sophisticated adult smile.

The huge boy looks at her with those shockingly familiar eyes rimmed with wheat-colored lashes. Wondering. In a dull way, wary. You've certainly grown since I last saw you, Mira adds humorously.

Once at her wedding she hoisted up this boy as he slept in a basket. A memory of that baby weight still resides somewhere in her right arm. And now he looks at her as if encountering a fabled monster. She knows that the Reivers have never forgiven her, and who knows what the boy has heard about her? She is the wicked aunt. A creature she always envisions as a smirking pantomime Dame with painted pink-and-white face, powdered hair, a beauty patch on her withered bosom. She feels a pang, though she knows nothing shows on her face. One thing wicked aunts know about is veneer. So Mira stands smiling, an elegant composed older woman on a street where she was once perilously young. Knowing that nothing is lost, that all times are one time. And knowing, though her daughter and nephew do not, that one reason they are standing casually embarrassed there on a street in Cambridge is because twenty years earlier, in a nearby garden, there was a happy ending.

1981 · MEMBERS OF THE WEDDING

Before Rome, before New York even, there is for Mira and Nick a certain June in Boston.

One of the blissful Junes of college towns, pastoral seasons of graduations and weddings, when the rank humidity of East Coast summers is still just a languorous softness in the air, which smells intoxicatingly of youth and the future and white linen and green leaves. Young life all channeled into civilized forms. Diplomas and weddings and infinite hope, and with this particular marriage, something resolved. An old wound healed.

The garden is attached to one of the old Radcliffe houses whose linoleum corridors are haunted by spirits of scholarly maidens who had to cram their studies and their furtive lovemaking into strict timetables. But the world has changed. By the opening of the nineteen eighties, boys and girls make love and ingest various chemicals at all hours in these halls.

The changed times are why these two families, the Wards and the Reivers, are in the garden together. Mingling in the maple shade, eating poached salmon and drinking toasts in an atmosphere of scared conviviality. The black Wards, of Philadelphia and Washington, and the white Reivers, of Rhode Island and Maine. So conspicuous in contrast when divided into the groom's side and bride's side in Memorial Church, that a mischievous cousin of the bride—herself about to marry a white boy from her class at Yale—says the place looks like a chessboard.

There have been the appropriate fairy-tale obstacles. Since the night at the beginning of senior year when Nick and Mira, struggling to set up camp in a high wind on Mt. Katahdin, watched their tent fly away, burst out laughing, and realized that there was nothing else to do but get married.

A decision that triggers veiled protests. Veiled because both families, more similar than they guess, are filled with suburban liberals, strong on justice, weekend work camps, peace, affirmative action, mown lawns, sensible shoes, a Quaker-Shaker, old-school, civil-rights ideal of fellowship. Indeed Nick's father, the small-town publisher, and Mira's dead father, the public school principal, both marched in Birmingham and Washington. Unaware that their blood would be mingled in the next generation.

And who is to say that this marriage isn't what they marched for?

But grandmothers fret that integration is one thing, marriage another. Letters fly, voicing qualms about how Nick or Mira will "fit in," about their future happiness, about the identity of their children. Nick is the butt of white-boy jokes and political needling from a self-conscious dreadlocked cousin of Mira's. And one of Nick's aunts, after a few too many Bloody Marys, effusively asks Mira what tribe she's from.

When the engagement is announced, Nick and Mira's friends torture them with cheesy ad-libs from *Guess Who's Coming to Dinner*: . . . Don't worry, Mother and Father, we don't want children, and we'll be living in Switzerland . . .

This mild Montague and Capulet fuss, as it is somehow intended to, cements the bond between Miranda Alice Ward and Nick Strong Reiver. But though they feel star-crossed, they never think of eloping. Beneath everything they are good middle-class kids, and they want their wedding.

And as the day approaches, the obstacles turn out to be about as solid as dragons made out of clouds.

Everything organized by the bride and groom, because the old folks have nothing to contribute anymore, except checks.

The wedding on this neutral university ground, far from the incense-filled arches of St. Michael's in Little Compton or the high, yellow Baptist gloom of New African in Philadelphia. In the soaring ecumenical space of Memorial Church, a place that suggests a utopian lecture hall.

The joint bachelor party, a tequila blast where the happy couple get knee-walking drunk and perform a double striptease to "Brick House."

The bride, glorious as the queen of Sheba with a rose in her hair, teetery high heels, and a yellowing muslin dress that once belonged to her grandmother.

Nick, reassuring everyone by how handsome, how steady, he looks in a suit.

The rumbling basso of Mira's uncle, a famous Congregational minister who flies in from Nairobi to perform the ceremony. His dour brown face and his strange pale eyes flickering with resignation over the young couple, as if he had seen it all before.

The swell of laughter in the church during the kiss, where Nick grabs Mira and lifts her up and bends her back as if he'll never let go. An old uncle of Nick's who teaches classics at Amherst calls out, *Hymen îo Hymen, Hymen!*

In the end, a wedding not very different from others held on campus. A strain for the bride and groom, who can hardly wait to grab their backpacks and take off for Maine and then Greece, where they'll spend a month lost to the world among dazzling islands, the blinding sea.

Yet for the others, most especially the relatives with qualms, something extraordinary happens after that theatrical kiss. The pleasant dormitory garden where tables are spread in the shade of the old maples becomes the setting for a pastorale. Mira and Nick, who have steeled themselves for anything from barbed politeness to a full-scale race riot, find themselves enclosed in a bubble of arcadian harmony. Where, like figures in a dynastic union, they shine like symbols of the general good.

A sense of liberation is in the air. The two families suddenly realize that they need nothing from each other. That the terrifying intimacy is the province of the young couple. So they can relax.

The Reivers notice that none of the Wards is dark-skinned, or fat, or dressed in loud colors, or possesses frightening ghetto accents. Several of them are distinguished people. That the Wards, puzzlingly, seem resigned and not at all jubilant about a marriage that twenty years before would have been unthinkable.

The Wards notice that the Reivers are not the lords of the earth. That neither are they limp-wristed white liberals who are so easy to despise. Nor the trash who lined the school steps, howling and spitting, in South Boston and Little Rock. One or two Reivers are plump, and several are badly dressed in a way that cannot be put down to New England parsimony.

Mira's famous uncle and Nick's father drink scotch and trade portentous gossip about Liberia and Somalia, and the foibles of K Street, and obscure think tanks.

Old Reiver aunts, overeducated at Bryn Mawr, swap reminiscences of their civil-rights days with old Ward aunts, overeducated at Spelman.

Mira's mother, in pleated chiffon, has drunk several glasses of Vouvray, shed a tear for her dead husband, and now sits in the shade with a lively old elementary school teacher, a distant Reiver cousin from Concord, happily exchanging tales of peril in inner-city classrooms.

Babies cry and are put to sleep, and children climb walls and trees.

Mira's normally sedate older sister, Faith, kicks off her shoes, pulls her dress down on her lovely shoulders, and flirts outrageously with Nick's younger brother, Teddy.

Nick's cousin, in a large Chinese hat, nurses her infant son. Who will later stand on a Cambridge street corner blushing at the sight of Mira.

A Chesapeake Bay retriever chases an Italian greyhound and knocks over a table full of glasses.

Nick's former crewmates from St. George's take Nick and Mira into the dormitory bathroom and present them with half an ounce of the finest Colombian.

The toasts include references to the poetry seminar that brought the happy pair together. Finally the old professor reads:

To the Nuptial bower
I led her blushing like the morn: all heav'n,
And happy constellations on that hour
Shed their selectest influence; the Earth
Gave sign of gratulation, and each Hill; Joyous the birds;
*   fresh Gales and gentle Airs*
Whisper'd it to the woods, and from thir wings
Flung Rose, flung odors from the spicy shrub
Disporting, til the amorous Bird of Night
Sung spousal, and bid haste the Ev'ning Star
On his Hill top, to light the bridal lamp.

He blinks in the sunlight, his bald head covered with age spots and his hooded eyes behind his reading glasses making him look like an ancient tortoise.

The bride and groom stand through this with a charming awkwardness, he in his blue suit and she in her yellowed wedding dress. Their weary young faces flushed from the drugs they have taken. They look tall, handsome, in a matching way that suggests that they are their own race. Twin stars in the sky. Too good for this wedding. Too good for anything, too rich for use. For a moment the eyes of the guests hurt from looking at them.

And then they are gone in jeans and T-shirts, rattling off to Maine in an old loaned MG. The bouquet thrown to Faith, who marries her high school sweetheart with much more traditional pomp six months later. Parents and friends embrace, a whirlwind of tears and confetti and rice.

THE GUESTS

Back in the garden, we suddenly acknowledge our own importance. And our relief. As if a strategic task has been accomplished with the sending off of those two in the old sports car. We savor our position in the shaded enclosure of the powerful university. Black and white chess pieces mingled in the waning hours of a June Saturday, when campus is shut down and the streets are quiet. Where the setting sun gives a festal golden tinge to every complexion, and there are still bottles of wine to finish. In circles we sit down on the grass and on the cheap university folding chairs. Heedless of our fancy clothes, which we'll soon take off, finding ourselves the same as ever. But now, brandy and cigars come out. We are infatuated with one another, young and old. Nobody wants to leave. And in fact, we sit and drink and talk about unimportant things until the impatient student waiters clear the tables and summer darkness falls. There is an odd feeling, a communal tipsiness, in the air, and suddenly everybody knows what it is: peace and— it must be—love.

5

NICK

2004 · WHITE SNAKE

The earliest dream he remembers is the Ferris wheel. Turning faster than the real Ferris wheel at Rocky Point, a buoyant speed that means happiness. And it holds cartoon animals: dogs, cats, mice, who are smiling and waving. Like the Japanese anime that enthralls his two younger daughters, or the crap plastic toys made by that deadshit Zenin. Nick must have started dreaming it when he was three or four, when his family was still in the old house on Moffatt Lane. He'd wake up feeling good, that things were in their place. But a few times, the dream changed. The image would blink out like a TV going off. And there'd be a black field with a white line across it that would suddenly convulse in pulsing rhythmic curves like a mechanical snake. Each time, he'd jolt into consciousness, not screaming but dumb, frozen with the terror of a world sliced into glaring extremes.

This memory comes to mind, strangely, as he sits with Maddie in a sleek overpriced Cambridge coffee shop, a few weeks into her freshman year.

Weird recollection to have when you're contemplating a gorgeous grown-up daughter who has just started Harvard. A moment rich with a thousand facets of feeling that offset the ordinary sinking sensation caused by tottering around one's old campus in that dreariest of supporting roles, a paterfamilias.

There is, for example, the smug paternal sense of completion, of having his child arrive at a conventional peak of success in the eyes of all the world. Then there is the wrench at seeing the face he's carried in his heart for eighteen years, of its changing forms suddenly distant, finished as a portrait in its womanly perfection.

And of course the disconcerting fact that this face is attached to a healthy pair of breasts, to a long-legged body almost embarrassingly ripe and exuberant that, along with a cascade of chestnut curls, turns every male head on the street.

Nick, who in London enjoys the usual expatriate addiction to scurrilous English tabloids, is aware—though he hopes Maddie is not—that everyone who looks at the two of them must wonder about their relationship. The lovely dark-eyed young woman and the tall blue-eyed man with graying fair hair whose clothes and bearing identify him as one of those who command in the world outside of academe. The captain of finance, still virile, who can claim any young beauty he wants. So—are they father and daughter, or lovers?

The thought tickles his vanity and at the same time makes him uneasy, so that he finds himself lecturing Maddie with extra firmness about the hazards of debit cards and the importance of learning to budget. She sits listening, poking holes in the froth of her cappuccino with the tip of one rather grubby fingernail, her face wearing a daughterly expression of loving indulgence, restrained exasperation. Rapt in thoughts far from debit cards. She teases him that when he lectures her in the ceremonial role of Dull Dad, all she has to do is wait for him to get bored and turn into Cool Dad, the Nick who takes her on tours through his old Clash and Dead Kennedys albums, who reminisces—editing out drink and drugs—about nights at the Rat, at Tunnel, at Danceteria and Trax. For years she has worshipped him uncritically, as daughters who see their divorced fathers on weekends and on vacation do.

Now, in his best Cool Dad manner, he asks, So how's the race thing on campus these days? Is everybody still obsessively culture-fair?

You wouldn't believe the political correctness, Dad. Some of the kids and some faculty are so snotty and aware and exclusive about our unique minority cultures that it's like the Civil Rights Act never happened. Some days I feel like getting dreads, and some days I just identify Italian.

You what? Nick feels oddly disturbed. But you're not Italian.

But I was born there, and it's my other language, and people think I'm Italian anyway. It's my business, isn't it, Daddy?

I guess it is, says Nick in a conciliatory tone, but inwardly disturbed, reflecting that this is one more thing that bitch Mira has to answer for.

He reaches out to take Maddie's hand, but she grabs her cup and stares dreamily out the window. I sometimes wonder, she says, if I made a big mistake coming to Harvard.

Nick sloshes his coffee. What do you mean?

Yeah it's the best. But sometimes this campus feels like there's no room for me. Like it's overcrowded. With you. With you and Mom.

That's where the white snake flashes into view, for an instant twisting mechanically in his peripheral vision as he looks around for help. Probably the fault of this pretentious café, so different from the battered beer-stinking booths of Cronin's, where he used to hang with his jock roommates. Back in the day, he recalls, this place was a Frenchified clothes store where a lot of cute girls worked in ankle-tie espadrilles. But now the air smells portentously of Ghanaian chocolate and gourmet bean blends, and the walls are laminated black and decorated with blowups of film noir scenes: shadows of venetian blinds, movie stars with tragic cheekbones, sleuths in creased fedoras.

A black-and-white cave of melodrama looking out on the clear September sky, and on the students shuffling up and down the brick street like angels in beggars' clothes.

Maddie is right: the past abides in university towns, no matter how transient the decor. He sees the truth of this as he looks into her unmarred face, where his own and Mira's features are inextricably blended. And says the most honest thing that Cool or Dull Dad has ever told her.

It might be true, Mad. I can't help you there. It's your world, you chose it, and now you have to make it fit.

1980 · ICE

How could a kid have a dream that was so bland? demands Mira. They're strolling back from the Brattle Theatre or lying in her Adams

House bed, Nick never afterward remembers. How can you have had a life that was so tranquil? It seems crazy to me. She pauses. I could hate you for a dream like that.

I'm white, it's my burden to be boring, he says, kissing her, grabbing her butt. Crude on purpose. He clowns for her as a white boy, it occurs to him, for the same occult reason black minstrels existed: to defuse suspicion. For love of her, he's always embarrassing himself, making dumb jokes, dancing ludicrously, burlesquing one of those sad white hipsters who high-five and quote Richard Pryor.

He doesn't tell her that he started having the snake dream after his brother Meade died from meningitis at seven years old. For the simple reason that he doesn't remember. Just as he was too young to remember Meade, the golden oldest son, except as a brief flux of joyful noise and light, and then a dark cave of absence around which his mother and father, in their agony, set up a valiant defensive structure of family life.

And Nick and his younger brother grew up in their rather threadbare clan of New England patricians with thrift and books and heirlooms and sufficient love, but always with the feeling that something essential was lost. That you had to compensate.

Now he says, I can't help it that I was happy. We climbed trees, we caught crabs, we pissed off the side of sailboats. Delivered papers for Dad in the summers. Waited for Mom to pull up at school in one of those big station wagons like barges. I thought Dick and Jane was a portrait of life.

And I was always freaked out by Dick and Jane, says Mira. They were exotic, so white and perfect. I wanted to be them. But my family was on a different planet. My sister, and I used to joke that we were the shadows of *Leave It to Beaver*. The grown-ups went on about love and brotherhood, but we lived in the suburbs like in a ghetto.

She tells him complicated childhood dreams. Strange animals jumping out of the woods, sea monsters washed up on tiny beaches. The comfortable fieldstone houses of her Mount Airy neighborhood suddenly opening eyes and glaring. Above all, a dream about being unmasked in a crowd. Having a Sleeping Beauty mask torn off to show an alien face, a shameful black face. While classmates from the Quaker school in Germantown, where she and Faith were two of three black students, look on, sniggering.

Nick listens to this and feels sick inside. His own loss, barely comprehended, seems insignificant. He thinks he could spend his life shielding her from dreams like that.

As vivid to him as dreams is the memory of how they first got together, one afternoon before poetry class.

A February sleet storm coats every tree with crystal and turns streets into skating rinks. Slipping and sliding, Nick and Mira meet on the threshold of a rambling Victorian frame house whose shabby opulence and smell of stale wood smoke and cat pee always reminds Nick of home in Little Compton. The house and classroom of a famous poetess, a plump feminist with the piping voice of a little girl.

Nick, lapsed jock, now English major with a medieval bent, writes muscular poems exploring Old English meter. About canoeing at night on the Swampscott River. About a dead dog he found in the rocks on Prudence Island, mummified by salt and sun into rawhide, legs fixed in a desperate swimming position. About being lost in fog in Ledbetter's Narrows. He knows something about his poems already: that they are good enough to get him into writing seminars, but not good enough to make him a poet.

But Mira, he thinks, might continue. Something about her breezy passionate bullshitting on Eliot and Pound, about her short verses that sometimes sound like specious translations from Lorca but other times transfix one's imagination like nails hammered in a board. She rejects with aplomb the famous poetess's insulting urgings that she write "something close to home."

About what?

About anger, for example. Your anger as a black woman.

The only time I feel real anger, says Mira calmly, is when I have to hear shit like that.

On the afternoon of the sleet storm, Nick is wearing a ski hat that has frozen into a helmet, but Mira is bareheaded, each curl of her mass of hair encased, like the twigs on the trees, in a rattling sheath of ice.

Amazing! says Nick, courage coming to him out of nowhere. May I? First bowing like Jeeves, and then reaching out gently to pull off the crystal beads that dissolve in his cold hands and run down into his sleeves. Her drenched hair a freezing cloud. She laughs up at him as her chapped wet cheeks glow. Around them the student winter smell of damp uncleaned down jackets. I've been meaning to tell you I like your name, he goes on.

Everybody thinks it's something unusual, but it's ordinary. Short for Miranda, to avoid horrible Randy. My dad used to teach high school English, and *The Tempest* was his favorite part of the AP curriculum. But I always thought Miranda was kind of a sap. Fell for the first guy she saw after Caliban.

If you think of it, Shakespeare's Miranda was just an overprotected only child. But speaking of names, mine's worse, from some points of view. When I was really little I thought I was named after Jolly Old St. Nicholas and I used to worry about living up to the title. You know, being nice instead of naughty.

Mira grins impudently. Nick's also another name for the Devil.

They look at each other. Mira sees blue eyes as direct as a fall sky. Nick sees dark eyes like the entrance to somewhere he has always wanted to go.

Nick notices he still has a tiny piece of ice in his hand. He puts it in his mouth, where it dissolves without any taste at all.

A thunder of feet on the porch and all the other aspiring poets in the class pour inside in a noisy frosted body like a polar expedition. And down the staircase in an oversize squaw dress creaks the poetess.

Who sees Nick and Mira and exclaims, Oh no—love. Not again. Not in my seminar!

MADDIE

Just one thing: *fuori dalle palle.* Get the hell out of my way. That's what all parents need to hear.

It gets on my nerves that they can't figure out that they're old and their lives are over. It annoys me that they can't speak, can't get it to-gether to tolerate each other for one weekend to deliver their only daughter to college, for fuck's sake. Most people's parents are divorced and it's not a big deal. I'm sick of being their messenger girl.

I'm prettier than Mom ever was. And less of a drama queen, less wacky and needy. She has to be told how hot she is every five minutes, which gets pathetic, and she flirts with my guy friends. As for Dad, I see that he's not a prince. No, he's just a dad with a slightly dorky crew cut, and I hate to say it but he's getting one of those pretentious faux British accents. He tries with the Cool Dad stuff and I do think it's awesome that he hung backstage with the Cars. But . . . but . . . but . . .

In the mirror I see a face that's not Reiver, not Ward. A face from anywhere. That's what they did to me: I'm American but European too. I'm neither black nor white. I've seen every episode of *Scooby-Doo* dubbed in Italian, and my idea of hell is tortellini in Boston or Chinese food in Milan.

Lots of my friends are mixed: half French, half Thai; half Russian, half Senegalese. It's cool, it makes you good-looking, and in a funny kind of way nothing can surprise you. Mom says I'm as pragmatic as a forty-year-old. That's just because I know what I want to do: study anthropology, and get married and stay that way. On a continent I choose.

I don't remember when they were together. Just a long time ago, when there was a dark patch spreading everywhere. When I was at the little school near the Colosseum.

But I grew up okay. How is that? It's like my eleventh-grade English teacher used to say when we'd fight in class about why the best stories were the sad ones: that hard times are like sculptor's tools and make meaningful shapes.

And when I think of Mom and Dad, I imagine a weird picture of them: skinny and naked under a stormy sky like two little kids at the beach. It makes me feel protective, and a little superior. My life is different, my Harvard is different.

I have to say, though, that a lot of kids here seem really young. They go on about getting carded and I was already drinking wine when I was eight.

6

ZENIN

Seven forty-five A.M. and Zenin stands in his bathroom shaving and watching a young woman across the river, a tributary of the Adige, that flows underneath his window.

Zenin's bathroom is the size of a squash court, full of alcoves for steaming and washing and massaging and evacuating the body, lined with travertine and oriental rugs on pale carpeting. Gold faucets and a flat-screen TV, and a number of mediocre seventeenth-century Venetian paintings, school of Canaletto, or shithouse school, as his girlfriend the antique dealer calls them. Despite her energetic efforts, the place remains as bland as a hotel suite, the only personal touch a forest of half-used miniature bottles of sample cosmetics, with which Zenin amuses himself by making odd mixtures.

He has eaten his laxative breakfast of caffellatte and stewed pear, and now stands scraping sparse white hairs off of his lean cheeks, with his mind, as usual, running on four distinct tracks. Two of them run in the vast yet hermetic universe of money and product and chance, incomprehensible to all but a few thousand people in the world but as familiar to Zenin as the curve of his own ass. Another absently replays the sorry spectacle of the previous evening's Manchester United–Milan match, when he and his friends wasted time by flying to England to see the Brits make fools of the Italians. And the fourth track is just watching the girl.

Not a pretty girl: the thirty-year-old daughter of the butcher whose shop is half visible in the brick alleyway beyond the weedy green stream. Across the small cobbled bridge where Zenin has installed a watchman to keep Gypsies and Albanian thieves away from his palace. The girl—Maria Grazia, Maria Caterina, some Maria name like that— whom Zenin has watched growing from a stolid ruddy child playing hopscotch on the paving stones to a stolid bleached blonde with a big bottom that stretches out the white work smocks she wears over tracksuit pants and nurse's clogs.

Every morning, with the aid of the butcher, a pale obese melancholic mountain of a man, the girl scrambles up a stepladder to tug open the aluminum shutter that hides realms of veal roasts and lambs' tongues and prosciutto. A graceless ceremony at which Zenin, in his opulence, through a rift in the double layer of swagged Venetian silk that the decorator thought a fitting setting for his nakedness, is faithfully present every morning when he is not traveling. The small scene is somehow linked to his bare mortal body, its long bony limbs growing daily more bristly and puckered with age, and his whole half-contemptuous affection for it.

No one would guess that Zenin, one of the industrial princes whose names sail like galleons through the financial pages, whose products have made this small city famous, that Zenin, who lives swaddled in Gobelins, Savonnerie, and tasteless but lush wall-to-wall carpeting in a Palladian villa purchased cannily in the seventies from the last direct heir in an ancient line that provided the Most Serene Republic with three doges, that Zenin is a voyeur of provincial life.

Yet unconsciously, obsessively he collects these glimpses of the butcher's daughter; of the old men conferring in dialect as they stroll, their caps pulled low over their brick-colored faces; of the old women with cropped hair, white as thistledown, pedaling bicycles with stumpy legs; nuns hurrying from Ospedale San Giuseppe; salesgirls with sunlamp tans and vulgar filmy black stockings, adjusting the brassieres and nightshirts in the window of the underwear shop beyond the butcher; the ancient cobbler who is unchanged from when Zenin was poor; the baker's wife with her necklace of gold coins; university kids on scooters, with their naïve tattoos and piercings on faces as callow as dabs of paste; some girls with such perfection of beauty as to make Zenin swear to himself.

But it isn't desire that drives him. No, it is the sense of place, of himself in the town where he was born and that he has never really left. With the noisy current of its swift brick-bound river that runs from the Dolomites to the Adriatic, the sound of the parish bells of San Carlo and San Tommaso eternally in dispute over the correct hour. The scene of his poverty and shame, where now everybody is richer because of him. Which has become one of the well-heeled small cities where it is said that Italian life is lived at its best. Where the new shopping malls and maxi-stores, with their parking lots and ugly Plexiglas roofs, are relegated to the outside of town. Where the old fish market is now a center for crafts fairs and computer-animation exhibits. And where the old-fashioned profanity-filled dialect spoken by Zenin's father and mother is praised as cultural heritage by eager local leftists.

A town where Zenin is still apart from everything, because that is his pathology: to be a penniless tourist in life, eternally deprived, unable to have anything for himself in any real sense. Though for a long time he has been as rich as a sultan in the Emilio Salgari novels he read as a boy. A billionaire who always feels like a beggar.

Yet still the city in its own way, along with the genius of Italian families and villages, accepts and sustains him. More than pride for an eccentric local tycoon, it is the shrugging Catholic indulgence that finds a place at the table for even madmen and criminals. Zenin, divorced and immoral, living misanthropically in the finest palace in the heart of the old city center, speeding through the narrow streets in his parvenu's Rolls-Royce or one of the less significant cars he adopts when worried about kidnapping, is regarded with the stony loyalty small towns reserve for their own. And his spying on town life is his loving reply.

Only once has he tried to explain this to anyone: to Mira, the American girl. And she looked at him so blankly that he understood that for her he will always be the sum of his travels.

C. 1962 · ZENIN'S MARRIAGE

Takes place in the early sixties, which in northern Italy will soon come to seem like the Middle Ages. A period after the war when mines from the Kesselring Line still dot the battered Veneto countryside and the Mantegna frescoes pulverized by Allied bombs still lie in flecks of colored plaster in the rubble of the Eremitani Church. When the Counts Manzano still occupy the castle on the Alto Sperone and are bowed to in the streets. When a bicycle is riches, and lice-ridden blond children steal bread and die of tuberculosis.

Zenin stands on the cathedral steps in a blizzard of confetti and applause, noisy tears from his crowd of sisters. Beside him, his bride, Cecilia, a provincial heiress and the town beauty. Nineteen, secretly pregnant, tall and stately in a column of satin as white as the marble of the statues at the high altar, her chubby adolescent cheeks flushed through a mask of pancake makeup below fair hair that has been backcombed according to the height of fashion into an airy monument like a Christmas yeast loaf.

A wedding that, though scorned by the nobility, is in some ways the wedding of the year. With an edge of social daring that goes with the reconstruction era. The bride is the only daughter of a canny local magnate whose plastic factories managed to both contract to the Italian Social Republic during the Badoglio confusion and qualify for Marshall Plan reconstruction grants afterward. A great leap for Zenin, the twenty-four-year-old "Tartar" with his primitive cheekbones and flat black eyes. Whose mother who was an eel-catching savage from Chioggia and whose father was a drunken peddler who beat his wife, did worse, they say, with his daughters, and died unmourned on the Russian front.

Yet there is something about Zenin that has impressed people since he was in short pants. Perhaps it is that stony face that hides a rapacious peasant mind and a cold ambition that belies his poorly dressed awkward figure. He is already the first in his family to achieve a university degree. Capped by a thesis that he paid a studious old maid to write, knowing even then that it was all bullshit.

Women feel his ruthlessness and pursue him. When he was ten, the tobacconist's red-haired daughter took him down by the railway embankment one evening during Carnival. Breathing a hot smell of Carnival fried dough in his face. Yanked up her skirt and put his hand on her. As if he didn't already know what was there, with all those girls at home.

By the time he begins to circle around his future wife, he knows exactly how easy it is for him.

So the tall morose youth fixes his single-minded attention on the rich beauty. In the street during the Saturday evening *passeggiata,* at Mass, during the few times a friend manages to wangle him entrance to the *circolo* where the middle-class kids play bridge. People snub him extra hard at the *circolo* because they sense that the distance is fast decreasing between the Tartar and themselves. And the heiress herself, fond of extravagant sentiments that she thinks of as aristocratic, yearning for a great love, comes to him like a bird charmed off a branch.

Her father considers having Zenin shot or horsewhipped, then quiets down when he finds out that she is pregnant like any factory girl—fruit of two Lido afternoons when she evaded cousins and maids to lose her virginity in the cabin of a friend's boat. The rich old man reflects that he could do worse than to have a son-in-law who seems able to work as hard as a mule and—he says privately to himself—to eat grass and shit gold. Better than a dim-witted aristocrat or a small-town playboy. Zenin is a fortune hunter, but one with balls who will make something out of what he gets.

Thus Zenin in one move achieves a beautiful teenage wife, a job, a honeymoon in Rome with a papal audience, and two hundred square meters floored in gleaming Verona marble composite in the most fashionable speculator's brand-new apartment building on the edge of town.

Standing on the church steps amid applause, feeling the corsetlike constriction of his wedding suit, magicked through some connection of his father-in-law from the legendary Zucchoni of Venice, he feels mildly astonished at the ease of his conquest, how it seems that he reached out his hand and grabbed a prize down from the top of the greased pole, what in old village fairs used to be called the *albero della cuccagna*—the Cockaigne, a prize that in the hungry days was usually a bundle of sausages, prosciutti, cheeses, and sweetmeats.

But behind his astonishment is the normal feeling he walks around with all the time. Of something missing. It opens onto a vision that serves at all times to add vastness to the landscape of cornfields and small villages of his world: a black mountain, a black lake that threatens to swallow him. A dark world of things lacking. His prize brightens it not even as much as a lantern or torch would: only as much, perhaps, as a firefly.

Non basta, he is thinking, without exactly forming the words. Not enough.

THE NEWSPAPER VENDOR

One *Gazzettino* and one *Sole Ventiquattro,* that's Zenin. That pimp-faced Portuguese majordomo comes to get the papers even if the old man is away in China. The newsstand is right here in the wall of the palazzo, so the joke is that Zenin should be paying me doorman's wages. I see him rushing back and forth like a bat out of hell in one of his fancy cars, and he always waves. Sometimes he stops by the *edicola* to check what the kids are buying among his promotional collections.

The story goes that he sneaks girls into the house late at night, but the only one I see these days is the signora from Verona, a nice woman, with the patience of a saint. He's not a monster, old Zenin, though they say he drove his wife crazy and then divorced her. My mother-in-law helped sew the wedding dress, and says that nobody had a figure like Zenin's wife back then. The prettiest breasts in the city, she always says. You'd think that would satisfy any man, but not old Zenin.

7

MIRA

───⌒───

A magazine editor from New York sends Mira an e-mail. It begins: "Miranda Ward, I want your life! Oh, to be a writer in Italy!"

The editor, a gay woman who seems to lead a pleasant existence in Chelsea with her partner and child, goes on to propose a piece on the Lovers' Walk of the Cinque Terre, but Mira is mesmerized by the opening lines. Of course she long ago discovered that every American, regardless of age, race, sex, and class, has the same maudlin soft spot for Italy. Street kids and hip-hop magnates believe that Italians are cooler than they are. Hardened travel snobs become humble and pliant when confronted with any hint of regional knowledge outside of Tuscany. The joke among Mira's expatriate friends is that the best thing about living here is coming back to the States and mentioning it.

But rarely has the contrast between cloudland and reality been so glaring as at the present, ten thirty on a wet October night as she sits at her kitchen table surrounded by shopping bags full of cat and dog food, trying to check her e-mail by candlelight. Candlelight because in Mira's beautiful old house—an early Renaissance villa that has belonged for generations to her second husband's family, a house that in Roman brick and slightly crumbling stucco does indeed incarnate the fantasies of magazine editors and anybody else stuck behind a desk in Manhattan—the lighting system begins to strobe whenever it rains.

Electricians come and poke around in the vaulted cellars and shrug, and Mira's husband, Vanni, who like all Italian husbands views his wife as an organic and moral extension of his house, is annoyed with Mira personally about the archaic wiring. Tonight he came home and said, with his usual sarcastic flourish, So, my darling, love of my life, light of my soul, you're up to your old tricks, I see.

Mira just stares at Vanni, who looks pompous and faintly stout in his business suit, his saturnine face glowing like a jack-o'-lantern through the candlelit dark. She thinks, Who is this man?

Her eight- and six-year-old sons are in bed, sullenly pursuing sleep after Mira broke up a battle that began during the blackout when Zoo, the younger, stepped on one of Stefano's customized Lego dragon boats. Stefano called Zoo *pezzo di merda* and socked him, which was when Mira stepped in, but the boys made so much noise that Vanni dashed upstairs to roar at them himself in time-honored paternal fashion, smashed more Lego, and then complained to Mira about the mess on the floor. What is the point of spending money on maids if the house is never in order, he asked, with that plaintive rhetorical intonation that means that he is about to reminisce about the legendary perfection of his Aunt Giusy's household in Cuneo, where the silverware shone like the sun, the linen rivaled Alpine snowfields, and the storeroom was a cornucopia of wild boar prosciutto, dried *chiodini* mushrooms, and ambrosial jams from recondite ancestral recipes.

And at that moment the phone rang and it was Maddie calling from Cambridge to bewail her crush on a sophomore from Yugoslavia. When Mira, with a touch of pedantry, reminded her daughter that Yugoslavia no longer exists and then said that she'd have to call Maddie back because the lights were out, Maddie shouted that Mira only cares about the stupid house, burst into tears, and then hung up.

So Mira, now seated at the kitchen table, feels inclined to pack up the low farce of her existence, and indeed all of Italy, and send it off to the envious editor.

What would be my Lake Isle? My one everlasting dream of *away*? she asks herself. The States, certainly. No children or men. Perhaps a nice cozy lesbian life, not in Manhattan, though. In a snug little upscale suburban condo, with wall-to-wall hemp carpeting and everything ordered online, though occasionally we'd hit the malls. There would be nothing European in our house, not even wine or olive oil. Nothing old at all except perhaps a notable collection of Victorian hair jewelry. Mira loses herself for a second or two in a reverie where instead of hiking the Cinque Terre, she is power walking the nature paths of a gated community with an empathetic companion named Bethany.

She hardly notices that the lights have come back on and that Vanni, quickly, efficiently, the way he can when he wants to, has made himself and her a cup of chamomile tea. When he sets it in front of her—in a cup and saucer, not in a slapdash American mug—she looks at him across a distance of reverie, as if he were a tiny passerby in the background of a television travelogue. And he looks back at her with the amused, forbearing air of truce that Mira knows means love, the long-lasting kind that remains after the fanfares of courtship have died down. In Italy and elsewhere.

It is true that Vanni is familiar with the panorama of Mira's past, the pretty and not so pretty parts. As she is with his. And that somehow, amazing as it seems at this moment, they have accumulated a past of their own. Created this particular world of house and family that is independent of anyone's fantasies.

Look here, Mira says, indicating the computer. There's a woman who wants to take my place.

Her husband leans over to study the screen, propping his chin comfortably on the crown of Mira's head and running his hand down the back of her jeans.

È carina? he asks. Is she good-looking?

1985 · IMPRESSIONS

Cities are like clothes, Mira writes in one of her first magazine articles from Italy. *Each has its own style, its own fabric and weight, each transforms you. . . . The fabric of Rome is heavy, rich and coarse at the same time, like a mixture of sackcloth and brocade. It weighs on you, the constant mixture of old and new, spendthrift beauty and grotesque ugliness. It rubs away any delicate illusions a foreigner might have, any Puritan squeamishness. Pasolini, the latest great profane poet of Rome, writes,* "La bellezza eccessiva di questa sovrapposizione de stili è un autentico shock al sistema nervoso"—"*The excessive beauty produced by this juxtaposition of styles is a genuine shock to the nervous system.*"

What Mira doesn't write is that she hates Rome. Feels a visceral resistance to it, as your body does when it is trying to fight off a disease. A fever that gives everything a red-tinted haze, that makes the tawny battered monuments in their magnificence feel like predators, just waiting, considering.

She writes nothing about it but feels it all the time as she and Nick shape their new life, which is that of all prosperous young expatriates. Working, taking their morning cappuccino and *cornetto* at the neighborhood bar, diligent with their Italian lessons, wandering the backstreets of the Ghetto, deciphering odd inscriptions and eating pizza in Testaccio with new friends who are all handsome young people like they are. American and Italian, from the banks and multinational companies, from the embassy, from the academy, from the Food and Agriculture Organization, funded by leading universities, farmed out by indulgent rich families.

She feels it as she and Nick walk home hand in hand late at night, perhaps from an outdoor movie at the Baths of Caracalla, a hilariously dubbed American movie they never would have seen at home, giggling about bad Italian rock and roll, their footsteps echoing in the narrow cobblestone streets, feeling that they own the city. Except that something in Mira tells her that lovers can own New York, can own Paris, but not Rome.

Other scenes she doesn't write about:

An old woman with thick black-penciled eyebrows and garish bleached hair is buying a tiger-striped brassiere with cutout nipples in a lingerie shop on Via Nazionale and having a good laugh with the saleswoman. My husband loves me in this stuff! she cackles. Keeps the whores away!

At a party on someone's terrace in Parioli, where everybody else— an international crowd of junior staff from the embassy and journalists—is wearing jeans, a blond Italian girl arrives in a silver cocktail dress. People whisper that she is a university student and the official mistress of a famous right-wing politician twice her age. She kisses the hostess, drinks a glass of wine, laughs and flirts. She is Mira's age, hard-eyed, with beautiful skin and an odd air of dignity. Mira studies her covertly, wondering, What does she know?

A cluster of African girls, stewardesses, actresses, students, friends of a Senegalese friend of Mira's, sit around a kitchen table in a Monteverde apartment, complaining about their Italian boyfriends. The infidelity of Italians, worse than Africans; their vanity; their obsession with sodomy; their lies; their awful families. Listening to this, Mira begins to feel strangely left out. She asks why they stay with these terrible men, and they tell her that Italians, when they are good, are the best. And they're not racist, they add. They're more obsessed with your being foreign than your being black. They tell her all this in gentle, patient voices, like someone explaining the facts of life to a child.

Mira visits a yoga class one afternoon in a palazzo near the Lungotevere that seems cavernous and gloomy, even for Rome. The instructress, a spry upper-class Englishwoman sitting cross-legged on a needlepoint rug, tells her that they are in Palazzo Cenci, where Beatrice Cenci murdered her father after he raped her. Can't you feel the blood and incest in the air? says the woman, smiling, gesturing around her living room.

And indescribable is the street world, the casual resonance between art and life. Botticelli angels in groups of high school girls, young Caravaggio toughs doing wheelies in suburban squares. How Mira begins to exist within the net of dialogue between men and women on the street, the endless conversation that goes on in every Latin country but has in Rome a touch of raucous fantasy. Mira gets used to attracting notice, to being called *mulatta, brasiliana, cubana,* or just *bellissima.*

She craves it and loathes herself for it, and could never explain it to Nick, though she used to tell him everything in New York.

No, there's a secret between her and every man on the street, a guilty secret connected to her mad escapade on the boat with Zenin. Which she sees now, with shame and fear, as a seizure, an outbreak of delirium, an early warning as to what can happen if she doesn't defend herself.

So Mira can't write or talk about these things. Or about the fact that Zenin, once a certain interval has passed, still calls her from time to time. With no explanations, no further propositions, but as if he had a certain right to call. Just a few minutes of idle chat that she knows she shouldn't tolerate. Yet she does.

She doesn't admit to herself that she is creating an alternate world in her imagination, separate from her official life, and from Nick. A labyrinth of tunnels and evasions buried so deep that Mira believes she can construct her love, her marriage, over it, the way accumulating centuries have laid down layers of streets and dwellings over the catacombs and mithraea of Rome.

THE LITERARY WIFE

We know the Reivers because we've lived in Montevecchio forever and we get to know every American who passes through Rome who has anything to do with writing. Gore Vidal calls my husband the official greeter and majordomo of the academy, which would have been a major insult coming from anyone but Gore, but the fact is that there have been evenings when I'm making *trenette* with pesto for Nadine Gordimer and Giorgio Bassani slips in the door and starts playing Transformers with our son, and we've had poets unwashed and washed and starched—Rome fellows and fellahin, as my husband likes to say, but there's no use playing at names, because it would be like a phone book, and I am keeping a diary, even if it will all be in the Novel, when my husband finds time to get back to it. But the Reivers are a pretty young couple, who look like they need a nanny. They tend to toddlerize each other—nicknames, playtime, cuddles—but I can tell it won't last because marriage, a long marriage, takes something different. I'm Polish Catholic, and I know that someone has to break their back and give way, and it really should be the woman, even if it is unfashionable to say it. This girl doesn't have it; maybe because she is colored, or black I should say, but I honestly don't think race has anything to do with it. She's just arrogant, full of herself without even knowing it, and at the same time horrifically ignorant, so that you just want to take her out to the kitchen and say, Honey, get your basket and go to market and learn from the old Italian ladies the way I did when we got here in the sixties. But she wouldn't get it. I remember her sitting at the table one night when some writer, a real one, was here and saying that she wanted to write a trashy novel. When we asked why, she said she wanted money and power, just right out like that, just to annoy everyone. And Nick Reiver just laughed and egged her on. I remember thinking that she's the kind of girl who gets in trouble in Italy.

8

ZENIN

2004 · GREEN EYES

It's twelve thirty in Milan, and Bocconi University students are stuffed as tight as a bunch of asparagus around the counter of the bar, waving receipts, clamoring for pizza, focaccia, puff pastry stuffed with *crema pasticciera,* all the carbohydrates necessary to keep young brains alert through the steely verbal cross-examinations that push them high through the ranks of the elite. Outside, streetcars strike blue sparks from wires in the rain, and inside is a cacophony of voices and cell-phone themes. Zenin sits at a corner table with an empty coffee cup in front of him, eyes scanning the crowd, occasionally contemplating some rain-soaked student beauty, but obviously waiting. Waiting with eagerness, with emotion, but for whom?

Ciao papà! Only in Italy would a twenty-year-old male college student shout out a greeting to a parent so joyously, shove his way through a crowd, and embrace his father with such thunderous energy right in front of his friends and classmates. Even so, the sight of his son—for it is his youngest child and only son, Daniele—has an extreme effect on Zenin. The blood rises in his face and the expression in his eyes, reflected in the steamy bar mirror, is beseeching, rapturous, almost dog-like in its adoration.

The fact is that he would do anything for Daniele. Whose birth and childhood were so tentative, dark, and confused, born as he was from a mother Zenin has never wanted to marry. Such was his cold fury at Tere, his former girlfriend from Udine, for trapping him into fatherhood once more, that he refused to see Daniele until the baby was five months old. But when he finally held the squirming baby in his arms and the child looked up at him with a sudden, huge toothless grin, Zenin felt a slow explosion of an emotion so intense that at first in his ignorant way he confused it with sex. But it was only love at first sight, strangest of all emotions to Zenin, that stranger in his own life. And then, so inexpertly that it seemed that the action should have been accompanied by a rusty creaking noise, Zenin smiled back.

Years later, Zenin sits watching Daniele, with strong white teeth, wolf down a focaccia stuffed with sliced tomato and cheese, sitting straight and tall as a lance in his quilted jacket and ridiculous oversize rapper's jeans. His young hawk's face eager and fresh beneath his fashionable Marine-style haircut, the green eyes of his Udinese mother brilliant and severe beneath his bristling straight dark brows. Zenin sees his own face there, his face bare of any suspicion, shame, hunger, ambition, as if he has been given a second chance to live in the world and enjoy it. *Un bravo ragazzo,* as everyone says. Well mannered, unspoiled—not like some of these little turds with rich daddies—getting on decently at school, has spent three seasons skiing for the Monte Rosa team. A son good almost beyond the hopes of any father. Except for what Zenin knows already: that Daniele is not forceful enough, not bloody-minded enough, not enough of a monster, perhaps, to take on all his father is going to leave him. And why the fuck should he be?

A car and driver are waiting for Zenin around the corner in Via Bligny, with the head of Zenin's own patent office already quietly fuming and looking at his watch, the big shots at the Camera di Commercio already expecting them down in the smoggy corridors of power near the Duomo. But Zenin sits as grateful as a lover for these snatched moments between Daniele's lectures, listening to him chatter about his projects. The Mille Miglia regatta from Trapani up to Trieste. A motorcycle trek with friends across the Libyan desert. All fabulous, *mitico,* except that Daniele's girl hates both ideas and they're fighting about it.

Zenin frowns. He's not impressed with his son's *fidanzata,* a prettyish half-Austrian daughter of a minor noble family from Vicenza, a girl a little too plump and serious for Zenin's taste. He wants to slap his son on the back, say something paternal and risqué, make a normal joke, the kind he'd make to any of his friends, to the effect that women, the bitches, are good for only one thing, but as usual his son awes him into circumspection.

He settles for making a clumsy joke about not getting married and settling down too soon, and the boy, unexpectedly serious, replies, But I could, Papa. I'm crazy in love. *Sono innamorato pazzo.* This is the first time I ever felt like this.

And Zenin feels something seize up in his chest, so that he wonders with his usual hypochondria if this is it, if he will end up a leaden corpse of an old man stretched out shamefully in this place of the young. He is tempted to phone his friend, the head of cardiology at the Umanitas Clinic. But then, looking at his son's shining eyes, he understands that it's only jealousy.

1985 · UNA BRAVA RAGAZZA

There comes a time, dear fellow, when chasing pussy just isn't enough, remarks Zenin's oldest and best friend, Macaco.

It's a May evening a couple of decades before Zenin sits listening to his son talk about love, and the two friends are driving through sunset fields to dinner in the hills above Asolo. Knights errant leaving the walled city in Zenin's Rolls-Royce—or at least Don Quixote and Sancho Panza. Zenin drives, a bit self-conscious about the stares the car draws along the country roads, while Macaco has propped his short legs up on the dashboard, his tuft of thinning blond hair standing up straight over his round impish face, which wears an air of resolute nonchalance. His name isn't really Macaco, but everyone has called him that ever since the priest in catechism class ordered him to stop behaving like a macaque monkey, and he even signs his newspaper columns with the nickname. The class was where he met Zenin and first made the tall gloomy kid in the fraying short pants laugh. He's been doing it ever since.

Now Macaco clasps his hands behind his head, settles back into the deep leather seat, and continues. Pay attention, Zenin. When this solemn moment comes—usually it's a few years after you've been separated and have been fucking around like crazy—then it's the moment of the nice girl. A good girl from a good family. *Una brava ragazza.* Not the only girl, of course. But an important girl for you.

They pass a battered brick shrine at a crossroads, the scene of some miracle or accident, where an old woman pauses on her bicycle for a minute to stare at the vision of the long gleaming green car. The few other cars on the small road move respectfully to the side as Zenin flashes through. In front of them, the road winds up into the darkening woods and vineyards.

Who is she? asks Zenin. Your cousin? What'd she pay you?

Macaco lazily tells Zenin to go back into his mother's belly the way he came out. It's a funny obscene expression in dialect, which makes Zenin shout with laughter. Zenin feels good, riding up into the cool rising damp of the spring hills, the plain below them filling with lights. The economic miracle is in full swing, and he has just set up a promotional deal with Mondadori that he knows in his bones is the affair of a lifetime.

Dinner is at a roadside inn on the outskirts of Conigliano, a place run by two old humpbacked sisters, where hunters used to go to fill up on polenta and sausage and the insipid but powerful *prosecco* of the area. Since then, rich people on their way to the mountains have made a cult of noisy dinners under the crocheted lampshades, swapping salty jokes with the sisters, who have added an ugly aluminium annex to the place.

The *brava ragazza* whom Macaco mentioned is there, of course, concealed in a thicket of mutual friends. She's Tere, short for Maria Teresa, a professor's daughter from Udine, not exactly Zenin's type, but with tanned, sporty good looks and large shallow-set green eyes that look both surly and vulnerable. The rest of the crowd is the usual mix of small-town playboys, the thirtyish breed who still live with their parents, and tennis-playing middle-class girls working languidly through ten-year university degrees. They are in awe of Zenin but at the same time despise him for his low origins, which his fortune is not yet quite vast enough to obscure. Zenin, a slippery bastard, has fucked several of the girls once, quickly, and they would all like to marry him and civilize his money, but it is clear that he's not going to be caught. Not a second time. Not with two daughters and his beautiful former wife (daughter of the *notaio* and the first divorced woman in their city) going around calling him a devil with an icy hell for a heart. But he must not be allowed to roam free, bestowing all that money on foreign models and Brazilian dancers. So tribal consensus has chosen Tere not as a sacrificial lamb but as a sort of lightning rod.

And they sit around the big table in a light that the crocheted lampshades brighten into a thick yellow glaze, eating not polenta on that warm evening but cold bean soup, and drinking *prosecco* until the women—pretty Veneto blondes, most of them—grow as flushed as courtesans in a Longhi painting. There is talk about unrest in Bosnia, just a few hundred miles past the Dolomites, which quickly shifts to talk of football and Formula One and the newest Spielberg movie followed by a high-flown discourse by Macaco on erotic friendship, which he illustrates with the story of the nun and the nearsighted hooker.

As they leave, Zenin invites Tere to come with him and some friends for a weekend in the Pontine Islands in his boat. She pushes back her hair with a tanned wrist and accepts in a light tone, but Zenin sees an avid flash in her eyes, and he likes it. He likes her being a part of this sporty, clubby group, and he likes the provincial greed in her that makes him feel at home. Perhaps Macaco is right and it is time for a nice girl.

MACACO

Let the small minds call me Zenin's toady, or pet Macaco, ass-kisser, *leccaculo*; the fact is I'm his only real friend. I was his friend before he had a cent, when we were both boys and my mother told me to keep away from him because he had bedbug bites suppurating on his legs. My family was a family of lawyers and we even have noble connections, and Zenin's family was trash, the father a drunk who beat his wife and probably messed with the daughters the way peasants did back then. Even then though there was something in the Tartar, and I felt proud for being able to winkle a smile out of such a sourpuss. I used to give him my *Tex* and *Diabolik* comics, and even my Salgari adventure books, though he isn't much for reading. He never reads my column on culture and sport in *Il Gazzettino,* and I've never bothered to tell him about the novel of provincial mores I am writing. But he does listen to my pearls of wisdom on how to enjoy life. Because the poor fellow really has a blind spot there—Musil's *The Man Without Qualities* in that one area. So I taught him the parvenu circuit of Regine's and Castel and Porto Cervo and Formula One, but also offbeat things like going to country *liscio* dance places or visiting the crazy old Marchese Dell'Olio who has a room in his Friuli castle with twenty bathtubs in it. Of course Zenin always pays for the dinners, the trips, the girls. He's the one with the money. But I've never asked him for a loan. Never had to—everyone knows whose friend I am.

9

NICK

2004 · A POSTCARD

Nick writes on a postcard to Maddie:

Dear First Daughter,

No comparisons, please! You may recognize the battered stone fellow on the front: Pasquino, one of the Roman godparents who watched over your toddler days. As always, he is stuck all over with papers scribbled with political doggerel. Your sisters call him Ape Man just like you did, but all the documents make your old dad think far too much about the office. We're here for a night on a whistle-stop half-term tour—Pompeii, Venice, Assisi, et al.—and the girls want to see where you were born. I think they're disappointed that we didn't live in ruins like the Forum cats. For me, that time seems as lost as old Pasquino's heyday. A peculiar pair of sandals that the womenfolk assure me you will understand will be arriving in the mail. Midterm news? Love from all of us and especially from Ancient Dad

The postcard is a small colored rectangle in his hand. Sitting at the desk in his bedroom at the Hassler, he feels like a god holding a portal onto another world. In the sitting room of the suite, his daughters Eliza and Julia, seven and four, are watching television and bouncing on the couch. Dhel comes out of the bathroom running a wooden comb through long wet strands of hair, her face mysteriously perfect and dry. Beautiful. Half Vietnamese, half Swiss, with a terse mid-Atlantic accent from a lifetime of diplomatic schools. And a touching dignity in her bearing, like a kid on best behavior.

Very Baedeker, she says of the hotel rooms, heavily upholstered, filled with nineteenth-century mahogany and engravings of antiquities and the general atmosphere of steam-heated comfort that spoke to the hearts of the stout Teutonic hoteliers who gave the hotel its name.

Perfect for a *cinq à sept,* he says, grabbing her towel-covered ass and pulling her toward him. As he does—and their heads turn automatically, parentally, toward their daughters in the next room—the question flies through his mind as to whether Mira ever came here with that scumbag. At various times in the past, he has imagined her in every hotel in Rome. An image of her face contorted with illicit pleasure in the Victorian gloom. A thought no sooner there than gone, a shadow of a bird. And he is holding his young second wife, who has skin as poreless as a child's, and who arranged this trip with her usual efficiency because she wants, in an ingenuous way, to overwrite his history with that of his new life.

She loves him and hates the thought of his having a past. As he is jealous of her old boyfriends, of lecherous City boys and the Oxbridge cybergeek artists she works with now. Yet what's the point of it all?

The engraving over the bed shows a cowherd napping against a funerary monument on the Appia Antica, the cow placidly pulling grass from the rotten masonry. What is that Browning poem, "Two in the Campagna?" ". . . memories that should be out of season, with the hot blood of youth, of love crossed long ago . . ."

What struck him while touring Herculaneum, three days ago, was how some pragmatic municipal gardener had planted the courtyards of the shattered villas with apple and pomegranate trees. All bearing fruit in the ruins.

It's not been hard to avoid Rome, a financial backwater, all these years. To avoid Italy. His family vacations on Formentera, on Nantucket, in Thailand, in Devon.

But now his little girls, almond-eyed angels, are splitting their sides over the Simpsons dubbed in Italian. From Piazza di Spagna down the Spanish Steps rises the noise of the crowd of shoppers and tourists, like the roar of far-off breakers. And he can smell the smell of Rome, unchanged, creeping in through the closed windows, through the hotel walls themselves. The smell of car exhaust, of frying, of a million perfumes applied daily over centuries by a vain populace, of sewage, of baking bread, of the dust of martyrs, of hope and despair.

And the postcard lies on the desk.

He hates this fucking town.

Come on, he says. Let's go hit Via Condotti. I haven't wasted enough money on you girls. And then we'll go eat some exploded artichokes the way they do it only here in the Eternal City.

And we didn't throw coins in the fountain yet, Daddy, says Eliza.

Yeah, come on, ladies, says Nick. Let's go be tourists.

1985 · TERRA DEGLI UOMINI

Guarda queste. Look at these.

The fruit-and-vegetable woman is not old but astonishingly ugly, with a black fright wig of a perm, a squat powerful body, and a bristly cragged face of almost North African swarthiness. She has paused in weighing eggplant for Nick, disappeared into the gloomy onion-scented fastness of her tiny shop on the corner of Via dei Serpenti, and emerged with her hand full of photographs.

Look—pictures of my daughter. Her accent is thick Roman, hardly different from dialect in all its harsh jangle, and her eyes in her dark weathered face shine an unnerving clear blue. For months, she has been selling big mottled *cuore di bue* tomatoes and broccoli rabe and figs and lemons and chopped-up fresh minestrone greens to Nick, who enjoys stopping by on his way home from work, to fill a list sketched out for him by Mira in the mornings. He enjoys the woman's looks, her speech that he is taking some trouble to untangle, the way he is gradually learning the back streets of Trastevere and Monte Mario.

But he hasn't thought that the woman might have been observing him as well, that he for her might also symbolize some new exotic landscape.

Now, as she slides the pictures into his hands, not snapshots but black-and-white prints that look almost professional, he gets a glimpse of how he must seem to her. Tall with his straight fair hair and a face that everyone in his office tells him looks as American as a baby's behind. In a Wall Street suit badly cut by Roman standards but made of expensive fabric. With the briefcase and the jaunty little sports car out front.

The photos show a very young blond girl, perhaps seventeen or eighteen, heavily made up, with lined, glossy lips. She is posed in a variety of conventional studio shots, in evening dresses and in bathing suits, her thick wavy mass of hair pulled up dramatically or flowing backward in a wind machine. It seems impossible that she could have come out of the old stump of the vegetable woman, but the girl stares out at him with the same clear eyes, with mischievous provocation. She is very beautiful, and in the last two photographs is bare-breasted, her pale nipples as round and precise as two coins.

Hot, thinks Nick, blushing slightly. *Bellissima,* he says, handing back the pictures to the fruit seller.

Keep them, she says.

No, no. No thanks.

She's gorgeous, isn't she? says the fruit seller, who is blushing herself, as mothers do when talking of a passionately adored child. A curious sight on that old, dark, coarse face. She wants to be a model.

Well, she should be.

Lei potrebbe aiutarla. You could help her, says the fruit seller. Looking at Nick as at a schoolboy who is particularly slow on the uptake.

Me? Nick is genuinely astonished.

You are an important man. A businessman. An American.

Always comes down to this, he thinks. Even buying vegetables for dinner.

Nick Reiver disapproves of himself. Not of his tranquil fuck-the-world inner self. Of himself as part of his tribe: the ruddy WASP freemasonry of men who know his father, who sit in Boston and Providence boardrooms with his uncles, who run the Ida Lewis Yacht Club, who burned the children of Cambodia, and whose toothy sons and daughters took up useful space in all the schools he ever went to. The Men in Charge, whose establishment power his father rejected in his own waffling dilettante career, if it can be called that, as small-town newspaperman and unpublished novelist, but freely took advantage of when it came to getting his sons into clubs and colleges.

Nick is under no illusions about what he bought into when he went to work in finance. He likes the money—money which was in short supply in the underheated rooms of the beautiful shabby Federal house in Little Compton, where he grew up. Given a choice, he might have tried to be a writer, but he has already been witness to his father's gentle bohemian failure. And so he watched with a benign detachment through the sixties and seventies as his rich older cousins took off for Maoist communes or teepees in Maine. Knowing that his role is to make up for a lack, to provide. Yet he hopes that somewhere underneath he is different from the men in charge and longs for people to understand this. He tried to demonstrate it to Mira's family and was amazed by their stony indifference. And the same happened earlier with the kids he tutored in the Providence Head Start project.

But Italy, as no place he has ever been, pushes Nick to act like one of the lords of the earth.

At the bank, in the group of junior account executives and vice presidents where he is the sole foreigner, the band of handsome full-blooded young males from all the provinces of Italy, who go out to the beach and the stadium in a happy pack like a group of young hunting dogs, he finds that men his age who happen to be rich and noble are pleased about it. If they aren't rich, they are striving cheerfully to marry an heiress. Nowhere does he see the pangs of liberal conscience that tormented boys like him in prep school and college.

There is no idea that there is something wrong with being on top, that one has to pay something back. Or at least be modest and guilty. In Italy, you can even, it seems, be both leftist and a happy snob.

Everybody, even the secretaries, even the men who wash the marble office steps, seems to feel that all is right with the world as Nick sweeps by in his suit and drives off in his shiny little car.

It is a corrupt feeling for this young American in Rome. There is an element of temptation in it, for him just to relax and be what he is.

Of course he says nothing about this to Mira.

But the atmosphere is beginning to work on him.

As now, in the shadowy little store, in the autumnal perfume of the grapes and cardoons and chestnuts that are just coming in from the *campagna*.

My daughter would be happy to meet you at any time, says the fruit seller.

She's lovely, certainly, but I'm a married man. The lame phrase sounds like Doris Day even in Italian, he thinks.

The woman bursts out in a hoarse laugh that shows her strong yellow teeth. *Che cazzo c'entra?* What the hell has that got to do with it? she demands.

THE FRUIT SELLER

And he goes off swinging his bag like a kid whose mother sent him to run an errand. Why do they all walk like babies, these Americans and Englishmen? I see the tourists going around wagging their big asses with their short pants and big white sport shoes looking like real cretins. Like they have no hair on their balls, and that's half the reason when they blunder in here I charge them double for rotten stuff that nobody with any sense would touch. But this boy is as polite and handsome as an angel, a rich man's son, obviously, bless him. He could be the twin of my daughter, *una ragazza d'oro,* a golden girl, even if she's too much of a fine lady to wreck her hands hauling crates and loading up the van with those sons of bitches down at the *mercati generali* depot at three in the morning. I do everything, I tell her, ever since her sodding father took up with that bitch who sells rags down at Porta Portese. And I'm as strong as a mule; I don't mind it, as long as she gets her beautician certificate. But the silly little cow wants to be an actress, and now we have the boyfriend hanging around all day, a worthless Sardinian who calls himself a theatrical agent, but who looks like a pimp, I tell him to his face. If she goes off with trash like that she could end up on the street or sold to some Arab or in one of those filthy films. So I do what I can to help her out. In this life, there's nothing

else, you need a *raccomandazione* to get ahead. You need someone rich
and important, a sponsor.

Shame that this boy is too young to understand. But *pazienza*. He'll
be a man when he learns a thing or two, I can see that. When he
leaves, I hand him his bag and say, *Sua moglie però dovrebbe prendersi
più cura di Lei*. Your wife should take better care of you. A gentleman
like you should not shop for vegetables.

10

MIRA

Toss the pods in the washtub, the artist says, nudging forward a big galvanized tin. It is a Sunday morning in May, and Mira is one of nine guests shelling peas in a castle courtyard. Busy leveling a mountain of waxy green pods among the coffee cups and remains of breakfast focaccia on a stone table shaded by a huge mulberry tree. In front of them unroll the budding vineyards of Monferrato. Behind rise two medieval towers restored in garish nineteenth-century brick, an arch wreathed in roses leading to high dim rooms encrusted with frayed opulence. Enthroned in the center are the lord and lady of the domain, an elderly pair of children's-book illustrators—white-haired, leftist, and famous. The guests are mainly literary and artistic Milanese in linen trousers and expensive snub-toed country shoes. Friends of Mira's husband, Vanni, who comes from the same kind of well-heeled bookish background. They exclaim over the freshness of the peas, which they will eat for lunch with homemade tagliatelle. Their children run screeching among the new cyclamens and old beech leaves of an overgrown allée, playing in and out of a rusted old camper propped up there, and Mira feels a wing of boredom brush her mind. She loves Vanni but has grown weary of the cloud-cuckoo-land, of these gatherings where he is in his element, weekends of political chatter and rustic pursuits, where the men are all terrible intellectual flirts and their beautiful emancipated wives trade lore on artisanal mozzarella or buckwheat pasta made by monks.

It was on a weekend like this, over ten years ago, at somebody's country house outside Lucca, that Mira first met Vanni, divorced, childless, ten years older than she. A lawyer with a snuffly upper-class Piedmontese accent and a pair of hooded gray eyes that could be cold and magisterial or as warm as a boy's. She was enthralled by his mixture of frivolous wit and obvious thunderstruck lust for her, as well as a kind of expansiveness that from the beginning seemed to propose not simply a love affair but a life together. A happy crowded existence that has allowed her to sink unexpected roots into a country where she had once felt like the heroine of a melodrama.

Still, the fact remains that she now finds these gatherings extraordinarily tedious. Just one of the small, sometimes inflammatory differences in taste that, it is said, add spice to marriage.

Already the chatter of her husband's friends around the table mingles the arcana of kitchen gardens with the usual scatological jokes about presidents and prime ministers. The details of the latest CIA-Mossad conspiracy. She has already heard the word *egemonia*—hegemony. Vanni says it, his voice grown playfully didactic as he gestures to make his point to a pretty museum directress with earrings like little chandeliers.

Soon, thinks Mira, she will have to pretend to check up on her perfectly contented sons. Or hide in the bathroom with her emergency book, *A Short Walk in the Hindu Kush*. How many bathrooms in run-down castles and beautifully restored farmhouses has she escaped to to read through tedious afternoons and evenings of politics? Castle bathrooms all look the same, like bathrooms in an Edwardian girls' school, with clunky English porcelain knobs and worn mahogany seats. Vanni doesn't ask anymore where she disappears to, just waggles his eyebrows like Groucho Marx when she returns.

Someone asks their host about ghosts in the castle. He admits to only one manifestation, a supernatural tug on his shirttail when he was digging in the old midden heap. And he was happy, he says, because it meant that there is something else. That he will meet his wife in the afterworld. His great love. He says it simply as his wife beams at him. Forty-seven years since they found each other, he says. Since they met as students clutching their portfolios in the offices of Einaudi. Mira looks at them, white-haired, like twins, almost sexless. Their adoration, their marriage, is legendary. Childless, they work together in adjoining studios in the Navigli district of Milan, nurturing a talented young crew of graphic designers who help them create the literary and television adventures of Leonardo, the plump pacifist hedgehog who has made them famous.

The host leaves the table for a minute, disappears into the kitchen garden, and returns with a handful of raspberries that he places ceremoniously in front of his wife. The first of the season, he announces, and the guests burst into spontaneous applause. You have to make a wish! someone shouts. Mira notices that, faced with all this connubial bliss, the younger husbands and wives avoid looking at each other. As she shields her glance from Vanni.

She zips open another pea pod, thinking, Well, these two old darlings found their work and they found their mate. That's what people are supposed to do in the world—not fumble with trial and error like most of us poor slobs. And, if you're lucky, I guess you end up in a castle, in the arms of your childhood sweetheart.

But then she remembers something she saw earlier during a tour of the castle. Upstairs in the garret that is remodeled into a gallery, a display of small ceramic statues modeled by the wife. The one art form she does without her husband. Twisted and frightening, real gargoyles. There is a small blue-glazed statue of a woman wound around with three serpents, her mouth opened in anguish or glee, it is impossible to tell.

1985 · WHAT THE CARDS SAY

Ma hai due uomini. You have two men, *ma petite.*

The fortune-teller, like many Italian ladies of a certain age, likes to interlard her conversation with genteel tag ends of French. But her voice as she studies the Tarot cards on the table is level, diagnostic, pitiless as that of a headmistress or hospital matron. She is Mira's neighbor and friend, an agoraphobic Bolognese gentlewoman of sixty, divorced and abandoned, who ekes out a living giving Italian lessons in her shadowy flat whose gold-flocked wallpaper is peeling in the corners, and what furniture remains unsold swathed in ghostly flowered sheets. Her face is that of a saint hooked on morphine: penciled eyebrows on a high waxen brow, thin gray hair pulled up into a grisette's knot, a huge pair of black eyes with a rim of white between the pupil and the lower lid that give them a deliquescent languor, an erotic victimized spirituality. She is rarely seen in the palazzo courtyard or the neighborhood, only as a shadowy figure in a dressing gown late in the sultry Roman summer afternoons, moving with a hose among her jungle of oversize balcony plants.

Nick calls her Madame S., for Eliot's Madame Sosostris, and gives her a wide berth as every sensible man does with his wife's loony friends. But Mira looks forward to the twice-a-week conversation sessions where she trades English for Italian, and readings of Leopardi and Manzoni have been swiftly abandoned for an exchange of life stories, and, of course, the cards. The Tarot pack has back designs that are almost obliterated and yellowed dirty edges so worn that they remind Mira of the hollowed marble steps of the old churches she has taken to visiting daily in the center of Rome. Her friend's hands, long-fingered, spotted with cooking burns over arthritic knuckles, are the color of church candles; they move over the cards with a gambler's ease, but also with a kind of wincing delicacy.

Twice, the cards have revealed small true things about Mira's life, before the older woman chuckles and sweeps them away to pour out the weak Ceylon tea that Mira suspects she lives on.

But today she pauses and says it. Two men. I saw it in the cards twice before, but I thought there was a mistake. But it is here again. *Gli Amanti, La Torre, e Il Diavolo.* The Lovers, the Tower and The Devil. With one swollen finger she taps the cards that, in the green gloom of the plants covering the windows, have the crude faded colors of the Sunday comics Mira read as a child.

If you mean a man who's my friend, besides Nick, I have several, Mira says slowly. Everybody my age does. In America.

You know what I mean, petite. There is a man sniffing around you, besides your husband, who is not a friend. Oh no, not friendly at all. In fact, he is a demon.

Mira doesn't scoff or laugh. In fact she feels a chill, though it is a hot May day. Feels the hair on her arms stand up like it does before a storm. There's nobody like that, she says. Only a man who calls me once in a while. Very rarely, once every few weeks. A man I met on a plane.

Italian?

Italian.

Mira says his name, and the older woman slowly folds her hands in a small arch over the cards and looks at her appraisingly. On the wall behind her hangs her one remaining painting: a vile portrait of Madame S. as a young wife, a showy Mediterranean beauty with rose-bud lips, a huge cantilevered bosom in aqua satin, vulgarly abundant falling curls, and the same drugged martyr's eyes. The painted young face and the ruined sixty-year-old face both regard Mira, as different as life and death. He's very rich, says Madame S. A moneybags. I see his commercials on television. Did you sleep with him?

Of course not! Another prickle goes through Mira as she recalls like a shameful dream her mad behavior on the boat, her madness in going there.

That is your good fortune. You must never have anything more to do with him. He is very dangerous for you. It is not a harmless flirtation.

Awkwardly and defiantly, Mira says there's no problem, that she only had lunch with him once, that she never expects to hear from him again, that she never thinks about him—a fib, this, because she does think about Zenin, wonders about him, when she sees Italian men on the street—that she loves Nick, which is true.

Madame S. smiles, as women always smile when they talk about Nick, then looks serious. Your husband is a boy, she says. You are both too young for your ages, but he is a boy. If you get involved with this man, it will kill him. Don't make that face—I don't mean *kill* literally. I mean destroy something important.

If Mira were older, she would tell Madame S. not to be ridiculous. But she sits staring down at the spotty linen tablecloth the color of aloes and knows it is all true. And she blurts out: *È troppo buono.* He's too good, Nick. Sometimes I feel like I was put on earth to hurt him. I even wrote it in my diary. Isn't that terrible?

Worse than thinking it is doing it. But you can choose not to. You must never see this man again, never talk to him. What does he say to you?

Mira giggles with a touch of schoolgirl conceit. He teases me and asks me to come away with him. To a different place each time. To the Aeolian Islands. To the Seychelles.

Balle, says the older woman, with a crispness that belies her portentous expression. Do you know that expression? It's a vulgar word for nonsense. He must be very weak to have to impress you like that. Weak but ruthless. I see it in the cards. And you are a silly girl for listening. What do you do all day?

I write, I study Italian, and I explore the city. And at night we go out. It's enough.

It's idleness—dangerous idleness. You are young, pretty, married with no children, no problems of money, nothing to tie you to the earth. Madame S.'s voice is clear of envy, but suddenly a shade fainter. And you will hear from that man again, I can guarantee that. He is the kind who never lets go of anything he wants, not even after years. And there is something in you that he wants.

He can have any woman he likes—models—

He can have prostitutes of various kinds, but a girl like you is harder than you think for a man like that to find. And the more I warn you, the more the idea interests you. I can tell. What a pity you're not a Catholic! But you can still pray to the Virgin for protection. And it may be that you will have a child soon, and that will put a stop to it. She gathers up the Tarot cards in one snap. Perhaps.

Later, when they exchange kisses and Mira is about to dart across the courtyard to her own apartment, the older woman adds, Don't ignore what I said. There is only one word for falling into the hands of that man: *l'abisso.* You can't guess what that means? She adds with a surprisingly mischievous flash of her black eyes. It's part of your lesson. Go find your dictionary!

And Mira, at home in her own beautiful apartment, where the

evening sunlight is falling in dusty rays on the carved and gilded furniture that isn't hers, obediently goes to the dictionary. *Abisso,* she finds: abyss.

MADAME S.

When I was eighteen back in Bologna, my parents married me off to a notary nearly three times my age, so I know all about hell in marriage. My husband was social-climbing Roman scum, a pig who could only have marital relations in perverted ways. *À chacun son goût!* He set me up in this apartment, filled it with Luigi Seidici and Napoleonic furniture got from God knows what black-market thievery and made me entertain his thuggish political friends, dressing me in Sorelle Fontana designs, when all the time I was bruised and scabbed underneath from where he used to pinch and burn me with cigarettes. He said if I told the priest I'd have to show evidence, and that would prove I was a whore. He left me with nothing and while I was waiting the seven years for the divorce to come through, the monster tried to have me charged not just with prostitution but with witchcraft as well. Because of the cards, of course, which is a family gift my mother and grandmother had, too. Even Padre Iacinto, the Jesuit missionary who sends me foreign students for lessons, tells me the cards are a mortal sin, so I put them away. But I had to bring them out again for the little American girl because I could feel something bad around her—a familiar stink of brimstone. Well, God punishes you through the cards by letting you see too much, and in these last months, I've watched those two young Americans the way you do when you know the end of a book or a television show. And of course she was already pregnant when I told her—that you don't need cards to see! But the child, poor little thing, makes no difference. I can see the outcome, and it turns my stomach.

11

NICK

~~

2005 · DEATH IN THE MORNING

Don't you ever answer the bloody fucking phone?

One of the hideous talents of middle age, thinks Nick in the very instant of answering his mobile and hearing his wife, Dhel, yelling at the other end, is that you can instantly classify hysterical phone calls. It has to do with the times, as well—when he first got to London, in the halcyon boring days of John Major's administration, before the World Trade Center attacks made cellphones messengers of mass disasters, such calls were almost exclusively personal. At some point one has gotten monstrously used to the call at two A.M., or in this case to the call in the black London cab stalled in morning traffic beside St. Paul's. This tone means death, catastrophe—but not, he can hear, of his family, his flesh and blood. And with a mixture of shock, pain, and shameful relief, he hears of the death in a car crash of Samuel Tsembani, one of his best friends in London. Samuel, Nigerian American, six years younger than Nick, Stanford MBA, going places at Goldman Sachs. The only person Nick knows in London who shares his passion for following mainland Chinese soccer leagues. Devoted family man and, as only Nick knew, tireless traveling fornicator. His older kids, a boy and a girl, were the age of Nick's younger girls, and Dhel and Sammy's gorgeous foul-mouthed Scottish wife, Mo, spent a lot of time talking math tutors and international versus British schools. The families dated each other as families with matching kids do, going to shows at the Natural History Museum and the V&A, buying junk at the Notting Hill and Camden Town markets, eating overpriced hot dogs and watching cartoons at the Electric. At a certain point early this morning, Sammy had kissed his beautiful brown kids and pregnant wife goodbye, and sped away from Holland Park in the testosterone-fueled E-Type Jag that they all teased him was too early acquired for a midlife crisis. Left as always at seven just to get in those Asian calls and before eight was dead against a sycamore amid the Turneresque February mists and ice of the Embankment.

Nick comforts Dhel, who is headed over to Holland Park to help out, cancels a nonessential appointment, fields the inquisitive All right, mate? of the cab driver, all the while feeling his nose stinging, tears leaking painlessly from the corner of his eyes like they do when sulfur levels are high in polluted air. Thinking that he parted with his friend in a mood of condemnation. Nine days ago when they'd met for lunch in a huge noisy City restaurant where public school boys lob bread rolls and howl for their meat, Sammy had told him about yet another Eastern European girl, this one a Czech he'd met at a German techno club, Tresor. And Nick had told him in essence that he was behaving like a jerk. Then Sammy looked at him over the table with those big seed-shaped Nigerian eyes and said, But I see these girls, and I melt. Melt, Nick, do you understand, man? Nick had gone away from the lunch with his mind, not his face, set in a prissy grimace. But now he thinks, Would it have been so hard to tell him you understood? You haven't been a saint your whole life, Nick Reiver. You've even been dumb enough to fool around once or twice on Dhel.

I melt. The words seem to him heartbreaking, precious evidence of live, flawed humanity. An epitaph for a man—a father and lover and friend and fucker who was and isn't anymore.

1985–86 · GOLDEN AGE

When happiness comes, observes the Australian writer Helen Garner, it is so thick and smooth and uneventful that it is like nothing at all.

Virginia Woolf describes it as a child hypnotized by a mirrored ball. G. K. Chesterton calls it a mystery. Tolstoy says, in essence, that it makes families boring. Whatever it is, it is the opposite of what the Chinese call "interesting times." History is shaped by war and pestilence and troublesome ideas, thinks Nick. Peace shapes nothing at all.

Still, there are scenes that remain from this time when Nick and Mira have learned the idiom, have learned how to live with each other in Rome. The time that lasts for two years at most but could be a thousand years, or just an hour. The untranscribable history of contentment.

Some examples:

The tail end of a Halloween party in their apartment, four A.M., the beautiful old rooms a battlefield strewn with plastic cups and empty bottles, everybody gone except for a few drunken diehards, a Scottish friend passed out on a couch. Music still playing: Fine Young Cannibals' "Johnny Come Home." And Nick and Mira are still dancing, because they can't stop. Nick is dressed as the Invisible Man, in an old tuxedo, with an Ace bandage wrapped around his face. Mira, six months pregnant, wears a moth-eaten black velvet evening dress from the Porta Portese flea market and a rubber gangster's mask. Nick, drunk, lurches over to grab his wife, as she squeals, Ow, careful!, and as he squeezes her against him he feels, for the first time, the strong kick of his child inside her. He almost shoves her away in his shock, and hears her laughing through her mask.

Nick's boss sends him to meet with a famous financier in Milan, a youngish man with white hair who in a few years will kill himself in a scandal but who now sits at lunch with Nick in a cinquecento palazzo with four smog-stained giants grappling on the façade. And talks slippery condescending nonsense until Nick says something quiet but accurate, and then the man turns his empty silver eyes on him, except they're no longer empty, but direct, like a key turning in a lock, and says, *È vero, sono tutte cazzate*—you're right, it's all bullshit—and Nick realizes that he is doing this, he is speaking this language, and he will never be outside again.

In the Parioli clinic, when he first holds his daughter Madeleine Rose and sees the Asian calm of the tiny round face, as mottled as a seashell, miniature fingers withered with their long immersion like the claws of a newly hatched prehistoric creature, he understands that this is bigger than anything. Not a miracle—as the nursing sisters whisper, in a rustling aura of starch and bleach—but a secret simultaneously perpetuated and resolved. How two can make a completely separate third. The fierce, almost electric independence that emanates from the slight weight he holds gingerly in his arms touches him even more than the expected weight of responsibility and the bonds of love. He looks over at Mira, who is sleeping, and sees that her face, worn beyond exhaustion, is identical to the one in his arms. Both of them with the anonymous dignity of statues around the city, minor ones, whose faces are almost obliterated by time.

But the scene that remains with Nick as a symbol of the improvised quality of these years when they were happy is from one hot June night when he takes Mira's mother on a tour of Rome in her nightgown. His mother-in-law has come over from Philadelphia to help with the baby, alternating comforting expertise with extreme aggression, as only a new grandmother can, when Nick declares that she has to see the city by moonlight. He overrides protests by Mira, by the lady herself, who is already in her nightgown—a voluminous cotton-polyester garment with printed rosebuds that Nick has already seen far too much of—and sweeps her off in the little open car.

He does this out of a lazy impulse of pity and a real fondness for the old girl, who's done nothing but change diapers since her arrival. But it quickly becomes an adventure for him as well. He is amazed by how fast—as fast as her daughter—this stout little olive-skinned gray-permed sixty-year-old widow lets her modesty go, leaning back cheerful and alert in her seat as if she always rides around foreign capitals in her sleepwear. Her excitement transforms for him the tourist route he's shown a dozen visiting relatives. Uniting into a single vision the yellow evening sky cut by veering swallows, the pines like thunderclouds on their trunks, the shattered monuments, the tight streets of shops and apartments, the hordes of nightwalkers, the piazzas overflowing with the roar and frying smells of outdoor restaurants, the flood tide of traffic and profanity in the big avenues. A waking dream that he sees through her eyes.

Rome, in her nightgown. Like an ad in a fifties magazine or the title of a paperback romance. In a sports car, with a white boy, the blond hair blowing on his forehead a forbidden desire since her Philadelphia girlhood. He takes her everywhere you can drive in Rome: the Appia Antica, where the tombs bite at the air like broken teeth; swirling along the huge arc passing the Forum, the Colosseum, the Baths of Caracalla, the Pyramid of Sestius, the pine-shrouded darkness where Keats lies guarded by the bones of other foreigners. They make quick illegal forays into Piazza Navona and Piazza del Popolo, Nick showing off his talent for wheedling *carabinieri.* They stop in Trastevere for ice cream and watermelon and *porchetta* sandwiches.

It gets late, but Nick is in no hurry. For a few minutes he feels that he is riding down Via Veneto with the most beautiful woman in the world beside him, laughing in her nightgown. Not even on the morning when his daughter was born, and he raced beside the Tiber before dawn with Mira groaning beside him, has he felt such a sense of his fate linked to his surroundings. And rarely has he felt so close to his wife as driving now with her mother beside him. An act of love? he wonders. Not really. An act of dream.

MIRA'S MOTHER

I always knew that Miranda would never keep him. Even in Rome with the baby, I knew. The wind in my hair, that golden boy. I should have been the one! And that foolish, undeserving, ungrateful girl, throwing the whole world away.

12

ZENIN

I'm getting too old for this, thinks Zenin, as he summons up a treble laugh, droops his wrist like a pansy, and blows a kiss in the direction of his Chinese associate, Brandon Hsu.

We will always be together, my darling! he says in English, and the entire tableful of Chinese and Italians roars with laughter at the ritual clowning of their two bosses.

They sit overlooking the hazy expanse of Lago Maggiore on the terrace of the Hotel Wellington, a Belle Epoque leviathan with five hundred rooms, curly iron balconies, and an almost industrial number of huge geraniums at each window—geraniums Zenin always finds himself counting and mentally trying to calculate the cost of, wholesale from the nursery. For the past twenty years, whenever Hsu sweeps through on his biannual trip to Europe, with his entourage of mistresses, secretaries, second and third in command, and lately, grown children, he pauses, between bouts of frenetic shopping at Italian designer outlets, for a few days of golf at this hotel. This place that Zenin considers the most boring and vulgar on earth—depressing too, because it looks like a retirement home, full of doddering old farts of all nationalities in navy jackets and white trousers.

By tradition, Zenin hosts the Chinese for at least one banquet. And he has long ago stopped being amused by the efforts of the Hong Kong contingent to mask their disgust at the taste of Parmesan and mozzarella, their subdued murmurs of apprehension about the rotten fish Italians eat, not hygienically chosen live from a tank, but two or three days dead. All this a reply to the nausea of his own staff when presented with feasts of shark fin and snake and jellyfish in Shenzhen and Shanghai. And traditionally, between toasts of ludicrously over-priced Barolo and Brunello and Rémy Martin, Zenin and Hsu demonstrate their business loyalty by hamming it up like two theatrical fags. *Kampai!*

Zenin knows he doesn't have to do it. Even his patient wifely girlfriend, the antique dealer from Verona, refuses to attend these gatherings, though she does guide the Chinese wives and mistresses on shopping sprees in Milan and Paris. But dozens of successful joint ventures that have earned Zenin the title of *il nuovo Marco Polo*—the new Marco Polo—in the business press have won Zenin's loyalty over twenty-five years and he caters to Hsu the way he'd never cater to a friend or a lover. Besides, he likes the old son of a bitch. The Chinese is the same age as he is but looks much younger—with his elevator shoes, his gangsterish Armani black shirts, his sleek hair, his round, intelligent porcine face unchanged since the day they met as hungry kids with a few good ideas. And though Zenin knows that the crafty bastard has been going behind his back for years, cheating on him with the Americans among others, he still feels affection for him. Envies him, even. For the Chinese, besides being fitter—he swims a mile every morning—seems to have settled tranquilly into a complex life that is an uncanny blend of tradition and mad contemporaneity. He enjoys his money, his vulgar hotels and clothes, his mistresses—who get younger and younger every year—and a vast family of siblings, children, and in-laws ruled by Hsu's mother, who back in Hong Kong still cooks his morning congee.

Now Hsu's astute, slightly swollen eyes study Zenin. More white hairs, my old friend, he says. Maybe you are worried about your family.

Zenin conceals his annoyance. Tell me your secret, he says.

Me? I have no secret. I keep my wife and change girlfriends all the time. He indicates his latest mistress, a lanky twenty-year-old covered in Gucci. Pretty, isn't she? But there is one thing. I choose them always from my province. That way they understand me, my food, my wife when she talks, my mother also. We respect each other, and we don't waste time. Perhaps that is the secret. Don't waste time on strange girls.

Zenin works up a smile and grabs his glass for another toast. Brandon, my precious, I learned that the hard way a long time ago.

1985–86 · TRICKED

In some ways Zenin hates women.

He especially hates it when they have their periods, the way it is with all his sisters in the old house in Boara. The atmosphere of mass secrecy—they all bleed at the same time—the suppressed moaning and groaning, martyred pale faces, stink of bodies and flux, stained cloths discreetly hung up to dry, the weird sense of occult power, a lunar army arrayed against him.

He hates certain things about his mother, her peasant face with its burst veins, her flinty eyes when she talks about *quella bestia del tuo papà*—your animal of a father.

He finds he hates his ex-wife Cecilia most of all when she talks about her love of French literature, which she sums up in an adoration of *Le petit prince*. Which in a sentimental voice she calls *il mio petit prince*—my petit prince.

He doesn't hate his two daughters but doesn't know what to do with them, whiny and reproachful even when they were small.

He hates, without knowing it, all beautiful girls for making him want them.

He hates secretaries and factory girls who get loud and drunk in pizzerias and bars on International Women's Day.

He hates many different women in many different ways, but rarely has he hated women in general as profoundly as when that nice girl Tere got herself pregnant with his son.

That's how he thinks of it: as almost an immaculate conception. The pleasure he finds in his brief relationship with Tere has been social, the comfort of feeling the approval of all of his friends, his family, the relaxing feeling of being a good fellow. He's entertained by the fact that she is one of those upper-middle-class Friuli girls with low hairlines and greenish eyes that watch you as attentively as a cat. Not gorgeous, but good-looking. He likes it that she's educated but tells jokes in dialect, knows her way around the stadium, how to talk to a maid, and what the right texture of *baccalà mantecato* is. He likes her streak of bourgeois slyness.

So he's outraged when it is used against him. The oldest dirty trick in the book, he thinks, regarding her with slowly increasing rage and incredulity until, red-eyed and sniveling, she confesses. And that yes, it is true that she lied when she said she was taking birth control pills. But it is a lie that grew out of the fact that she adores him. Another lie, he knows, in which he can hear the massed chorus of women's voices—his mother, her mother, his sisters, all the women in the city, all the respectable women in the world who have been in on the plot to get him back in harness. To get him married again, to this girl who did of course use a trollop's trick, but one every Italian mother knows is allowable in the case of a very difficult, very rich man. And Tere isn't a secretary or a model, but a nice girl from a good family.

He stands staring at her tearful face above an absurd reindeer-print sweater—they've been skiing at his house in the Dolomites, decorated by his ex-wife in Tyrolean flounces. It is New Year's Day, and he realized the night before, celebrating in a mountain refuge with the usual group of friends, that he is getting sick of her. Now he wishes he'd shoved her off a glacier. Kill all these *puttane,* he thinks, baffled by his own stupidity, which had plopped him in the center of a traditionally undistinguished group, worse than cuckolds. *Coglioni.* Dickheads. Dupes.

BRANDON HSU

My old friend and partner Zenin is the one white man I know who does business like the Chinese. But he has never enjoyed life.

TERE'S MOTHER

I told the poor girl to be strong, to wait, to pray and be patient and that rascal would come around. No one, not even the devil himself, can resist a baby.

13

MIRA

High noon in the supermarket parking lot, and Mira stands chatting with the toothless Moroccan boy who's helping her with the bags. Part of the gang of North Africans who hang out near the island of mock America—Blockbuster, Media World, McDonald's, acres of Japanese cars—set here on the Piedmont plain in view of the Alps. He says he's sixteen, though she doesn't believe it, and he's not really toothless; just his upper front teeth are rotted down to the gums. His name is Bakhid, and every time he sees her, he demands a cellphone.

You should be thinking about school, Bakhid. Not phones.

Vado a scuola. A volte. I go to school sometimes, he says, flashing those pitiful teeth at her in an Artful Dodger grin. And Mira sees from the still babyish contours of his face under the pimply malnourished skin that he is probably about twelve. She wants to take him home and wash him and raise him with her sons. She feels a pang when she sees him hoist the plastic grocery bags bulging with cereals and mini-mozzarellas and the fruits and vegetables he needs. Once he laughed as he helped her load a pumpkin, and said that back in his village his mother cooks it with couscous.

She pays him triple, three euros instead of one, and in his presence feels personally responsible for American foreign policy. But he and his little band of ragamuffin friends always flash her a thumbs-up and call out, USA bravo!

Don't sentimentalize those boys, her brother-in-law, a Lega Padana conservative, tells her. They are part of an invading immigrant army that little by little is colonizing Italy. The new Muslim state, that's us. Free health care, welfare, education, protection from the law—the fools down in Rome treat them better than Italians. One day we'll wake up to muezzins in St. Peter's.

Study hard, Bakhid, says Mira, giving him the coins, and noticing that he is wearing a grubby Juventus soccer shirt and a pair of Reeboks.

Ciao, Signora America! he says cheerfully, grabbing the shopping cart and skidding off with it like a scooter. Next time the cellphone, okay?

1986 · MOVIES

Once in a while, Mira watches old movies on Italian television at nine in the morning. It's her little secret, her willful dissipation of some of the hours she reserves so carefully for writing. Nick leaves for the office, Tree, the Filipina housekeeper, wheels young Maddie off to the street markets or the park, and Mira turns on the computer, glances at the article in progress, and then drifts out of the study, coffee mug in hand, to sit in front of the television, a portal. Still foggy from interrupted nights with the baby, she steps into the gray-and-black world of early Fellini and Rossellini and a dozen minor directors, whose scrambling creativity and inspired use of scanty resources shine through sentimental plots and stock dialogue as records of an age when the gods of cinema walked the soundstages of Cinecittà. Films from the fifties so un-Hollywood, so embarrassingly old-fashioned to Italians that they appear only on television, only at this godless hour.

She sits cross-legged on the rug, too close to the screen, feeling the images flowing through the dark rambling apartment, illuminating its gilded beams and tarnished mirrors and claw-footed furniture; flowing into the morning city outside, so that Rome itself takes on the attributes of the film characters: the architectural shadows under Anna

Magnani's eyes, Alberto Sordi's baroque nose, the flat white oracular mask that is Totò's face.

One morning she watches a melancholy Cinderella tale: a young shopgirl freshly arrived in Rome from a poor Veneto village takes a walk one night and meets a young Roman count who writes poetry in a wing of his family's decayed palazzo. He falls madly in love with her innocent beauty, and she comes to live with him. But the idyll wanes as the girl learns to move in high society, and finally, greedy for more than poetry, she runs off with his playboy friend. The movie, full of dusty half-light, cathedral bells, and the bare despoiled piazzas of the postwar era, is called *L'amore a Roma*—*Love in Rome*.

When Mira sees it she knows it's a sign she will hear from Zenin again, and a few weeks later, he calls. It is a gray April morning, the air pressing down over the city, and she has abandoned work to watch a Don Camillo movie. Don Camillo has won a skirmish with his old foe, the Communist mayor of the village, and is taking off his cassock for a celebratory swim in the river, when the phone rings.

Don't hang up on me, Zenin says.

She hasn't spoken to him for a over a year, since before Maddie was born. He called one morning and Mira said that she was pregnant, that she was very happy, and that she never wanted him to call her again. And she hung up the phone, as she had always wanted to do with Zenin. Feeling strong, pleased with herself, wondering at the ease of sealing off that underground passage.

And as the hectic, absorbing months pass that transform first her body and then her whole pattern of life, as she undergoes the dazzling recognition, studying her daughter's small perfect face, that a newborn child is yet another occasion to fall in love, as she and Nick fumble through the domestic alarums, the conventional terrors, the rituals of feeding and care, and take Maddie out into the city to the rambunctious chorus of admiration with which Romans greet babies, Mira has hardly any time to note a strange absence at the edge of her thoughts. A tiny indefinable lack. Like an almost invisible black spot at the corner of her vision. Or a pinhole that lets darkness leak in.

She begins to feel it only when she gets back to work again and begins her clandestine mornings with the movies. And when she notices, it spreads like an inkblot. Not regret for Zenin, exactly—more regret for the fact of Zenin. An odd kind of nostalgia for things that never happened, for a presence that, like these old movies, opens a door on another dimension. A place where late-night footsteps echo in foreign streets and you hold your breath, perishing to know what comes next.

And when he calls this morning, she clutches the phone with a peculiarly feminine feeling of triumph.

Ho detto di non chiamarmi, she says, feeling each hard word on her lips, distinct as a subtitle. I said not to call me.

Please don't hang up. Please. Zenin has abandoned his faintly risible English and speaks to her in Italian.

Mira is silent, but the silence is acquiescent, expectancy hanging in the air like the clouds hanging over the domes and belfrys of the city. She realizes that her breath is shallow, as if she's been running. That she feels more awake than she's felt for months. That she loves hearing him beg.

I'm in Rome, says Zenin. I have to see you. I came only for you. Have lunch with me. Please don't say no.

On the television screen, Don Camillo leads a heroic village force to sandbag the levees of the surging Po River, his cassock sleeves rolled up to show off his muscular forearms, as the soundtrack blares hysterical neorealist music. But to Mira the music sounds like a pennywhistle. She has plunged into a different plot, one where a woman puts on a black dress—a black linen dress designed to show that she is sophisticated, a foreigner who at last has learned how to dress like an Italian, just as she has learned the idiom—and strolls out into the Roman crowds, where men turn to look at her. To have lunch in a restaurant that smells of money with a man whose eyes look dead but ask the kind of question that sets her blood tearing through her veins. The only question worth answering: What can happen?

All right, says Mira. I'll come. Once, and then never again.

BAKHID

The American lady looks like somebody from my country but she drives a fat shiny jeep like all the Italians and she talks like the ladies from the Servizi Sociali. Study, study, and then we have to memorize the poem "Quant'è bella la margherita," but they don't understand we are men already, we know sharia law and about the da'wa. And we know Italian: *va'a fa'nculo, stronzo, puttana.* The American gives more money than the others, but Raschid gets it. We hide coins in our shoes, in the sides of our cheeks, even up our asses, but that shark gets it all every time, he goes through us like a rake in the back of the truck when he picks us up at the parking lot every night. *Balanaye, Sermata!* he says. You little turds chat rubbish to me and you'll find my fist so far up your ass I'll wave hello out of your mouth, and there goes your *permesso di soggiorno.* Raschid is my cousin from Essaouira and has a room near Porta Palazzo where we all sleep, eleven or twelve of us, and shoot out the door if the *questura* police come in the courtyard. Below is the phone center where all the *stranieri*—the foreigners—Albanians, Romanians, Moldavians, those black Ivory Coast *ajam,* and the Chinese, everybody lines up to call international in the booths, but we don't have money. If I had a cellphone I'd get a special card to talk to my mother and sisters. I'd be a big man with my friends if I had a phone, and I'd find a way to hide it from Raschid.

14

NICK

You know, New York is dating badly, says Nick to his cousin Garcia. The two are eating brunch outdoors at the corner of Houston and West streets, gazing across the cobblestones at the SoHo Club, where even on Sunday at noon a couple of limos wait glistening like beached whales in the sun of one of those overheated Manhattan spring days when downtown girls roll up their capris to toast their moon-white knees.

Typical expat pontification, says his cousin, wrinkling up her choir-boy's face, which has retained its freshness below her graying crew cut. Garcia is a nickname for Grace, a closet Deadhead who edits a chil-dren's magazine, who is the closest thing Nick has to a sister. Now she scarfs a huge piece of his blueberry muffin.

Although, she adds, Gertrude Stein once wrote that America is the oldest country in the world. But perhaps you would like to explicate, Mr. Fitzgerald, or Mr. Eliot, or is it Mr. James?

There's nothing to explain. Every time I come for work or play I re-alize it bores the crap out of me.

Sounds like you're the dated one, my boy. Perhaps it's time to check testosterone levels.

Fuck off, Garcia. Nick, grumpy from jet lag and nonstop meetings, wouldn't take this shit from anyone but Garcia, who's been a confidant ever since they were thirteen and used to sit out in a dinghy all summer in Maine arguing about the juxtaposition of Sartre and Joe Orton in the lyrics of Adam Ant.

No, no—he goes on. I was thinking about it as I walked down Sixth Avenue to get here. Sun on brick. Stasis. Deserted shop fronts. It was like a museum piece. It was—quaint. And not just Sunday morning. I feel it even when I'm working. A kind of ongoing nostalgia. Frozen in time. Like stepping into a Hopper painting.

And London is so exquisitely vibrant, right? Garcia's tone is defensive, as if she intuits that Nick sees her as another New York museum piece, the trustafarian editor living at Pitt and Delancey with her obese lover, Carol, and two herniated cats. She straightens her Ozzfest T-shirt, which has a cleverly mended tear on the sleeve, and Nick remembers how, back in her thirties, her goth phase seemed to drag on forever. He doesn't quote to her what an English art critic said about Hopper: that Hopper created a new type of pictorial heroism, the heroism of failure. "At some point in its cultural stalling, the world began to confuse inertia, impotence, poky hotel rooms and losers with things to look up to. A world view made and exported from America."

Instead, Nick says, London is a total mess—overpriced, filthy, and more girl gangs than the Bronx. But it's awake. It's got that future buzz that Asian cities have. It's America that's asleep. We're at war, but we're lost in a provincial daze.

So you're not coming back to live in the States anytime soon. Mumsy and Carol and everybody are always asking.

You know the answer to that, Garce. No. I have a life. Dhel and the girls, school, work, friends. For the foreseeable future, the U.K. is where we are. And I like it.

Do you even feel American anymore?

I feel more American than ever before. Nobody lets you forget it. Not since we started colonizing Iraq. And you see stuff better from a distance. I can despise Bush and the neocons better if I'm despising Blair and Labour at the same time. Like having bifocals. Look at this face—Nick thrusts out his chin and leans close to Garcia. Does this look like the face of one who deserts the core values of his native land?

Hmmm.

Have I developed a reprehensible Yankee-Brit accent? Have I shirked my sacred paternal trust to make my three daughters into Red Sox fans? Have I denied them exposure to the Cars? To the Sugar Hill Gang? To Pop-Tarts?

Okay, okay, says Garcia. You've convinced me that you're the same homegrown asshole we've always loved. Now can we order some marble cheesecake? And refresh my memory, before that place was the SoHo Club, wasn't it some place you got thrown out of?

No, I got thrown out of Trax. Teddy and I. What I was trying to remember was where we stumbled on that drag festival.

Wigstock. Tompkins Square. I thought I'd walked onto a John Waters set.

And they start retracing the night landscape of the eighties until Garcia says, You know, I was thinking about what you said before. Don't you think that all the quaintness, the feeling of being frozen in time is because there's that big gap in the downtown skyline? The sun's out, years have passed since nine-eleven, but we're still breathing corpses. And sometimes late at night, it's bizarre, but I think I see the outline of the towers. The lights and everything, like ghosts—architectural phantoms. So Nicko, I think you should have a little compassion for your old town. Everybody knows that you can't just move along when you've had your guts blown out.

Garcia props her chin on her hand, stares owlishly at Nick, and adds in a mock-seductive whisper, Come on. You know you can't do without us.

1986 · THIEVES

Surfacing from an entrancing dream where he's playing electric guitar like a crossover genius in front of a classical orchestra—he can see his own head and jamming fingers gleam in the spotlight—Nick realizes that for once it's not his baby daughter who woke him.

It's Mira kneeling by the long bedroom window, peering outside through the velvet curtain, and calling him in a whisper. And when he joins her, he sees the reason: two men climbing the wrought-iron gate that shuts off the alley alongside their house from Via Panisperna. Silhouettes that drop down with silent ease, like acrobats. After the *portiere's* chained Vespa, or looking for an unlocked window. Break-ins are so common in Rome that all their friends have stories, but this is the first time for Nick. On impulse, he speaks through the open window into the dank alley in a quiet, conversational tone.

Che cazzo fate laggiù? What the fuck are you doing down there?

The perfection of his Roman accent—he notices irrelevantly—is astounding, and so is the effect of his words on the thieves, who immediately back up jerkily like a video rewinding and fling themselves over the fence. In a minute there is just the alley—a noisome crack between buildings, home to a colony of feral cats who thrive on leftover pasta tossed down by the neighbors. That and the disturbed air of a warm March night.

Mira giggles and throws her arms around him. You drove them away, you brave boy.

We should call the carabinieri.

Why should we? Do you want noise and questions and bureaucracy? Let 'em alone, our skinny little thieves.

But they might come back.

No, I don't think so. Mira speaks in a tone Nick has never heard before, absent, yet strangely indulgent. She's never a coward, but it surprises him that she's so casual about this.

How—he asks—how'd you see them anyway?

Oh, I was awake, says Mira with a yawn. Staring out of the window, communing with my coven of cats. Then they showed up over the fence like Mimes from Hell.

Still that curious tone in her voice, as alien to her husband as a strange smell on her skin. Amused and detached as if she were—he fumbles for the idea—not quite there. As if she herself, standing there so solid in her T-shirt and underpants, were really outside in the dark. As if in a dream he glimpses her naked, shadowed, in league with the thieves. Yet he's still half asleep and there's nothing to ask, is there? Nothing there, like the tingling absence left by a ghost, or a vanished intruder.

In the next room, little Maddie wakes up with a grumbling wail, and against all good pediatric advice, her young parents bring her into bed with them and they fall asleep curled up all three together in a moist stalky tangle of flesh that smells like nothing else in the world but family and safety. And the next day they tell Rocco, the *portiere*, who nails a spiral of barbed wire above the gate.

But much later, when Nick looks back to trace the beginnings of venom and suspicion, it is always that night he returns to, the night when the fear of robbers is eclipsed by one brief flash of certainty that he doesn't know Mira—his chosen love, his best friend, his wife— at all.

GARCIA

My first memory of Nick is of an incredibly blond kid who was an incredibly slow and methodical eater—he'd be there at the table of his parents' place up in Maine, forking up baked bean after baked bean for what seemed like hours after the rest of us cousins were allowed to get up. Eating calmly like Buddha would eat if Buddha ate baked beans. I think he ate so slowly because he was studying his food—he wanted to understand how everything worked, not scientifically, but in a humanistic way. Just like he'd spend hours drawing up the exact formations of Waterloo with those old lead soldiers that belonged to Uncle Jake. And later on, working out the precise scansion of passages from *Beowulf* and *The Wanderer*. But he wasn't one of those weird control-freak boys. He just wanted to know and see everything, and even fix everything. Brilliantly, but like a brilliant amateur who needed to cover all the bases. Maybe because they lost Meade, the oldest son, and Nick felt he had to make up for that. We always knew that he'd be the one to replenish the family coffers.

Anyway, for a little kid he was exceptionally kind. I remember once in Little Compton when we were about six or seven, I was climbing a tree in a dress and ripped this huge hole in my underpants, and he just lent me a pair of his, first closing up the pee flap with a safety pin. He was never a prig—he was deep into sex and drugs and rock and roll when we were teenagers—and somehow I always saw him as the ultimate American character, like Huck Finn. So I'm always taken aback when we meet up in New York and I see this slightly jaded multilingual Citizen of the World. Carol calls him the Wandering Wasp. But he's still playing those war games, fooling around with literature—I always think business types are so much more poetic than those money-grubbing real writers I have to deal with—and he's got what looks like a domestic idyll over in London, so maybe the distance is what he was after all the time. After all, there were generations of sea captains in the family. Captains and missionaries.

15

ZENIN

2005 · CONFIDENTIAL

Cocco, did you ever love any of your women? whispers Zenin's sister, Maria Cristina. She is dying of cancer, and so entitled to ask the kinds of questions that ordinarily lead Zenin to throw up a hasty wall of subterfuge. As she is entitled to call him Cocco, his hated family nickname coined by the string of sisters, one that reminds him of stinking outdoor toilets and the sweet American potatoes they ate all winter after the war. Cocco is a mocking abbreviation of *cocco della mamma,* Mama's darling.

Of course, he mumbles, as he sits beside her trying not to look at her. Her skeletal face that under the gray stubble on her scalp looks startlingly like a boyhood photo he has seen of their father, in Sunday clothes somewhere in Istria. Her large blue eyes that as a teenager she flashed around far too boldly at the boys in town. She is the youngest sister, the arty 1968-style revolutionary. His least favorite sister, if truth be told, always lecturing him condescendingly about Gramsci, Lenin, Marcuse, Fanon, arguing in favor of the Red Brigades even when he, her capitalist-pig brother, was getting death threats. And not too proud later on to request a cushy job in the company for her husband, a brainless nobleman with politics further left than hers. But now, as he is about to lose her, as she has become an insoluble problem, she has become agonizingly precious.

They are sitting in a room as large and luxurious as a hotel suite, in a clinic overlooking a lake in Switzerland. They've called in and dispensed with therapies radical and traditional from all around the world. Veronese from the Istituto Tumori, the raw-foods man from Basel, the brilliant young Turk from Sloan-Kettering. All have been inspired, bribed, urged along by Zenin's money but have run up against the indisputable fact of cells that want to die. No one knows whether it will be three months or six. And the baffled rage built up in Zenin's cold heart, rage at impotence before a simple reality that makes meaningless the empire he has torn out of poverty and the past, makes this dying sister—a shape formed out of his blood, of the dust of his countryside—into something to be clutched as best he can.

Of course he says nothing about this to Maria Cristina, simply sits and stares at his big restless freckled hands while steely twilight rises on the lake and his ninny of a brother-in-law types something on a computer in the corner. But when her unexpected question comes, it links her curiously enough with women in his past for whom he has felt the same bafflement in helplessness and jealous clutching. One is Tere, the mother of his son. Another is the American girl, Mira. He thinks of them now, and it helps him sit on at the side of his wasted, breastless sister.

I've loved one or two, he says.

1986 · SAHARA SAND

The unpleasantness of the sirocco on the March afternoon when Mira and Zenin finally get together. Well, everyone knows what a sirocco is. Even people who have never been to Italy can talk about the sirocco, as they can about San Francisco fog or Bangkok smog: red grains of Sahara sand whirled like a biblical plague across the Mediterranean and up the peninsula in a demonic current of air that, like the mistral and the foehn, causes migraines, murders, and suicides before breaking in a burst of blood-colored rain. Everyone knows about the sirocco, which is as commonplace as falling in love.

Nick is immune to it as some people are.

Mira feels that her skull is being flayed from the inside, that she is breathing in the rubble of entire barbaric civilizations reduced to dust.

Zenin, the hypochondriac, dislikes it because it lowers his already low blood pressure.

In the leaden light of noon, Mira, head throbbing, takes a taxi to a fashionable restaurant among the umbrella pines of the Pincio and walks in high heels up the gravel path, past a Roman bust so worn with handling that it looks like a clown. Someone, with Magic Marker, has added a grinning mouth and a penis for a nose. Zenin, seated on the terrace, watches her arrive. With satisfaction, he observes the taxi driver's eyes burning into her legs, sees the headwaiter defer, and watches her pass a table of Roman men, all tanned hides and silk and sunglasses, who look her over and say, *Che bona! Bona* means "sexy" in Roman dialect, but it comes from the same root as the word *good.*

Mira is right and good in this world because she has put on lipstick and high heels, and a short linen dress with a decent cut and a mustard-colored sash. Has become a luxury item as unmistakable as a black limousine. Zenin can't imagine how much a masquerade this is. How different this Rome is from her own world only a few blocks away, of waking up with Nick and Maddie, of pushing a stroller out to the street market, of tapping frantically at the computer, of English language playgroups in the park, of nights of pizza and Fulbright fellows.

Zenin rises to greet her with a kiss on each cheek. *Sei cresciuta,* he says teasingly. You grew up. You learned Italian. And you're learning how to dress.

They sit ignoring the Pincio view spread below: domes, rooftops, antennae, and leafy terraces, all strangely vivid in the bilious light. And they eat a long heavy meal, a spring menu because it's nearly Easter. Risotto with *puntarelle,* asparagus, fried artichokes, suckling lamb, white wine from the Castelli Romani. Zenin dips pieces of tough Roman bread into olive oil and tells Mira about the peasants who hunt *puntarelle*—fern shoots—and sprouting dandelions in the countryside around his town, and jokes about the American soldiers from the base near Vicenza and the crazy things they order in restaurants. And he's pleased, he says, to see that Mira is as greedy as ever.

Neither of them feels the slightest bit awkward. And neither says anything about what has happened in their lives in the nearly two years since they've seen each other. Their ludicrous improbable false start gives them an odd feeling of having a past together.

He knew when she said she would meet him that she'd sleep with him. All that remains now is to follow the current. He reaches across the table and crushes her hand in his.

As they finish their coffee and rise to leave, Zenin is aware that all over the restaurant with its huge terra-cotta vases of orange trees and oleander, men are staring, envying him, wanting her. Even the head-waiter with his slicked white hair and smirking eunuch's face. Neither Zenin nor Mira is even slightly drunk, yet as they walk out, the heavy sirocco air on the terrace, under the Pincio pines, lying over the roofs of the city, seems to slow down their movements. Full of dust and ghosts of the famous people who have been there, and pretty women like Mira who leave the table to go to hotels with men in the haunted afternoon. Full of lust and exhaustion.

And soon Zenin sits on a hotel bed, making no move to undress or embrace Mira, and commands, *Spogliati.* Take off your clothes. I want to see you.

He's brought her to the d'Inghilterra in Via Bocca di Leone. The classic Baedeker hotel, where rich friends of Nick's and Mira's parents stay. But Zenin and Mira meet no one because they've entered through a side door where an elevator leads to a small two-room apartment lined in red velvet.

A big low bed with a formal cover of red damask. Gold-framed botanical prints that no one has ever looked at. Dark nineteenth-century cupboards where no one ever puts away anything. A slippery Empire couch that no one ever uses except to fling clothes onto or to perform sexual acrobatics too complicated for the bed. A seventies-looking giant television and a glistening white marble bathroom. Windows shuttered, bolted, draped blind with silk. It's the kind of room Mira and Nick would giggle at, trade ironic comments about Victorian porn. Couldn't you just see Nanà here—or Chéri, or Odette? Jokes to disguise their uneasiness at the straightforward eroticism of the suite, its banal power. It exists for one purpose only and is the color of blood, of valentines, of Babylon. It lies hidden deep in the city like a heart in a human breast. And faintly, from the cobblestone maze of shopping streets outside, rises the sound of the river of tourists flowing by.

Zenin—who has chosen the place because none of his friends go there—thinks it's overpriced but correct.

And now with a feeling of profound satisfaction—because he loves above all things to be paid back—he watches as Mira obeys him and cancels out the moment when she flung her clothes off on his boat.

Calmly, without theatricality, she takes off the linen dress, the small undergarments that she knew would be seen when she put them on, and stands naked in front of him in her high-heeled shoes. Doesn't pose, just stands. And as she does so, a strange thing happens to Zenin, something that never happens outside of the instincts he uses to do his deals: he sees things through her eyes as well as his own. Feels her mixture of excitement and shame at standing there stripped in front of the tall man with the expensive, badly fitting suit. How brazenly pleased she is to show her body, unmarked by childbirth except for heavier breasts. Feels just for a second how much she has set aside to come to him. She knows that there will never be another moment like this, where she stands presented and beheld. That she will never be as powerful, and that part of the reason is that she is doing something she thinks is wrong. She feels as if she has come to the center of her life, to the center of a wood in which all the leaves on the trees are eyes. Or to the hidden center, the secret heart she has been searching for in the labyrinth of Rome.

She puts out a hand and touches his face and Zenin feels himself tremble. He shuts off the light and in the hotel blackout begins to tear at his clothes.

And fucking her is, as he knew it would be, like a reconciliation. Like two enemies surrendering in the same instant. Violent and silent recognition there in the dark. Her body is so young, so smooth, though a child has passed through it. Like a weapon or a piece of perfect machinery. And Zenin, who has begun to brood about middle age, about his miserable, stressful tycoon's life, to worry about impotence, realizes that deep inside, without even knowing it, Mira loathes him. And because of this he'll be able to be excited by her for a long time.

And then it is five o'clock, and like dozens of other women who have spent afternoons in that room, Mira has to leap out of bed and race in a taxi back to her life. Cheeks burning, thighs chafed, repeating to herself, Is that all it is? Then I can do it. I can be two people.

And Zenin, sitting on the Fiumicino runway, puts the thought of her aside as he makes phone call after phone call, waiting for the all clear for takeoff to Venice, staring at the sudden gusting sirocco rain that leaves windows in the plane coated with splashes of red sand.

THE HEADWAITER

Ammazzalo, these two-bit industrialists think their balls are made of twenty-four-carat gold, strutting around with their whores. But they're nothing. I remember nights right here when Pignatelli was trying to get a leg over Ava Gardner, when there was Rossellini, whom we boys all called Tino, who was already fucking around on Bergman, there was Gianni of Capri, there was that juicy piece of ass Marisa Allasio, there was Niarchos, Kirk Douglas, Lollobrigida, the lot. Those were people who knew what fucking was. People with style. Those were the days.

16

MIRA

Mira holds her breath as she opens a small mahogany drawer. Her husband, Vanni, is away helping his politician chums cobble a new leftist alliance in Bologna, and she's downtown in his office after their home computer crashed. His cheerful secretary promptly went to lunch after ensconcing Mira behind Vanni's desk, where she sits observed only by the burnished leather-bound volumes of *L'Encyclopedia legale malintoppi,* an ugly but valuable Casorati watercolor, and a series of exotic vacation photographs featuring Mira and the kids; boats; palm trees; Vanni and his fishing cronies with a gargantuan blood-daubed tuna. So in the stillness of this summer afternoon, Mira has license to pry, which she indulges with the same gut-clenching thrill she used to have as a teenager snooping through her best friend's brother's stash of porn and grass. She's not searching for anything in particular. She doesn't suspect Vanni of fooling around, nor does she not suspect him. But she's lived in Italy long enough to know that men here require occasional supervision.

The drawer holds the rubbish he collects on his travels: airline cosmetics, bits of jade, counterfeit wristwatches, business cards with Japanese names. She rummages further, realizing that she's holding her breath with a treasure hunter's anticipation. And in the very back, she finds two snapshots. One shows a reclining woman with thin lips and a tanned skeptical face. She is wearing an orange head scarf, the bottom half of a bikini, and two lobsters—uncooked, freshly caught, the mottled brown of the Mediterranean rock lobster—are carefully arranged over her large, flaccid bare breasts. The second photo is of Vanni grinning merrily, lounging on the trampoline of a catamaran, flanked by the woman in the orange scarf and a pretty black girl with hair in a pixie cut. Her husband looks paunchy and sunburned in his bathing trunks, and is wearing a piratical bandanna. The two women are topless and decked in lobsters as in the earlier picture, and Vanni holds up a fifth lobster as if toasting with a champagne glass. The snapshots are very poor quality, and Mira at first thinks that they record antics from before she met Vanni, but the date on the back is early last July. Exactly when she and the boys were in San Francisco.

She puts the photos in her bag and leaves the office. She drives across the river at the Gran Madre bridge, stops her car beside a yellow glass recycling bin, tears up the snapshots, and throws them away among the broken bottles. The street is deserted, magpies circling overhead.

The next day, she tells her friend Rachel about it as they are drinking coffee outside near the Madama Cristina street market. Rachel, who is English and has a loud, posh voice, laughs so hard about the lobsters that all the other coffee drinkers—market vendors and Senegalese trinket sellers and old Piedmontese housewives with bulging plastic bags—turn around and stare.

I know, says Mira.

The most ludicrous, the most pathetic, gasps Rachel. She ruffles her spiky hair. How could you possibly confront him about anything so silly?

I can't, says Mira. I thought about it all last night and I don't think I can let on that I was snooping for such a ridiculous result. Maybe I've just lived in Italy too long, but I find it hard to take it seriously. Poor Vanni, anyway. He loves me, and he's feeling old. This could be his red Porsche.

He is devoted, Rachel agrees. Obviously still fancies the hell out of you. As well he should, because you're a beautiful woman. How long have you two been married again?

Nine years.

Are you faithful to him?

Rachel! You'd be the first one to know if I weren't. I love Vanni, and frankly the idea of sneaking around again is kind of nauseating.

Is he jealous?

Yeah, he sulks at the mention of Nick or any ex-sweethearts. Makes rude noises when Zenin's ads come on TV.

How very touching. Do you think he fucked those two tarts?

Maybe a bump in the night. I don't think there was much else. I remember now he was in Riccione spearfishing on his cousin's boat—that asshole Michele. Michele always has slutty girls hanging around. He's got a harem of students and research assistants. So Vanni might have let himself go. But a serious affair has a different feeling about it. We all know that.

Oh, we certainly do. I've been through it all with sodding Gianfilippo.

My God, those girls' faces were pained. Can you imagine—lobsters on your tits. Crustacean porn, like a bad dream out of a Dalí painting. Only a man—an obsessive fisherman—would come up with that idea! Here Mira breaks down, and the two women explode into giggles.

Stop, there's coffee coming out of my nose, chokes Rachel. Did you put the pictures back?

No, I stole them and threw them into a street bin. He won't dare ask for them, and it serves him right. I tore them up—do you know how hard it is to shred photos by hand? A face or a lobster kept coming out whole.

Stop it, you're making me hysterical.

And the funny thing is, says Mira, the whole time I was sitting there beside that disgusting trash bin, ripping them to shreds, the radio was playing "Sexual Healing." Rachel, do you think I'm crazy laughing my head off like this?

No, sweetie. Just grown up. I must say that as I get older, life does tend to look less like romance and more like a farce. But let me ask you something, Mira. Wouldn't you have been disappointed to poke around in his desk and find nothing?

Probably, yes.

Aren't you pleased that it was something so astoundingly, so cosmi-
cally foolish?

Definitely yes.

Well, there you are, then.

Where? asks Mira. But she's laughing again, and she knows what
her friend means.

1986 · GOBLIN FRUIT

It's like a drug. You can handle it.

After she's been seeing Zenin for about six months, Mira starts to
spend a lot of her time telling herself that a person can be two people.
She takes dawn runs up to Villa Borghese and repeats it to herself like
a mantra.

This is life. This is what people do.

Down the deserted Corso, past steel-shuttered shop fronts, in
streets where damp stone exudes a bridal freshness that by eight
o'clock will be the teeming traffic-scented miasma of the Centro
Storico. Across Piazza di Spagna, where airport buses stand idling as
parties of Japanese file silently aboard. Past the graffiti-covered stone
fountain, up the slippery cascade of steps, feeling muscles straining in
her legs as she passes Keats's house, Villa Farnese; the shaggy palms
and giant golden walls glowing in the daybreak, breaking a sweat as she
pauses for a heartbeat to view the carpet of the city spread out in the
pink-and-brown dawn while swallows cut through the pale air loosing
their frail whistles. Then the cool air of the Borghese pines, where
mosquitoes, Coke cans, and condoms linger from the night before, and
she joins other runners flitting like spirits in the rising damp.

You can handle it. This is what people do: This is what women do
in books.

Like so many others, she has discovered how fatally easy it is to divide a life. Two hearts, two souls in one body. A little like being pregnant.

It's like a drug. You always handle drugs well. You can stop this
when you like. A few more times and then enough. You'll go back to
having one life, and no one will be hurt.

And later in the day, when she's finished work and takes Maddie to play under the chestnut trees of the Quirinale Gardens, she leafs through books she has brought in her backpack along with her daughter's apple juice and crackers. As she watches the children run like colorful sparks of life in the dusty unkempt little playground and the carabinieri trucks stationed in front of the smog-blackened presidential palace, she searches for company in literature.

"Natasha . . . was only aware of being borne irrevocably away again into that strange and senseless world so remote from her old one, a world in which there was no knowing what was good and what was bad, what was sensible and what was folly.

"Stefania R. had been married for a couple of years and had never thought of being unfaithful to her husband. To be sure, in her life as a married woman there was a kind of expectation, the awareness that something was still lacking for her. It was like a continuation of her expectations as a girl, as if for her the complete emergence from her minority had not yet occurred. . . . Was it adultery she had been awaiting?"

Meanwhile, Maddie, in overalls and a blouse with an embroidered collar, might be squatting with a friend in the dust near the battered sliding board, her curly brown head bent over some horse chestnuts they are arranging in a circle. Repeating in a bossy voice, *Così, mettilo così!* At almost two years old her face is cherubic, and in museums she reaches out to stone putti as if toward a mirror. From time to time she darts back to Mira to demand a drink or show a treasure or climb up on her mother's knees. The shape of her face is Nick's.

When Mira feels her daughter's soft resilient flesh she feels a lurch of adoration in her stomach, an ache in her breasts as if they were still full of milk. It brings up the image of Nick, freshly showered with his hair in wet spikes, dancing her and Maddie around the big Victorian bathroom as he did just the night before. Clowning around to Rick James's "Super Freak." The bathroom steamed up, the gorgeous little girl screeching with glee, flushed with her bath, her head swathed in a towel. Mira herself, bare to the waist, tits jiggling. Shrieks, giggles, the smell of diapers, shampoo, freshly scrubbed skin. Gilt mist of evening lamps, the pure essence of family passion.

Yet then the scene changes and she sees herself as she was with Zenin that first time, exhibiting herself naked in high heels as he sits fully clothed on the bed, looking at her as if judging a piece of horse-flesh. The foreign man who observes her, has somehow acquired her. If she thinks of Zenin—which she has begun to do unwillingly many times a day—she shivers and her cunt throbs as if her heart had tumbled down there. Yet she knows this terrible power she is beginning to sense is not in the sex, not in the fucking they do in the red suite, with the footsteps and voices of Rome echoing around them.

She knows this because she can still make love to Nick, squeezing images of Zenin into a tiny white dot on the surface of her mind that almost disappears like the last molecules of light on a television screen. That's depraved, she thinks. A whore's trick.

No, depraved is what she does with Zenin. The lover who does not try to please her, but who wants something badly from her. Making love to that lanky body that seems so much older than any she has ever touched before. In the blackout, the intense shameful pleasure of kisses that seem to drain her. The weary weight of his long limbs, a weight she somehow associates with his money. The foreign smell of him, a popular aftershave Mira has smelled in airports and along shopping streets in Rome. The scent makes her imagine a village of color-less houses in the early morning beside a flat sea. Worst of all is listening to him talk as they sit at lunch at restaurants around Rome: his clumsy jokes, his bragging about car or boat races he sponsors, about flying planes to places full of sand or snow, where other rich people gather. A tiny rational part of her notes sardonically how impressed she is, how she is unfaithful not just to Nick but to herself.

Afterward she always swears to herself that it's the last time. And then in a week or two he calls and she meets him at the d'Inghilterra. Dressing and arriving with that shiver of desire, like a bad child who likes her punishment.

She's appalled by her own behavior but not enough to stop. Because if she's honest she realizes that there is something there made to mea-sure for her, Mira. Something Nick, with his open blue gaze, can't see.

So she sits scanning her books at the playground. As shafts of dusty light strike down through the club-shaped leaves of the old chestnuts and children shriek and au pairs gossip and young Roman mothers come and go in tight skirts and high heels.

"Perhaps there was a world where people could act on whims, where deeds could detach themselves cleanly from all notion of consequences."

"For as the Freynshhe booke sayth, the quene and sir Lancelot were togydirs. And whether they were abed oother at other manner of disportis, me lyst not thereof make no mention, for love that tyme was nat as loveys nowadayes."

It's like a drug, you can handle it, Mira tells herself. You can do this and then stop it and nothing will get lost.

RACHEL

It's a bit of a religion being a foreign woman in Italy. I should know because I've been in this bloody country for eighteen years. Perhaps a better word is a *cult,* like Scientology. There are distinct stages. Girls arrive and they go slightly mad—think they've died and gone to a heaven of real men. Because I think Italians do the Latin courtship thing better than Spaniards or anybody else—all *spumante* and roses and making you feel like you're a natural woman Aretha-style. And the *meridionali* especially are spunky little fuckers. The nice politically correct English or American blokes you went to university with look a bit contralto by contrast. And then you settle down and find out that Romeo is fucking everybody—but everybody—else, and that his family is a pain in the arse besides. There's always some large disillusionment, and perhaps you get bitter and leave. But if you get through that phase, you settle down and start making a life. You start having a laugh at things. Italian women don't because they're genetically programmed to know what we have to learn. Mira's at the laughing stage because she knows she's all right. Vanni's a lovely man, though a bit short and intello-leftist for my taste. What the hell does it matter if he likes a bit of lobster on the side?

17

NICK

2005 · AN OBITUARY

The usual end-of-August pickup in the news, as if history were actually a trudging wage slave, bound to the convention of a fixed summer holiday. After a few relaxing weeks of paparazzi essays on the great and near great caught in absurd vacation mode—in cowboy hats and bikinis and giant hip-hop shorts; topless; bottomless; bulging; bejeweled; on the wrong beach with the wrong partner—suddenly the less great, the insignificant, are once again in the headlines, dying in their anonymous international swarms. In exploding aircraft, in sudden bursts of suicidal flesh and blood over the dun-colored grit of the petroleum lands, in floods and plagues and pitifully overcrowded trucks and ships of refugees heading toward dubious hope. In the sudden efflorescence of headlines, the small death notice is almost lost. But Nick catches sight of it.

The old girl is dead, he says to his wife.

He and Dhel are home in bed on a Sunday afternoon, alternately making love, reading the papers, and dripping cold sesame noodles on the duvet. A rare, almost unheard of, treat. The closed curtains making the Notting Hill daylight into twilight, the air conditioner providing a bracing chill, and Ben Harper, turned down low on MTV, singing in an annoying reggae whisper about changing the world. The two little girls, Julia and Eliza, are visiting Dhel's mother in Zurich, leaving the high white rooms of the family flat in Chepstow Villas resounding with their absence. Nick got in last night from Singapore and now revels in what his friend Vakhil has dubbed *uxory*—the thrill you get when you screw your wife in your own sheets after weeks of hotels. Ulysses knew about it.

What old girl? asks Dhel, tapping at her computer, where she is looking at shoes and also checking an installation proposed for one of her artists at a museum in Japan. The queen, Joan Collins, or your ex-wife?

Nick decides to pass over this last remark. None of the three, he says, tugging gently at her long soft hair. An old woman in Italy. You met Lodovico, the Lehman Brothers guy. Well, it's his great-aunt, the Princess Caetanae. Famous in politics back in her day. They call her a pope maker, say she was Mussolini's lover before she switched sides.

And did you get to know her?

Not well, Nick says honestly. But I went to tea with her once or twice. She liked me. She even gave me advice. This was in Rome, a long time ago.

Of course it was in Rome, says his wife, yanking her hair out of his hand. I can always tell, because you get that sound in your voice.

1986 · THE BLACK PRINCESS

Che bel giovanotto. What a beautiful young man.

This old woman, wheelchair bound, whose series of names—one of them is Medici—rolls out like a pageant of Roman and Florentine history, makes a compliment sound like a knighthood. Wrapped in a cashmere shawl, she sparkles at Nick with a hard flirtatious topaz gaze as he sits at tea with her and her grandnephew Lodovico, the most aristocratic and dimmest of his colleagues at the bank. The room around them is full of floral chintz and potted azaleas like Nan Reiver's sitting room back in Newport, but here the windows look out with a proprietorial air upon the crowds and autumn colors of Campo de' Fiori, which since Guelph and Ghibelline days has been the property of the princess's family. And on the ceiling above the chintz, frescoed giants struggle, as they do throughout the vast marble gloom of the palace.

Inferior nineteenth-century copy, says the princess, nodding at the ceiling. We're in the attic here. I thought it was more amusing, cozier, to leave it unrestored.

Nick can tell that she has never needed to be beautiful. A leathery tanned chinless face with a nose like a griffin's beak and an exquisitely styled crest of silver hair. She wears gold earrings that look the size of bucklers, a huge signet ring on her mannish hands, and is famous among the famous in Italy. *La principessa nera,* they call her, last of the old papal black aristocracy, a bipartisan political string puller, a chivier of financiers and heads of state, leader of the old guard who scorned the upstart Savoy monarchy, a maverick who once defied her Fascist family to support the partisans. Lover, depending on whom you talk to, of everyone from Mussolini to Fidel Castro. She is also, Lodovico tells him, money mad, slippery as an eel. Poor brainless Lodovico sits through an hour of teasing and cross-examination every week to safe-guard his inheritance.

But now the old woman plays at flattering Nick. You make me think of a Wagnerian hero. That high forehead of a *preux chevalier.* Or per-haps young Lochinvar. You came out of the West. Her English is per-fect, and she is charmed when Nick, the teacher's pet, supplies the next line of the poem. They sip weak tea and eat tiny stale rounds of pizza *bianca,* and in Roman dialect she remarks to Lodovico that this is the first friend he has brought her who has any charm.

All this goes to Nick's head more than if she were gorgeous and young. She knows New England well and had a fourth cousin who married a Lodge. She asks about Nick's wife, and the yellow eyes grow piercing when Nick explains that Mira is African American. *Avevi pro-prio bisogno di sposarla, figlio mio?* Forgive an old woman's bluntness, but did you really need to marry her? My brother certainly didn't marry every pretty black piece he came across in Abyssinia. But Americans are different, and I'm sure she worships you.

Lodovico gives a bray of laughter. No, he worships her!

The princess does not seem to change expression, but wrinkles fan out suddenly around her heavy eyebrows. They tell me my advice is worth something, and I'm going to give you some. It is this: Never worship your wife. Here in Rome, we know that marriage, like everything else, is a game of power. Take it seriously, and arrange, with constant vigilance, to have the power, or she'll make a fool of you. *È sei troppo bello per giocare al cornuto contento*—you're too good-looking to play the happy cuckold.

Afterward, when Nick has been warned by several Italian and foreign friends about the princess's propensity for picking up well-bred young foreigners for use in her real estate maneuverings—she owns hundreds of apartments and thousands of acres in Lazio and Tuscany—after she has urged him to return for tea and given him the freedom of the family archive, he wonders how he sat there and let her say those things. But she says them with a mixture of mischief and genuine ribald goodwill, smiling at him with teeth as crooked and brown ₋as those of the old vegetable vendor. As if she likes him and is telling the truth as near as she can come to it. Which, it turns out, she is.

PRINCIPESSA CAETANAE

A very pretty boy, and not stupid either. Just ten or fifteen years ago, I would have taken him from that wife of his and made something out of him. But I'm too old for lovers now, and *entre nous,* breeding Jack Russell terriers is more amusing than breaking in a protégé *in bianco*— without going to bed with him. So let him go. What eyes and shoulders, though—makes that fool Lodovico look like the inbred scarecrow that he is.

18

ZENIN

2005 · ON THE BEACH

Tropical Zenin, shaded by palm fronds, roasted by equatorial sun, wearing baggy pink hibiscus-print shorts, learns of the death of the old princess several days late, in one of the starched array of Italian newspapers handed him with morning coffee and a theatrical salaam by an attendant in a fez who speaks with a suspiciously Neapolitan accent.

He is vacationing in a famous Indian Ocean hotel, palatially thatched, redolent of ylang-ylang, its pools and beach dotted with Russian billionaires and a few movie stars. Pissed off because he was bullied into coming here by his girlfriend, Mariella, instead of staying comfortably on his boat in the Balearics. And because he has found himself in that most horrific of situations, the August hotel vacation with middle-aged friends. While the wives—most of them old trouts hardly fit for bathing suits—go on cultural outings to Arab ruins and spend endless hours in esoteric spa treatments, the husbands go deep-sea fishing, play *scopone*, discuss Viagra, and eye the girls on the beach. Zenin is irritated that the Russian tycoons—most of whom look like kids, and who could buy and sell him—have wives or resident whores who are infinitely better-looking than Mariella. She's gotten leathery and bores the tits off him by rattling on about the Dalai Lama.

And the combination of mangoes and too much seafood gives him the runs.

His mood isn't improved by the news. He knew the old girl from Cortina, where she had a Hapsburgian chalet—kitschy furniture made out of antlers, with polychrome ceilings transferred from a defunct family castle. She was a horrific snob but, like many aristocrats from threadbare families, no slouch when it came to latching onto money. You had to respect that. It had even flattered him when she cultivated his acquaintance to push a few dodgy real estate deals in Rome and Sardinia, deals of staggering size and ineptitude that he quickly figured out had to do with the political tentacles of Fininvest and the tanned, smiling dwarf Berlusconi.

She'd even placed a few of her ugly nieces in his path—an enormous honor—hinting that she'd be able to overlook his low birth and divorce and pull Vatican strings for an annulment. That failing, she had been kind about his son, Daniele, when news of the boy's birth was choice gossip among Zenin's friends. No, he'd liked her—that eagle's face, the hooded eyes that went straight through you and could turn opaque and impudent like a street urchin's, that steely flirtatiousness that could, without warning, loose a gust of invective in dialect. She was Rome itself, high and low.

He throws down the paper and stares out past the wicker lounges and tall wooden statues, past the bougainville, the huge blue-and-white umbrellas, and the bronzed bathers on the sugar-white expanse of beach and the blank tropical sea. A little Mauritian girl in a ruffled nylon dress, one of the few locals who occasionally slip past the hotel guards, runs by and glances at him with a face that shocks him with its beauty. A black angel, who for some reason makes him think of the princess, of his dying sister, of time he is losing or has lost. I want, thinks Zenin, to go home. What the fuck am I waiting for? He picks up his cellphone and punches a number.

1986 · REVELATIONS

I have to tell you something, Zenin says to Mira.

They met in the late morning, went immediately to bed, and now are eating lunch at the Casino Valadier. The ornate Belle Epoque pavilion with its well-heeled vulgar clientele ignoring the city view, like Mira and Zenin, from adulterers' camouflage among potted palms. Prices like the worst tourist trap, yet decent food. Mira and Zenin have discovered a shared passion for fish, and years later the older Mira will wonder how an illicit romance could have been constructed on mountains of fried sardines.

What do you need to confess? That you're married too?

Mira is wearing a white dress that looks cheap to Zenin—he will, he thinks, have to buy her some proper clothes—but that shows off her figure. She is smiling, at the high tide of any happiness she'll ever have with Zenin, desiring, desired, but still detached. Believing that she can pick up this mystery in her hand and put it down when she likes, unscathed. But now Zenin takes the first step toward changing it all.

No, married is one thing I am not. But I have a child.

I knew that. Two girls, at university, aren't they?

No, I mean a young child. A boy just a little older than your daughter. A year and six months.

She puts down her fork. How can that be?

He shrugs. A girl I met about the same time I met you. Italian, of course. A professor's daughter from Udine.

He is staring at her arms as he tells the story, at her long bones and tender skin that call up all the fascination of the body that he has possessed in many positions and will soon possess again. Half distracted, he lays aside his usual caution and sketches for her the fights, the hysterics, the family councils, the bribes.

I offered her a million dollars to have an abortion, he says, forgetting himself. His face is suffused with a dull flush. But she knew better, bargained on the fact that I'd fall in love with the boy. And I did.

Is he beautiful?

Beautiful. A midget with his hair cut down to zero, running and laughing . . .

Mira says all the right things, how wonderful it is for Zenin, describes the passion she feels for that darting spark of life, her own daughter, Maddie. Disconcerted, she resorts to a feminine social manner, a ladylike enthusiasm that she has never used before in her life. Then asks carefully if the boy and his mother live with Zenin.

He gives a harsh laugh. No, I bought them a house in their own city, in Udine. They are very well taken care of.

And the mother, what is she to you?

To me she is like an ex-wife, someone I have no interest in. But naturally she wants nothing more than to marry me.

And will you?

I would never marry her. Never. Zenin's eyes blaze coldly. She tricked me, and that would mean that she had won.

Well. They stare at each other over melting glasses of *sgroppino*, lemon ice whipped with vodka, that the waiter has placed in front of them. The nearly empty restaurant with its tarnished fin de siècle frivolity seems to have expanded around their two small figures like a big pink balloon.

Zenin feels obscurely relieved. Yet he has not added an important fact, for the simple reason that he is not aware of it. It is that the strange bitter-edged belated passion he feels for his infant son has a counterpart in the growing possessiveness he feels for Mira.

As for Mira, she feels as she used to when she was small on summer afternoons back in Philadelphia, when masses of electricity rolled in clouds overhead. The devil is moving his furniture, the devil is beating his wife, her parents would say. The sense of huge domestic motions in a gigantic occult world. She cannot grasp the ins and outs of risk and vendetta in what she has heard. How a man and a woman could bargain over a child's life. She has not had time to wonder yet what connection it all has to her. Yet she understands instinctively that such information contaminates.

Zenin reads it in her eyes and it excites him. Let's go back to the hotel, he says. There's still time.

HONORINE — THE LITTLE MAURITIAN GIRL ON THE BEACH

Maman m'a dit jamais aller sur la plage près de l'hôtel à Fosse des Biches. My mother said never walk on the hotel beach near the tourists because the guards will chase me and the *wasa*, the foreigners, are the kind that do bad things to little black girls. But Laurencine and Saida and I sneak in anyway and ask for bonbons, and sometimes they give them to us because they are very rich. But this man looks old and very sad and not the kind who gives candy, and he looks at me in a hungry way that makes me afraid that he might steal or even try to eat me up, so I pick up my feet and dash along in the water and don't stop until I'm near the rocks at Baie de la Cratère even though the new dress is all wet.

19

MIRA

2005 · THANKS

We have a ninety-six-year-old woman here, Mira tells the emergency-room receptionist. We think she's had a seizure. We've been waiting nearly forty minutes.

Keeping her bootless rage in check as the nurse presents one insurance form after another. Resisting the urge to scream about the barbarism of this bureaucracy compared to Italy or any place else with decent public health care.

It's late Thanksgiving night in Philadelphia, cold and gusty with dervishes of leaves in the streets, cloud wrack racing over stars. Mira and the boys have flown over from Turin and Maddie has come from Boston for a family reunion at Mira's sister's, Faith's, house in Mount Airy. And as happens once or twice in every family, the feast has finished up in the hospital. Great-aunt Sissie got dizzy after the pumpkin pie. It sounds, thinks Mira, like a bad television script. But families are bad scripts. And welcome back home.

Leaning on Faith's shoulder, the old woman's puckered face looks yellow-green under the wincing fluorescent lights, her white hair so carefully styled at the beginning of the evening now standing on end like stiff flames. The pleated wool skirt of her suit rucked up to show a Chantilly-lace border on a satin slip. Tall, withered, and spotted, but unbent by age, with a peremptory Tidewater voice, Aunt Sissie is a preacher's daughter from Suffolk, Virginia. A former belle at Spelman who, like so many women in Mira's family, went on to teach elementary school. But Sissie's epic career spanned the exodus of Jews and Italians from Philadelphia's row-house neighborhoods, postwar black migration, urban decay, and gentrification. She began with McGuffey readers and ended with *Sesame Street*.

Like some fabulous old tree in a shrinking forest, she has outlived Faith and Mira's parents, is in fact the last of the southern-born throng of ancient female relatives who loomed so large at childhood holiday tables that Faith and Mira privately referred to them as Aunthenge.

I wet myself, Sissie murmurs now to her grandnieces, stretched on a gurney in the little observation room as shiny and bleak as a supermarket. I'm so ashamed, she adds in a whisper. And Mira's heart turns over. The only thing she can think to do is to grasp Sissie's hand—exactly, she realizes too late, as she used to do when she was little and wanted comfort herself.

But Faith speaks up. Don't you be ashamed, she says in the empowering tone she has developed as assistant head and director of diversity studies at a girls private day school. Then adds with just the right therapeutic hint of provocation, You changed our diapers and wiped our asses when we were babies too many times to be embarrassed about a little piss now.

Aunt Sissie rallies enough to give a thread of a laugh and tell Faith to watch her language. And Mira looks with her usual grudging respect at her handsome sister, two years older and of course ever worthy in a crisis. You can see it in her neatly cropped graying hair, her combination of African jewelry and suburban cashmere, her general headmistressy air of affirmation and substance.

It's hard to believe that when Mira and Faith were little they used to pee together, sitting backed up on the same toilet seat like a pair of spoons, giggling, bodies feeling as if there were no boundary of skin between them. Sisters, dressed like twins in velveteen coats for Sunday at New African, counting each other's mosquito bites in the lake-smelling summer darkness of the cabin down in the New Jersey Pine Barrens, stomping shoulder to shoulder in defensive formation near the bad boys' turf of the playground at Germantown Friends.

Sisters. And like all pairs of sisters, with that curious distinction of chosen territories: the *mappa mundi* boundary drawn between the civilized world of the responsible sister and the "here be dragons" realm of the sister who wanders off.

Mira stopped confiding in Faith when she was about nine and realized that every secret flowed through a permeable membrane in Faith and ended up with their mother. And that Faith thought this was the natural order of things.

Faith went to Penn, married the son of family friends, and settled in a fieldstone Colonial just six blocks from the house where she and Mira grew up. Nowadays she arrives on trips to Italy knowing the exact layout of Chianti country, armed with floor plans of art galleries and lists of vintages to acquire.

But Faith doesn't cook, that's a comfort, thinks Mira. Something in her sister's idiosyncratic interpretation of feminism has kept her from following the Ward maternal tradition of working all day and sweating nobly over a fragrant stove all evening. Thanksgiving in her grand fire-lit dining room, with frozen supermarket turkey, greens, and succotash sent in from some neo soul-food caterer, is the usual anticlimax, superimposed on memories of the epic feasts the Aunthenge collective used to start preparing in September. As usual, Faith's husband, Raymond—an attorney who looks like Malcolm X but is actually a proselytizing Republican—needles Mira about politics. When Mira praises the rainbow peace banners displayed in Rome, Turin, and Milan, he gulps his pie and says, Honey, you stopped being black a long time ago. You going to stop being American now?

Up yours, Ray, says Mira. Mildly, because they have this argument every year.

Just then, slowly and heavily, Aunt Sissie slumps sideways in her chair.

Now Mira and Faith pass the usual hospital vigil, in garishly lit intimacy, the old woman dozing in between scans and incursions of nurses and irritable young doctors on holiday call.

The two sisters developed a choreographed expertise at being in hospitals together five years before, when their mother died of a cerebral hemorrhage. Faith is provident, magisterial, and Mira imitates

Faith. They take turns moving into and out of the room, calling Faith's house to give updates to Raymond, and overseas to Vanni, and checking on the children. The hospital is in Chestnut Hill, and Mira imagines the November wind tossing the oaks and beeches of the surrounding estates of the rich, whirling trash in the North Philadelphia slums, sweeping over the Atlantic coast, the mountains, the prairies, the whole vast slumbering country that still smells of roast turkey. Raking the cold sky where dawn is drifting eastward from Italy. Mira feels homesick for Vanni, for the warmth of their bed, for the creaks and chill and wood-smoke smell of the old villa above Turin. Strange to feel homesick in the place where you were born.

Aunt Sissie falls asleep, and Faith describes in an undertone how the old woman constantly forgets her medication and refuses assisted care. She's as stubborn as a mule. Worse than Mom was. I stop by every day, but sometimes I miss something.

Faith, I can't even think of the right way to thank you for everything you've done for Sissie. And that goes for Mom, too.

Faith looks more irritated than pleased. I don't need any thanks, she says, fiddling with an earring. I just do what there is to do. Because some people go away, and some stay and cope. Oh, that came out wrong, Mir. I mean that I'm the one who lives here, and you—

She stops as Aunt Sissie opens her eyes for a minute. The old woman's eyes, bluish with cataracts, look eerily large, set in nests of wrinkled skin that resembles cracked clay. She hardly looks human to Mira but rather like some ancient all-knowing extraterrestrial creature. She studies the sisters for a minute, adjusting the drip on her emaciated arm. And Mira and Faith stare back, transfixed the way they used to be years ago when she'd catch them giving each other Indian burns in church.

I love you girls, Aunt Sissie whispers.

1986 · CLOTHES

One day Zenin buys Mira some clothes. He goes to the most stylish shop in the city, a place owned by a cousin to whom he once loaned a lot of money. All the rich provincial women shop here, including his ex-wife, his sisters, and Tere, mother of his son.

Is she blond or dark, *dottore?* asks the shop assistant.

Dark. About so high. Size, slender.

Then I suggest, *dottore—*

Zenin suppresses a grin as mountains of clothes appear. Day and evening suits and dresses, belts, bags, shoes. All with the deep glow of expensive fabric or glittering with the fake gems and embroidered gold that designers have loved in the last few seasons. His cousin, sly bastard, must be trying to work off his debt in one blow. Yet it pleases Zenin to say yes or no, to heap up millions of lire worth of clothes until the envious eyes of the shopgirl grow round like cartoon characters. He's worked so hard all his life that he's never before indulged in the simple millionaire's pastime of dressing his mistress.

The next time he sees Mira, after they make love, he says, I brought you a present.

Her body stiffens. No. I said no presents.

It's nothing at all. Just look.

Mira is willfully ignorant of fashion for someone who has lived in New York. She buys cheap clothes from whatever shop catches her eye, or goes around in T-shirts left over from college. She looks at the Roman women traversing cobblestone streets in short skirts, fitted jackets, and high heels as using an idiom that just doesn't translate.

Now, naked except for a pair of underpants, she stands staring at a huge square suitcase covered with a web of gold initials. She knows the design means money, but apart from that it leaves her feeling curiously illiterate.

Go on, open it, says Zenin.

When she sees the clothes, she can't think of anything to say. Part of her wants to slam a fist into Zenin's face and walk out. But another part makes her lift the suitcase lid like a child opens a toy chest and plunge her hands into the layers packed in tissue paper inside. She's never felt anything like it. Satin, wool, leather, cashmere, and velvet packed together like a dense new element. Soft, so soft. And rising from it an almost imperceptible fragrance: the smell of luxury. She thinks of Ali Baba, of all plunderers dipping their hands for the first time into treasure, and she never wants to take her hands away. And at the same time, she feels trapped, for the first time understanding what it means to belong to Zenin.

He stands beside her and pulls out a suit. Put it on. Please.

He helps her, zipping the skirt and buttoning the jacket as if she were a child. Then leads her to the mirror. Look.

The suit is made of wool, not the wool of school uniforms and ski sweaters but soft as the pelt of a mythical animal. Feather-light, lined in slippery silk, it clasps her as if it has known her all her life, as if it loves her. And it is red, not the valentine red of the Hotel d'Inghilterra walls where they spent their first few times together, but what Mira sees as a perfect red. Not warm, not cold, the red of brides in medieval pictures, the *rosso porpora* of cardinals' robes.

And the girl she sees in the mirror is transformed into a girl in an advertisment, in a dream, a girl framed by old cities and the triumphant illusion of an unknown place. A girl like those she has seen stepping into and out of shops on Via Condotti. A girl certainly not like her natural self, but mesmerizing.

Valentino, says Zenin. Indifferent to his own appearance, he knows the name of all objects, all products and styles, that the world associates with status. Most of the women he knows live for these things. Beg for them. Mira's savage ignorance—like a Wild West Indian, he jokes to himself—has annoyed him and made him feel vaguely powerless. Now, watching her fall under the spell of the red suit, he experiences the same satisfaction a trainer might feel who has managed to bridle a half-broken colt. Satisfaction mingled with slight pity. He hands her a pair of black silk shoes with stiletto heels and the transformation is complete.

He pulls out a velvet dress. Try this now. Versace.

And Mira obeys, pinning up her wild hair, not taking her eyes off the girl in the mirror.

They work their way through the layers in the suitcase. The shopgirls have guessed well; the clothes might have been made for her. Zenin dresses and undresses her like a ladies' maid. And as he does, he teaches her the names of the designers. Fendi, Missoni, Montana, Alaia.

Laughing, despising herself, she repeats the names, because he is so earnest, almost religious about it, because he has never before been so tender and attentive.

Later he says, I'll have the hotel send the suitcase to your house. In the morning, when your husband isn't there.

You're mad. I can't take these clothes home.

They're yours. You can find a place to hide them. Or—Zenin pauses—do you want me to throw them away?

Mira is silent.

A few days later, she drags the suitcase out from under the bed in the spare room to show a girlfriend. The friend is a voice student from South Africa, with skin the color of dark plums; a Methodist, fat and beautiful and preachy. She lives in a hostel near Via Prenestina and has been scolding Mira ever since Mira confessed about Zenin one afternoon. You have a good-looking husband who loves you, her friend is saying as Mira unzips the suitcase. What do you need with an old Italian man? A dirty old rich man? You should send this stuff right back.

Just look, says Mira.

Her friend looks, plunges her hands in, as Mira did, gently unfolds the red suit. She is quiet for a moment, touching a pair of shoes, a coat, a satin bag. Then she lets out her breath and looks Mira straight in the eye. An unreadable, purely feminine look.

Keep it, she says.

FAITH

Once when my sister was about seven and I was nine, she shoved a piece of soap in her ear. It was after dinner in the summer, and Mom and Dad were sitting outside in the backyard reading the paper and I was just settling down to watch TV because it was Mira's turn to clear the table, when Mira starts howling from the powder room and it turned out that the crazy girl had tried to smell a piece of Yardley soap through her ear. Then Mom has to rush her to Temple emergency room and I end up with the dishes. I don't want to play the good girl—bad girl, Martha–Mary Magdalene routine, but this is so typical. She was always flighty and nosy, always getting in a fix and out of her re-sponsibilities.

I was the prettier one, everybody said. The one who behaved her-self.

When we played, Mira was always a buccaneer or a treasure hunter or James Bond.

And we won't even go into when we were teenagers and those sex poems she published in the creative-writing magazine.

She married Nick, and of course it imploded, because holding on to your first marriage requires backbone. But Mira married a white boy and went off to Italy as one of her adventures and then got bored when she found out it was work like anything else.

That's how I see it, anyway, though she never talks about what hap-pened. But I'm sure whatever it was, it was her fault.

I read my sister's books and articles, I do. If they're suitable, I even recommend them to the school librarian, though I have a nagging sus-picion that one day she'll make fun of me in one of them. Make fun of good old American Faith, Hope, and Charity, as she used to call me.

Anyway, how it goes is that she swans in from Europe for a holiday here or a funeral there. And I get on with things. She's settled down, I admit, and has a lovely family now with that nice guy Vanni—who must have the patience of Job. But whenever I'm talking to my stu-dents or my own daughters about inner strength and serious goals, about morality, I have an opposite example in the back of my mind, and that's Mira.

20

NICK

2005 · VERDE

Dude, this is awesome, says Nick's brother, LT. You did this?

Yes, I, the Lord almighty, snapped my fingers and it came into being. No, doofus, I told you it's a client.

LT, short for Little Teddy, in some circles known as Tedward the Unsteady, widens his protuberant pale eyes in mock alarm as he has done since he was a hyperactive four-year-old and Nick at seven threatened to shove him off the Sunfish. Nowadays he's three inches taller than Nick, a former varsity wrestler, not fat but tanklike—as only American athletes get, thinks Nick—lighthearted, foul-mouthed, and balding. And he should still be on Ritalin.

The brothers met up in Shanghai last night, and now push their way into a packed cocktail crowd under green lights in the Grand Hyatt ballroom. The launch of a new gin. A mountain of green bottles forms the centerpiece of the room, with a dancing laser show of emerald helixes above and green strobe lights zooming against black velvet walls. The pretty crowd is part expat, but mainly tireless South China social troopers, old and new orders of tai tais fluttering their designer labels like knights' standards. Nick sees the beverage company CEO for Asia and the gorgeous Singaporean PR director holding court over by the bar with the SAP Mendocino software guy, besides a half-dozen friends and acquaintances of his from Beijing and Guangzhou. The ty-coons, as expected, have stayed home.

I think I figured out that the theme is green, says LT, swilling his second glass of the specially created cocktail.

The drink's called Green Icon. Cheesy, but effective. And there are supposed to be green icons displayed around the room. A Buccellati emerald, a famous jade Buddha, a piece of Wimbledon—

A leprechaun's ass? Shit, there is some serious pussy going on. And not just Chinese. What's with all the icy blondes?

Second-string Russian models. There's a direct pipeline from Byelorussia.

That is some ill pussy. And I dig the phat French house beat. Seventies Eurotrash discos always rock.

Nick watches LT's round yellow head with its pink bald spot bobbing above the crowd as he toddles off toward the bar, and wonders as always how it is that a middle-aged white American male can talk dated preppie hip-hop and live. Even in China, where middle-class teenagers are just exiting their Ol' Dirty Bastard phase. But Teddy, a hedonist since he was a fat towheaded toddler gobbling stolen Milk Duds, gets away with it, the way he gets away with everything without even using irony, through the simple pleasure he takes in anything that is not his. Other people's girlfriends, other people's cars, drugs, music, and money. Ex–St. George's stoner, kicked out of Colby for pasting his bare ass on the wrong windshield; ex-manager for a defunct white rap group—thus the jargon—ex-manager of a failed Provençal restaurant in Napa Valley; now curiously solvent from a mysteriously successful Internet business he has set up to buy and sell classic cars.

Now he's shown up in China and announced to Nick over dinner—Nick's treat—at Sens & Bund that he's leaving his long-suffering girlfriend, Morag, to marry a Dutch dermatologist he met when he sold her an Aston Martin that once belonged to a minor television actor. They're madly in love. She wants a big white wedding at the Santa Clara Auberge du Soleil. And a honeymoon in Tuscany.

Nick protests. You just can't marry somebody you met five minutes ago when you sold her a car.

Not just a car. An Aston Martin DB4. The altar of true love.

And what about poor Morag? She put up with all your shit over the years and gets dumped? Teddy, you're not exactly marriage material. You're over forty and you've fucked most of the female population of North America.

As did you, my brother, retorts LT equably. In your prime, working your way around your bouts of fidelity. Everything on two legs and some, dare I say, on four. It's about moving on from one phase to another. I never thought I'd be into heavy metal, but now I'm listening to German progressive stuff. Queensryche. Dream Theater. Like that. By the way, did you know that the Nazis invented the first sexbot? Kronhild, they called her, and she was Aryan and anatomically correct. Isn't that wild?

You can't argue with Little Teddy. When Nick calls Dhel from his hotel room, she scolds him. Anyone would think you're jealous, she says.

It drives me crazy when fools go on about love.

Who are you to judge what's love and who's a fool? demands his wife from all those thousands of miles away. All of his girlfriends and wives have always had a weak spot for LT.

Now Nick watches as his enormous sibling surges out of the crowd with two glasses of Green Icon held high. His face is shining the way it used to when he successfully pilfered something of Nick's.

Come on, best man, drink to me, says LT. Toast my bride and the future. In green. *Verde, como te quiero verde*—how the fuck does that Spanish poem go?

Nick grabs the glass. First, to the bridegroom, he says.

1986 · VINES, WATER, CASTLE

If she's acting like a bitch, screw around a bit and clear your head. Then you can decide whether to keep her, kick her out, or kill her.

This advice comes from Nick's friend Lorenzo, a union lawyer in his forties sometimes called Lorenzaccio for his evil tongue and sometimes Rambo for his habit of toting a machete as he leads Sunday jaunts along lost Etruscan roads.

Seven thirty in the morning, the July sun already blinding over the Sabine hills, and the two have run four kilometers down the dusty road from the farmhouse Mira and Nick have rented. This summer, which will be their last together, they are spending on the slopes of Lago di Bracciano. Bracciano, liquid eye of an extinct volcano, rimmed in gritty black beaches and tourist restaurants specializing in eels, is said to be haunted like all the lakes in Latinium. Beautiful beyond hope with its hazy blue depths and vine-covered slopes, the Orsini castle crouched at one end like a beast at a watering hole. The lake has a disorienting simultaneous feeling about it, as if time were blurred and a million past and future lives floated in its atmosphere, without the gross material weight that is history in Rome. Popes, dukes, Partisans, Roman generals, Samnite guerrillas, Etruscan kings, Swiss tourists, all present, all unimportant. As if a series of transparent stage sets have been laid one over the other, giving the landscape in every direction a shimmer, like something seen through tears.

Nick and Lorenzo have run through the standing wheat and faded poppies and the bullrushes that lie along the shore path. Here they pause, sheeted with sweat at their halfway point, in the shade of a fig tree that sits on a spit of land that extends into the water that is already beginning to be dotted by sails in the distance. Among the wasps and the ferment of the ripe black figs hanging on the branches and rotting on the ground, they piss, gulp water, jump into the lake, and swim a few strokes before starting back. Nick marveling privately at the energy contained in the older man's small hairy potbellied body.

Lorenzo never stops talking when he runs, his bearded simian face turning delicate maroon as he lectures Nick about everything from the weeping Heraclitus to the latest scandals in the Craxi government. About ancient and modern heroes: the bloody last stand of the Italic League rebels against the war machine of Sulla's legions at Sentinum; Di Pietro nowadays, battering at the tawdry gilt fortress constructed by the villains of Tangentopoli. Talks as well with lubricious anatomical specificity about the women he is seeing (this summer, a surgeon's wife from Modena, convent educated, insatiable).

But this is the first time he has commented on the marriage of his two young friends—*i neonati,* the Newborns, as he calls them privately—though anyone can see that the marriage is poised at that interesting brink of dissolution that attracts spectators, scavengers. Noble rot.

The Newborns' vacation house—decorated with slightly too much toile de Jouy by a niece of the old princess—brings to life the American dream of Italian pastorale.

Platters of pasta and fava beans devoured in the pergola shade of a baroque vine. Moonlight vigils to watch the wild boar come snuffling out of the forest to raid the kitchen garden. Ethnological trips to country dance halls; to Communist unity festivals; to local gastronomic celebrations of every type, from strawberries to snails; to Gubbio for the phallic festival race of Sant'Ubaldo; to Orte for the mating dance of sacred portraits.

Then there is the peasant family on the property, who in spite of their blaring Berlusconi television, speak a brambly dialect—surely related to pre-Latin Oscan or Sabellian—and make satisfying feudal references to "his excellency, the prince." Above all there is the view, the intrusive beauty of the sweep of vines, water, castle. Nick commutes to work through the traffic of the Cassia each day, while Mira writes in an earwiggy but atmospheric tower room.

Their small daughter, terra-cotta brown in the sunlight, squealing with joy as she rolls about with a litter of white Maremmano puppies. The cheap Frascati, the mild drugs, the daring talk, the flirting, the self-conscious nudity. An ever-changing cast of houseguests, young Americans with expensive teeth and resonant fellowships, minor artists and musicians, aristocratic Roman and Tuscan riffraff in quilted shooting vests.

A happy, wise, and good world, thinks Lorenzo, who has rented out his own country house to rich Swedes and so visits the Newborns almost every weekend. But with something rotten behind it, as is always the case. *Et ego in arcadia*. And you don't have to look too far. He likes Mira, who is smart and a nice little piece, but he sees that she's got that hard bloom on her that means that she is putting horns on her husband. Who loves her. The odd thing is that she loves him too.

Hence Lorenzaccio's charitable and diplomatic suggestion.

Nick is still ass-deep in the lake, his old washed-out Harvard running shorts ballooning ridiculously in the murky water around his waist. His wet torso, the older man enviously notes, has the lapidary symmetry of an old statue. It glistens in the sun, the soaked scanty chest hair dripping downward in a V. Ah, youth. Silly twat, Mira.

Lorenzo doesn't know what result he expects from this kind of fatherly meddling. Tears, perhaps, or a punch in the face. Or a tight Puritan smile.

But Nick surprises him. First by waiting to reply like a seasoned negotiator, after pulling one big foot after another out of the suck of the slimy black lake mud and deliberately wringing out the sides of his shorts, once he stands in the buzzing shade of the fig tree.

Then he looks directly at Lorenzo, who flinches for a moment at the acuteness of that look. Saxon blue, surely, as he has thought many times, as clear as the eyes of Pope Gregory's angels. But with a stony desolation to it and something more: a calm rigor, a decisiveness that sends a thought like a chill through Lorenzo—that he has underestimated this American kid.

Lorenzaccio, caro mio, says Nick. *Perché non fare cazzi tuoi?* Why don't you mind your own fucking business?

LORENZO

He's no fool. And if I'm not mistaken, a man already.

21

ZENIN

2005 · HOME RELAX

Not a bad idea, muses Zenin, shifting one bare leg over another as he lies propped up on a motte of hotel pillows. He is in Frankfurt, in the lunar luxury of a suite in a tubular modern hotel. A hotel with chromotherapy and ionized air and polished stones piled in the corners of its rooms. Watching one of his favorite movies, *Amici miei,* with Tognazzi and Noiret, on RAI satellite. But now the plasma television, wide as his outstretched arms, has switched to an infomercial with color and detail as hyperreal as a video game. A big blue massaging armchair, where a weary but excited-looking man in a business suit is sitting and talking while his face jiggles. The man on the screen has made the mistake of putting on hair gel, and Zenin, with schadenfreude, watches the man's young but balding scalp gleam under the lights. The new Home Relax, the man shouts. Like living with a shiatsu master!

What bullshit, Zenin thinks, as the price flashes on the screen. *Che cazzate.* We could make them for under thirty euros in Harbin. Problem is the containers. He knows he could produce them and make a success out of the whole thing, but does he care? Does he need to work anymore? To get any richer? He could hand the project on a plate to Tonio, his inept son-in-law, who would as usual fumble and drop it.

No, he, Zenin, would have to take care of it himself. He sighs melodramatically. Seeing ways to make money, he has come to realize, is a talent he was born with and other people weren't, like a dog who can hear sounds inaudible to human ears. And does he give a shit anymore?

The girl comes out of the bathroom at the far end of the suite, and he presses the mute button, leaving the blue armchair and the gesturing man on the screen. Stop, he says, and the girl freezes as if he has pushed a button to control her too. Turn around and then walk slowly, says Zenin. I want to look at you.

He requested a Russian girl and supposes that she is one, since he overheard her in the bathroom gabbling on a cellphone in Slavic gutturals. Yet she speaks some Italian, as almost all of them do. Very young, possibly a teenager. Tall and almost inhumanly perfect, as if she had just been created in that instant to lope toward him in maroon underpants and high heels. Nipples a faint lavender on lunar skin. Short platinum spikes of hair.

Are you from Moscow? he asks, as she gets closer.

No, Suzdahl. A holy city. City of churches.

He has nothing to say to that, so he makes a crude joke about vodka as he stands in front of her and she drops to her knees. Occasionally she angles her head to look up at him, and the progress of his pleasure is almost derailed by those fierce pale eyes and elfin hair.

Her body is so uncanny that he toys with the idea of taking her downstairs to dinner to impress Mario, his *amministratore delegato*, also in the hotel. And the tedious but essential German flunkies, Hammerschmidt and Thun. Take her out to a disco, perhaps, as they have done hundreds of times with hundreds of girls. But then, between gulps of Red Bull, the Russian girl says, *Adoro uomini italiani.* I love Italian men. Take me to Italy. And he knows it is time to get rid of her.

When the door has clicked shut and he has torn up the business card she gave him, he climbs back into bed for a nap before dinner. Home Relax, he sees, with an odd feeling of contentment, is still on the screen, and he turns out the light and watches the blue armchair shiver as he dozes off.

1986 · A GOOD BALANCE

This is one of the happiest times in Zenin's life. The instinctive alter ego that makes his fortune—in a series of twilit precise visions that anticipate fads, show the way to transform an almost imperceptible playground novelty into mass desire—is striding ahead with gigantic confidence. Provincial caution and tightfistedness keep him from overextending himself in the deceptive prosperity of those years, while hubris sends his chief rivals, the Fillia brothers, down in flames. He makes the deal of a lifetime with the biggest confectionary company in Europe. He's begun nosing around for production sites in China and Eastern Europe, because that's the way the wind is blowing. He buys himself a bigger boat and his first jet and a chunk of the Grand Prix.

And as another kind of luxury, he tells Mira he loves her. That means he feels he owns her and that he gets intense pleasure from fucking her, not the least because she still feels distant to him. For Zenin at this point she is still the American writer, adrift in a rarefied atmosphere where he is out of place. His Gulfstream and her work writing travel pieces means that they can meet often. For a day, an afternoon, a night. Not just in Rome. In Venice, Paris, Vienna, Budapest, Vienna, Monte Carlo.

He's pleased with her beauty, which he has helped her make over in a dramatic yet conventional way, so that other rich men in airports and hotels turn around to look at her. He knows it's a mistake, but it relaxes him to talk to her about love, to watch the transforming effect it has on her foreign intellectual haughtiness. He doesn't actually want her to leave her husband—poor long-suffering fellow about whom he is not curious, but with whom he feels a sort of fraternal bond. Still, he suggests it.

The other side of the coin is his young son, Daniele. The child born of a mercenary speculation who is now the dearest thing in his life. Zenin's mother and sisters adore the little green-eyed boy whose existence was concealed from them for the first months of his life. The whole town now knows that moneybags Zenin has a son with a professor's daughter from Udine. Every weekend the boy and his mother come to stay at Zenin's big house on the river. They spend vacations on Zenin's boat or at his place in the Dolomites, and Zenin, who sleeps occasionally with Tere, enjoys these visits enormously. When the little boy with his funny red-cheeked squinting face runs up to him shouting Papà! Zenin feels all barriers collapse inside him. No woman ever made him feel like this.

So at the same time Zenin is exploring romantic possession with Mira, he is also exploring the mysterious land of paternal love. While Mira's family is withering, Zenin is, for the first time, coming to understand the joys of domesticity.

In a complacent moment, he remarks to Mira with his usual crude humor that it's a pity he can't be Muslim and marry two women at once. He's expecting a laugh, but Mira for the first time screams at him.

He stares at her coldly. And a few days later he goes to bed with a Brazilian girl he meets at a Formula One trial. After a while, these minor escapes from love become a habit. They give him a feeling his life is well balanced.

DANIELE

One of the first things I remember is Mamma dragging me out of Papà's big house on the river, pushing me into the big green car with the leather smell and driving away so fast through the Centro Storico that she scraped a fender. She was crying and shaking as she drove, and her hair was all over her head like snakes. There had been some kind of a fight about a fur coat, a coat so big and fluffy that when Papà gave it to her I made everybody laugh by asking whether it was a bearskin. Other people were there, Nonna, aunts, and cousins, and then it was just us. It must have been Christmas because I remember silver paper and *panettone*. And Mamma was happy at first and then she began talking louder and then she threw the big coat on the floor and shouted that if he couldn't give it to her with love, she wouldn't take it. *Niente elemosina!* she was screaming. *Niente tangente!* No charity, no bribes. And also, *Pensiamoci al bambino!* It was a refrain screeched in a terrible seagull's voice that I heard all through the time I was small. Think about the child. The child everyone had to think about was me.

My asshole cousin, Sandro the bully, used to tell me, *Siete zingari*—that we were gypsies, Mamma and I. Because we always seemed to be in the car racing back and forth between Udine and Papà's town. Or heading up to Cortina or to the Venice airport to fly somewhere to where the boat was. Though we had a home and a dog, it always seemed that we were moving, running in those days, and I associated our gypsy life with those terrible fights, with the fact that Papà didn't live with us, with the dark cloud of mystery that descended whenever I heard Mamma crying, the mystery that cleared up when I first heard the word I had to punch off Sandro's lips: *bastardo*.

It all seems a long time ago, those scenes. I heard from another cousin who heard Zia Clara gossiping that things were bad because Papà had a woman for a while that he was serious about. A foreign woman, an American. But that affair broke up and he never said anything about it.

Nowadays they get along, Papà and Mamma. They see each other and crack jokes at every family baptism, and they squabbled over the apartment I wanted to buy on the Zatteri in Venice like an old couple who have been married for twenty-five years. Papa always has his girlfriends, and when I was at school, Mamma had a fiancé for a long time, an osteopath from Asolo.

Everyone teases me for being Papà's favorite, and they ask me if I'm going to run the company. I say I'll do whatever Papà wants.

Neither Mamma nor Papà likes my girlfriend, but that's my business. She's part of the family now, and that's what counts in the end. We're getting married after I hand in my thesis next spring. Papà offered me the Shanghai office, but Caterina was born in Vicenza and wants to stay near her parents. So we'll start off here and buy a house in the hills when we have children. It feels good to stay put when you grew up as a gypsy.

22

MIRA

2005 · A CONTRAST

Just after Christmas, Mira has two dreams on the same night.

In the first, she is marrying Nick for the second time. They've met somewhere, and with a strange detached tenderness, he has taken her back. He is still the boy she knew, yet older, powerful, with something mysterious about him, and he wears a strange antique gold watch. There is something unsettling about his tenderness toward her, his lack of anger. She wants to ask what will become of his wife, Dhel, of his young daughters in London, but doesn't. They are going to be married again with both families present in a rambling New England house like his family's summer place in Maine. But Mira realizes she has only a pair of dirty jeans to wear. It doesn't matter to Nick and his family—they beg her to get married as she is—but she has a vision of herself in a beautiful cream-colored gown, and asks for just two hours to go to the mall. She sets out and in the flicker of an eye finds herself on a dark steamer like a banana boat, in neorealist black and white. She has become an Italian heroine like Anna Magnani, screaming and collapsing on deck as a dark man approaches her with a knife. And she knows it was all foreseen and planned.

In the second dream she gives an excuse to her husband, Vanni, and goes off for an illicit evening with a close family friend, the husband of one of those lifelong couples who are perfect for each other.

He takes her to a small, luxurious hotel in the center of Turin, obviously a local institution for well-heeled affairs. The lovemaking is pleasurable, but more pleasurable still is the feeling of security in the arms of this family friend, who she knows will never leave his wife. Mira derives great enjoyment from the sight of his shiny expensive shoes in the opulent Edwardian furnishings of the hotel, which are just like the rich dark interior of his car. At one in the morning, she leaps out of bed to slink guiltily home, trying to invent excuses for her husband, but when she arrives, Vanni just pats her hand and says, Don't fret. I know you've been with Edoardo; he called me so I wouldn't worry. He kisses her affectionately and they go to bed and Mira lies awake with relief and fear at the revelation of a world in which everything is safe, upholstered, rich, predictable. . . .

Both dreams leave her with the feeling of being permanently marked.

The contrast is important, she writes in her journal. Yet what is it, exactly? Is it the contrast between youth, when everything is a knife thrust, and middle age, when everything is cushioned with relativity? Or is it the contrast between the American I was and the European I have become?

1986 · HOUSE OF ZENIN

Mira spends the night at Zenin's house. It's easy; she's been interviewing on location on a television movie set in a grand Palladian villa near Asolo. Zenin sends a car to take her to Venice, where they meet for dinner at Harry's Bar. She walks into the buzz of the packed low-ceilinged room that always manages to seem more exciting than other places, and feels the stone and water maze that is Venice at night enfolding her like a black rose. She and Nick went to Harry's once and felt like tourists, exiled at an upstairs table. Now Cipriani himself waits on her, his long doughy face tender and deferential as he swaps jokes in dialect with Zenin. With them are Zenin's friend Macaco and Macaco's very young girlfriend, a Padua law student and a tennis champion. The girl has frizzy blond hair and bolts down a plate of squid risotto before going off to the bathroom to vomit. Mira likes Macaco, who flirts as easily as a gay man. When she asks how he met his girlfriend, he shrugs one plump shoulder and says, She's an heirloom—I had an affair with her mother first.

After midnight, Zenin drives her to his home from Piazzale Roma in his Porsche, tearing through cornfields as flat as Iowa until they reach the ramparts of a medieval city, wind through narrow streets, and drive through a silently opening gate. Afterward, for the rest of her life, she remembers that the brass knobs on the double front door are in the shape of turbaned Moors.

He takes her through his huge, empty house, turning on lights. She makes admiring noises at Gobelin tapestries, polychrome wood Madonnas, multifoliate Venetian chandeliers, acres of Aubusson and Savonnerie, a grand piano that twangs disconsolately out of tune when she touches a key. Privately she thinks the house looks like a hotel with its overstuffed furniture and big televisions in every room. A hotel without clients, growing dowdy in its luxury, the loneliest house she has ever been in. It used to belong to a prince, he tells her, and was the mainland residence of a family that produced six doges.

How did you first make your money? she asks him later, when she has seen the gold taps in his bathroom and lies in the acreage of his bed, which faces another immense television.

Zenin sighs. I sold encyclopedias and plastic goods door-to-door, village-to-village. In my father's old Giulietta. You can't imagine the humiliation.

It's love, thinks Mira as she falls asleep.

But later she wakes up in darkness, shaking. She thinks she hears Maddie crying, reaches out for Nick, then orients herself. In the complete blackness of a room shuttered in the European way so that no breath of air enters. A room like a vault. A foreign prison. And in the pitiless clarity that comes at these moments, she knows it is no use going to Zenin for comfort. Zenin, who sleeps with his big body curled rigidly in one corner of the vast bed. So she lies there, unable to pull even one illusion over her terror of what she has called into being. And knowing, too, that the remark about humilation is the truest thing Zenin will ever say to her.

The next day, Zenin leaves early for London and has Mira driven back to the film set at Asolo.

THE ASSISTANT DIRECTOR

She's been a hit among the cast and crew, a pretty young journalist with a lot more on the ball than most of the magazine morons the publicist brings around. Fluent in Italian, pleasantly ironic in the questions she asks, wandering through the formal gardens and the trailers and the frescoed halls with her little tape recorder, jotting down notes in the back of an old copy of *Crime and Punishment*.

23

NICK

2005 · ARIA

Nick chats online with his friend Kip, a medievalist at Case Western who has built his reputation on the Fourth Crusade. Nick has been fascinated since boyhood by the tale of the crusaders who started out from Venice to crush the infidel in Egypt, but were manipulated by Enrico Dandolo, the blind doge of Venice, to sail on Constantinople and sack the great Christian treasure house that was Byzantium. In between jokes that Dandolo was an early neoconservative and Kip's incomprehensible musings about religious recidivism among Janissaries, they both reflect on the naked power of the story, which is one of revenge. As a young envoy to Byzantium, Dandolo had his eyes put out by imperial order during a period of anti-Venetian violence. Decades later, as an old man, he returned to gut Constantinople with fire and sword, swept its treasures off to his land, and put a whore on the holy throne of Hagia Sophia.

The whole thing is an opera, says Nick's friend. The symmetry of it. You know he had himself buried in Hagia Sophia. Eastern Orthodox Christians spit on his grave.

A few weeks later, Nick dreams about the blind doge. The doge is dressed not in medieval clothes, but in an eighteenth-century Casanovan cloak and tricorne, with a beaked priapic carnival mask. And he is walking with Nick through the misty late-night alleys of

Venice, across bridges, along canals, through piazzas that Nick has never seen. Though he is blind, he gives Nick a tour, indicating half-ruined ancient constructions on either side, and even a Chinese shrine built of jade like a giant snuff bottle. They begin to hurry because they must get to a ship. And Nick feels the doge dragging him along with an iron grip like that of the Old Man of the Sea. They are no longer in Venice but in Constantinople, a set of Byzantine domes like pillows in the mist, long smudges of fire on the horizon. And at some point the doge has started singing the first words of the aria from *Rigoletto* in a wobbly countertenor: *Vendetta, tremenda vendetta!* Then he pulls off his mask to show his empty sockets. Singing in the same horrible voice—an eye for an eye . . .

Nick struggles to get away from the fire and the approaching soldiers and the sight of that monstrous blind singing face, and wakes up to find himself covered with sweat and fighting with one of the four slablike pillows on the bed in his room at the White Swan Hotel in Guangzhou. He gets up and goes to the bathroom and stares at his naked cadaverous self in the greenish fluorescent light. Stares with a masochistic appreciation, possible only at three A.M. in a Chinese hotel bathroom smelling faintly of mildew, at sad orchidaceous genitals, baggy slit eyes, porcupine hair, and incipient potbelly. The sights and sounds of the dream have not receded—as in very few dreams, the images remain hard and clear, and he feels his defenseless physical self contained in it like a tortoise in a shell. The feeling he understands very clearly is an anger so ravenous, so voracious for revenge, that the razing of a city, the sack of a civilization, is nothing.

Venice, he thinks.

Then he says aloud, I should have killed that fucking bastard. I should have cut off his balls and shoved them down his throat.

He is left feeling drained and vaguely ashamed, as if he has had a wet dream. And relieved that Dhel is not with him. He turns on CNN and watches the market reports and the news. A mine explosion in China. A car bomb in Israel. Women and children hunted through caves in the Sudan. American soldiers staked out on rooftops against a sand-colored glare. He just watches the pain of the world flash by, without having obscene conversations out loud with heads of state, as he usually does when he is alone in hotel rooms. After a while he is able to sleep.

1987 · THE PROCESS

People fall in love in an instant, but it takes longer to fall out of love.

Mira and Nick no longer fuck, but in the night when they are asleep they move toward each other and fall into a desperate embrace like two drowning people. Their pulses synchronize, their anguish lifts. Mira's devouring thoughts of Zenin, Nick's willful blindness, all of it departs with heavy wing strokes, leaving husband and wife sleeping embraced. The babes in the wood, huddled together against cold and death. All the lies, the contrived arguments, the discussions where he demands to know what is going on and she says nothing, nothing; all the circling hostility that makes unhappy families just as boring as happy ones—all this lifts in a few magical nighttime hours. Sometimes Maddie climbs out of her bed in the next room and sneaks in with her mother and father, so they wake up in the morning with her damp curly head and solid warm body squeezed between them, proof of their connection.

And they still laugh together. There's still their shared culture, the fact that they were born in America in the same year, played the same playground games, watched the same commercials, felt the same boredom in families that, though of different races, shared the same blithe suburban hopes for their children. They still laugh at Italy.

At the television special on the fattest family in Italy, where the mother gravely describes cooking four kilos of spaghetti a day.

At Italian heavy-metal music.

At Italian porn-film titles, like *Anal Vices of Sister Benedetta.*

At a Roman waiter, elegant and grave, walking out of a restaurant bearing a tray of leftovers, followed by a line of cats, their tails ceremoniously aloft.

When they laugh together, Nick feels a glimmer of hope and Mira feels roused momentarily out of a dream. There's no place for humor in the places Zenin brings her to. When she laughs, she looks timidly at

Nick with something curiously beseeching in her eyes. But after a minute she turns away.

And that happens as well when they wake up entwined in the bed. Pretending to be asleep, to be stirring, Mira pulls back from that intolerable warmth. And he pulls back too. And then they yawn and say unimportant things without looking at each other. And Mira gets up and digs for her running shoes in the big dark armoire, the Bluebeard's closet that conceals her guilt, the clothes that Zenin has given her. Their day begins with a retreat.

No one would guess that in the old bedroom with its beamed ceiling in the center of Rome, in their American bed, they had been braided together, breathing like one person. That in the middle of that bed, almost every night, there was a truce, as on battlefields when Christmas flares are set up on no-man's-land, and both sides down their guns for a day.

KIP EISENBERG

My research focus these days is kinship patterns and marriage settlements with particular emphasis on the documents in the Dandolo clan archive, but I've gotta admit off the record that the core story still turns me into a seventh-grader. I get shivers thinking about the old guy with his eyes ripped out brooding for decades, looking eastward over the Adriatic. And what did he feel after he'd put a prostitute on the patriarch's throne? After he'd stolen the bones of half the apostles and burned Eastern glories of Christendom to the ground? After they carried off the bronze horses and the Theotokos of Nicopeia? Was it enough for him? Is anything ever enough?

24

ZENIN

Zio, is it true that you had an affair with Brigitte Bardot? asks Zenin's nephew, a pain-in-the-ass Bocconi University graduate.

The annoying thing about getting old, thinks Zenin, about becoming the undisputed ruler, the *zio* or *nonno*—uncle or grandfather—in the family, is that if you've had any kind of interesting life, you become a goddamned legend. A legend is a fossil. A fossilized turd. He gives an inward snicker, looks gravely at the Zenin clan gathered twenty-seven strong around his sister's vast dining table. It's a *cresima*, confirmation, luncheon for his favorite niece, a nine-year-old monkey who is the only child to have inherited Zenin's Mongolian cheekbones, and who now bounces joyously in her seat fondling a string of pearls he's given her.

Twenty-seven sitting at a table. Including:

Zenin's two daughters, neither of whom has their mother's translucent blond beauty, and who have, in their mid-thirties, become tweedy matrons with flat pumps. One brainy, one horsey, both with a long-cultivated air of patient reproach toward their father.

Their husbands, his sons-in-law, interchangeable scions of local impecunious nobility, expert mountaineers and glacier skiers, useless in the office.

Their six children, Zenin's grandchildren, a mannerly blond swarm in Tyrolean sweaters, who after lunch will attack Zenin, pull his ears, rifle his pockets for chewing gum and drag him off to play James Bond on the PlayStation.

Zenin's adored son, Daniele, home for the weekend from Milan. As handsome and unassuming as usual, occupying his cherished niche in the family with the naturalness of a shepherd boy playing a flute in the woods.

Caterina, Daniele's girlfriend, a pretty, rather bovine girl of eighteen, conservatively dressed, serenely ignoring the fact that no one thinks she's good enough for Daniele.

Daniele's mother, Tere, the *brava ragazza* who tried unsuccessfully for so long to marry Zenin and is now completely absorbed into the family, looking tanned and attractive in a well-cut jacket and Sicilian coral jewelry.

Zenin's present girlfriend, Mariella, the jolly blond antique dealer, who has cunningly forged an alliance with Tere, with whom she is discussing chakras while blowing smoke rings in Zenin's direction.

Zenin's mother, ninety-four years old, spooning up *pastina in brodo* at one end of the long table, her dyed hair pinched up in a frail helmet, her cataracts covered by a pair of purplish sunglasses that make her look like an insect. Occasionally hissing an order at the Croatian nurse who sits beside her.

Zenin's three younger sisters, called from time immemorial *Le Tre Grazie*—the Three Graces—though only one of them is called Grazia. Not triplets, but inseparable—identical blue-eyed crop-haired ladies who together run a private animal shelter and a natural-foods store.

Their husbands, who work for Zenin. One of them, his marketing director, actually knows what he's doing.

Zenin's oldest sister, Betta, recently widowed, looking like a dowager empress with her crest of thick white hair, her large black-clad frame and huge pearls. Her face red from too much wine, her expression absent as she expertly directs the two Sri Lankan housekeepers in white jackets and gloves who are serving an enormous dish of semolina and béchamel sauce.

A horde of nieces and nephews ranging from toddlers to university students. All of them good-looking. Cheerful, tall, healthy, with thick hair, strong teeth. Products of seaside summers and winters skiing in the pure air of the Dolomites. Confident, well-mannered, filling their end of the table with a subdued chirping of laughter and pranks between cousins. Sometimes Zenin looks them over when they are gathered like this and thinks about lice, boils, runny noses, bluish bare knees, and the stink of the courtyard toilet when he was growing up. When polenta with a little sugar was a treat.

It gives him a curious mixture of pride and suffocation to sit here as the center, the defining force of this huge visible structure of family and wealth. The modern suburban villa of his sister, with the oriental rugs and every surface covered with silver wedding favors. They are an extension of him, like his factories, his offices and workers, the landscape, the city where he grew up. Yet at the same time they bore the tits off him with their dependency and demands, with the transparent hopes of the younger males to unseat a sclerotic Zenin and snatch his power.

And there is always something between him and his family, the same curious wall that keeps him apart and alone wherever he goes.

He takes a sip of wine, and in reply to his nephew's question starts to brag. No, it was Danielle Darrieux. I met her in Cortina when we were all stuck there during the big snowstorm of 1970. Four meters of snow and no electricity. Agnelli was there, and Vedova, the father not the son, and two of the Niarchoses.

But Papa got the girl! exclaims his younger daughter, in a fond tone.

Zenin looks around and sees that everyone—his son, his mother, his girlfriend—is looking at him with the same affectionate indulgence with which they looked earlier at the newest baby and the confirmation girl in her white lace dress. The alarming thing is how his family, his land, and his past, accept everything, even the worst parts of him. So it is impossible, as he learned long ago, to ever free himself.

A fucking legend, he thinks.

Later, when coffee is being served, his eldest daughter walks up to him with her youngest child, a two-year-old girl, and places her on his shoulders. Go on, give her a ride, shout his relatives. Act like a real grandfather for once!

1987 · ASTONISHING

Zenin becomes demanding. Finds improbable ways to contact Mira, to put his mark on her. Telephone calls from his secretary, who pretends to be Mira's friend, tickets waiting for her at the airport, elaborate presents, jewelry, a sable coat. Each time they meet he talks to her of love and marriage, without really asking her to marry him. Everything he does is designed to detach her from her husband and family, yet he has no exact plans for a future with her. It is visiting her, as she lingers in this space of tension and desperation between two worlds, that excites him. It doesn't occur to him that the greatest part of his attraction to her is that he is damaging her, and that she seems worth damaging.

She is his escape, his cloak of invisibility, and he still loves to astonish her. With his jet, with the excuse of her work, he is able to fly her to his home, or to far-off places for a day or night or a weekend.

Some places where they go:

To the Grand Prix in Budapest and Monte Carlo.

To a hunt ball in Northumberland.

To Paris, to London, to New York.

To a bar mitzvah in Tel Aviv.

To Biarritz.

These trips to such far-flung glamorous places are oddly similar. Always rushed, with cars and taxis dashing to and from small airports or heliports. Fat silk tassels on the keys of hotel suites that all resemble, in their anonymous opulence, their gilt and pelmets, the furnishings in Zenin's own house. Expensive shops where salesgirls assess Mira with the diluted professional envy born of constant exposure to rich men dressing pretty younger women. Expensive dinners, either in gastronomic temples with silver plate covers or in rustic inns where owners with deferential chumminess recommend course after course of overpriced peasant fare. Parties, clubs, piano bars, all the places where rich people come to be rich together and steal other's women and talk about where they will see each other next. Each place with the same mixture of hip-hop and classic soul and Europop. They always play "Reckless" by Afrika Bambaataa.

They fuck, they eat, they dance, they buy clothes for Mira, they fuck again, they leave.

Zenin, who travels with only a razor and a toothbrush and a clean shirt, enjoys packing Mira's suitcase. Folding the clothes neatly in categories the way his mother used to do for him many years before. After this peculiar little ritual, he delivers Mira back to her own world. And he goes off feeling strong and excited by his power to snatch a woman out of one dimension and place her into another. By the fact that, though she tries to conceal it, she is amazed.

MEGAN — A SALESGIRL

Shawn and the other girls say it's that French actor, and I'm like, come on guys, real celebs get appointments, and are you so ignorant that you can't tell French from Italian? I'm considered the store intellectual and they kind of like it when I give them a hard time. Rodeo Drive is crawling with Eurotrash and most of our walk-ins are older, rich French, Italian, or German tourists trying to impress their younger wives or girlfriends or some chick they picked up here in LA. This tall guy in serious need of a haircut strolls in and orders up the leather Alaia skirt and peplum jacket for his girlfriend who looks sort of Puerto Rican and has a cute figure even if she does have to go pee before she can zip the skirt. And she models it for him and looks great, but he's busy checking out all the rest of us sales assistants in our Alaia and Versace like we're some harem he gets included in the price of the suit. And then he pays in cash the way the Italians and the Colombian drug dealers do, and though he's quite low key about it, you can tell he's getting off on everybody seeing the size of the roll he's got in his pocket. It's a classic, all these men behave like that. I'm taking notes, and once I get into film school I'm going to do a short film just called "Fitting."

<h1 style="text-align:center">25</h1>

<h1 style="text-align:center">MIRA</h1>

2006 · MOTHER'S GLASS

Eighties theme parties, says Mira with gloomy relish. They're high on my list of stuff not to dwell on.

Hate to break it to you, Ma, but we have nineties parties too.

Maddie's home on spring break and she and her mother are rooting through old clothes. They've dragged two huge battered Chinese lacquer chests into the middle of Mira's bedroom and popped the locks, releasing into the bright afternoon a powerful stink of camphor and the almost imperceptible musty smell of fabric that is turning historic.

From the open windows come the shouts of Maddie's half brothers up on the hill where they are building a fort in a dry creek bed. High, screechy little-boy voices that seem to ring against the cloudless sky. It's early March, the bare woods still dusty gray and brown except for a carpet of wild garlic and trillium and the odd primrose. Dust motes dance in the sunlit air of the bedroom, with its iron bed and hundreds of books, and Mira can see herself and Maddie framed, backlit, in the speckled depths of the pier glass over the fireplace.

This green-and-black print is awesome. Look how full the skirt is.

This was Little Granny's from the fifties. Come to think of it, I wore this to a party myself when I was about your age. Mira remembers standing in the living room back in Mount Airy, hauling in the velvet belt, glancing smugly at her mother, who would never wear the dress again.

Only now does she connect the moment with a photograph of her mother at sixteen or seventeen, caught swinging her foot on a stoop in North Philadelphia, dressed for some Girls' High theatrical in a lace dress made for Mira's grandmother.

A basic pleasure, she thinks, to put on the old lady's dress and steal the past. Or is it stealing the future? How does the sonnet go? "Thou art thy mother's glass . . ."

A few things—a couple of linen sheaths from the sixties, a gold lamé fifties evening gown from Neiman-Marcus—Mira keeps in her closet and wears with the proper vintage irony. But these trunks she keeps stored away, rarely opened except to dump in more camphor once a year. They mainly hold the clothes Zenin bought for her, hidden now as when she was married to Nick. Vanni makes fun of them and calls the sable coat vulgar.

Maddie pulls the tissue paper off the red suit, which to Mira seems to have taken on the antique tints of the faded brocades in her bedroom. Gorgeous, breathes Maddie. I remember this one. I thought you were, like, a goddess.

You were too little to remember this. And I never wore it around you.

Yeah, you did once.

Maddie puts on the suit. She is taller, with bigger breasts and bones than Mira. A Valkyrie, high school varsity crew, with her mass of curls and the same seraphic face she had as a child. Nick's face. Unlike Mira, Maddie has beauty that does not come and go. In the pitiless equinoctial light she is like an unadorned fact. And Mira's heart, as always, contracts with a mixture of pride and envy.

But the suit, which barely buttons over her breasts, makes Maddie all curves, like a Vargas cartoon. She and Mira burst out laughing.

Let's be honest, says Maddie. I look like a ho.

Well—says Mira.

And I always wondered, Mom, Maddie adds, not missing a beat. What did it feel like when you wore this.

Mira has one of those maternal moments where one doesn't bolt but just stops. She thinks, We've done the discussion, many times, and this question now is just what it seems. And she says, You know I can't actually remember. The girl in that suit. Except that I wanted to be someone else so badly and I was running after it so hard that I didn't have very much fun.

Silence, as her daughter unwraps an extravagant short ruffled evening dress, also red. Mira recalls that Zenin bought it for her in Paris, that he insisted on it. Now the ruffles look flat and dull, like poppies in July.

So now you have more fun?

Yes.

Even though you're, um, a lot older?

You mean dead and buried, don't you? says Mira teasingly. Getting older isn't so bad.

Maddie looks at her incredulously.

You don't want the same things you did. You don't care so desperately. It's like being able to see in two directions at once. Knowing things makes up for a lot.

Maddie continues to look at her as if she's speaking a different language. So there is nothing to do but to give Maddie a big kiss. As Mira does so, she sees, reflected in the dusty glass, the mother embracing the daughter, who stares straight ahead at the vision of herself in red.

1987 · DISCO CLONE

It's scary enough on the lips of Nancy Sinatra, but when Cristina Monet sings her eighties version of "Is That All There Is?" backed up by her Disco Clones, you feel the oxygen rushing out of the atmosphere, the world shrink-wrapped around you.

Mira looks at herself in a bathroom at the Paris Ritz and notices she's getting uglier. She's been swimming in a mosaic pool that has Europop playing underwater. Alone, because Zenin has an appointment. Now she stands dripping on marble and takes a good look at herself in the fawning peach-colored light around the mirror. She's observed that her clothes have begun to hang loose on her, and now she sees that her face has grown sallow and beakish and her hair on both sides of her forehead is thinning, just where horns would be if she were a devil. And she's not even doing drugs.

She's starting to look like a junkie, even in luxury lighting, and she knows it is because she can't eat or sleep because inside her there is something like a cord twisting tight so that her lips are drawn back in a rictus; her eyes are bulging like a trapped animal and she seems to be constantly trembling, though no one else seems to see it. Zenin calls her beautiful, wants her more and more. Mira's days away from him are simply a counting of minutes and seconds until their next meeting.

And there's this feeling that is devouring her flesh. She knows it's not just guilt or hopeless love. It is something far more profound, the stress of struggling upstream against her whole nature. The knowledge, in body and spirit, that she is traveling *à rebours*. Against the grain. She won't help herself, but she can't stop her body from telling the truth.

At the Budapest Grand Prix, the doppler roar of the engines seems to increase the scorching heat, Eastern European midsummer heat enveloping a raw new track carved out of pastureland that still smells of the previous occupant, a collective dairy farm. Mira thinks that the candy-colored cars, the astronaut drivers, the ant swarms of mechanics in the pits all resemble the most monotonous kind of arcade game. But one of the cars, the Lotus, has Zenin's name printed on it, and at the sponsors' dinners she shakes the steel hands of the famous drivers and feels the hair on her body prickle from the charge of sex and death and money.

Girls are everywhere. In the sponsors' tent, a Brazilian runs up and throws her arms around Zenin. She has giant tortoiseshell earrings and hair down to her ass. Hey Brazil, he says.

The girl gives one of those white-toothed Brazilian grins. Suddenly she grabs Mira's left hand and loooks at her wedding and engagement rings. What's this—are you engaged to Zenin? she asks in a different voice.

No, says Mira, and the girl's manner is once again chummy and informal. She tells Mira that she is a correspondent for a racing paper, that she follows Formula One all over the world.

Mira tells the girl she is a magazine writer, and the girl winks and sticks out her breasts. I guess we're in the same business, she says in a relaxed and friendly tone.

The north of England, early on an October afternoon. On the motorway leading away from the small airport outside Newcastle, a man drives a Range Rover while singing "Barbara Allan." He is a short, white-haired, bowlegged Englishman with red cheeks and eyes shaped like caraway seeds, and he's driving Mira and Zenin and Zenin's friend Macaco to a country hotel where they will attend a dinner and a ball given by one of Zenin's British clients.

The white-haired man is not a chauffeur, but an office employee of Zenin's client who appears to know Zenin and Macaco from previous visits. Though they use first names with each other, the two Italians have ignored the driver since they left the airport and talk loudly in Italian about the Milan-Inter game of the night before. The man's mellow tenor warbling of the old ballad is a mild protest against monumental rudeness, Mira thinks. She loves "Barbara Allan," a favorite solo of folk-minded counselors at the Quaker summer camps she attended as a child, and hearing it as they drive through bronze woods and dun-colored rolling fields that recall western Pennsylvania fills her with unexpected nostalgia.

When it comes to the last chorus, she can't help chiming in: "O mother, mother, make my bed, / O make it soft and narrow . . ."

Well sung! exclaims the white-haired man, and he and Mira finish the song together. "My love has died for me today / I'll die for him tomorrow."

Macaco and Zenin stare. You're embarrassing me, hisses Zenin.

Later, as she shakes hands with the Englishman and thanks him for the ride, the man looks at her keenly and says in a swift undertone, My dear, you're too good for these people.

This is all on film somewhere. Mira dancing in the Tel Aviv Hilton at the bar mitzvah of Liberman's son. Plump, glum Liberman, Zenin's partner from London. Who stands beside Zenin as the snaking line of women dances by to an orchestra that suddenly sounds like a village band. Gorgeous wives and daughters, flown in from London, Paris, Sydney, Buenos Aires. Big-haired women with bodies maintained like formal gardens, encrusted in couture flounces and gilding and planetary jewels. Mira is wearing the red dress that she will shake out ruefully with her daughter in fifteen years' time, and she is giggling, recalling her folk-dancing lessons from school, enjoying the fact that all these cosmopolitan beauties have kicked off their high heels and are tearing around the ballroom like shtetl wives and maidens.

All weekend Mira's been poking fun at Zenin, who has never even heard of a bar mitzvah and looks ridiculous with a kippah perched precariously on his shaggy head. They see nothing of Tel Aviv and spend their time between the hotel pool and a dozen parties.

Later, an entertainment is announced and a pair of Brazilian dancers appear. Dressed in transparent body stockings over jeweled pasties and tangas, they do an acrobatic samba during which their brown stocky bodies seem to expand and contract like rubber bands, and then one gets on her hands and knees and the other pretends to ride her around the floor like a pony, beating her bottom with a little jeweled whip. The crowd explodes into laughter and applause, and then the bar mitzvah boy, Liberman's son, blushing violet, is pushed out onto the floor, and while everyone claps, he bestrides the smiling girl and rides her around the circle. Then Liberman does the same thing. And then Liberman's father, who has a long gray beard and a noble patriarchal brow but seems very agile, gets down on his hands and knees and lets the two girls pretend to ride him—walking straddle-legged on the tips of their toes—and flick his buttocks with the little whip, and the shouts and laughter from the guests becomes a roar.

Zenin, bored by the chanted Hebrew longueurs of the religious ceremony he was forced to attend earlier, now brightens up, thinks that it's hilarious, and that Liberman certainly knows how to throw a party.

Mira stands in the cheering crowd, studies the dancers, who seem happy and quite professional, and wonders if she's missing something.

This feeling returns when she and Zenin are leaving Israel and are questioned at the airport by El Al security officials.

What is this man to you? demands a beautiful tanned young woman in a military uniform. How long have you known him? Are you married or divorced? If you are still married, where is your husband? Who is this man? What is he to you?

Mira gropes for answers. All the while seeing Zenin replying serenely to his interrogator in the booth up ahead. Not daring to imagine what he might be saying.

LIBERMAN

A cold fish, Zenin. A shark, really, though he has been a great friend over the years. When we met, when he needed a partner for Favolosi, I was still in my winklepickers and we were both thin enough to fit in those wasp-waisted seventies sport jackets, and Zenin was trying out wearing a big gold watch on his cuff, like Agnelli. That was two stone ago for me, though Zenin hasn't plumped. My wife, Jen, calls him the Beanstalk, says he is the kind who never gets sick or dies early, just dries out and rattles, like a weed in a field. We used to argue over who was poorer growing up, me in the East End or him eating dead horse in that village of his near Venice. He is always the same, a genius at what he does, hardly a word to say for himself, a born thief, though he comes by what he has with cleaner hands than most Italians. He comes to see us once or twice a year, at the place in Essex first and now in Oxfordshire and Marbella. And both my wives and I have spent holidays on the boat. Gin palace, plane, houses, he has them all, though he doesn't seem to enjoy them much. Women too. When I was younger and liked a bit of skirt, it used to put me out just the least bit, of an evening at Tramp, that the birds would be all over him. It wasn't the dago accent or the money he spent—he was never mean—it was something they called mystery. Bollocks, I say. Anyway, he has had some beauties. Beautiful first wife, beautiful Australian girlfriend. Though he didn't seem to enjoy any of them much. Then he suddenly announces he has a baby son, and we assume he'll marry the girl. But no. That's because he's a stalk, says my wife. No heart. Shame, really.

At Alex's bar mitzvah—beautiful affair, the kind you remember when you're lying in hospital with the respirator going—he shows up with yet another of his girls, a good-looking skinny brunette that looked as if she had some colored blood. A smart girl, classy, a writer, Zenin says, bragging. Harvard girl. I told her I have two girls and Alex at St. Paul's, and you don't get smarter than that in London. The girl talked to my Jen, and it turns out that she's still married to somebody else. I wanted to tell her not to leave anybody for Zenin, says Jenny. But would it do any good? Mystery! I'll give you mystery up the arse!

26

NICK

2005 · FROG'S END

Maybe the echo of this was always here. Nick walks through Froggy House, his family vacation place in Maine, videotaping as he goes. Not echo, he thinks. What's the word for future echo? The sense in the present of what will be? *Resonance*? Too New Agey. *Premonition*? *Presentiment*? Too specific.

There's no word, yet it seems he's right in thinking that the decades of summers in this house were always backlit by this act, the last one. Where Nick, bundled like a pneumatic mummy in layers of Patagonia down—years of London winters have not prepared him for the bone-gnawing chill of a Downeast April, and the house, an original saltbox disfigured by postwar restructuring, is only theoretically winterized— walks brandishing a lens at the geography of his childhood with the slow wary gait of a special forces soldier on recon.

How many times in his life in England have his thoughts wandered through these rooms, picked up this view of the cove, handled a memory steeped in wood smoke and ionized pine and salt air, then let it drop.

The kitchen, ludicrously small by today's standards, its collection of Julia Child amber with age, its curtain of indestructible orange-and-white Marimekko cotton hiding the under-sink plumbing in what they teased his mother for calling "the Provençal manner."

The hallway with his father's discolored collages of wine labels, his shelf of warped *Goon Show* records, his wistful, oddly feminine sketches of Camden Harbor, a cracked snapshot of Nick and Teddy in foul-weather gear, smiling like losers.

The sitting room with its giant stone fireplace better suited to a ski lodge, its drafty picture window that looks out past squat Bullfrog Rock onto the cove, a flat corrugated stretch of sapphire where he and his father used to sit in the dinghy hooking dogfish, hoping for flounder.

The boathouse, damaged by Hurricane Charley, and the jetty where he and Garcia used to hang out listening to the Fall and the Dead Kennedys and arguing about whether *cunt* could be used as a verb.

The three Cooper family houses called Widowstown on the opposite shore, which for a whole summer he conned four-year-old Teddy into believing was China.

The Sex Bathroom, scene of epic masturbation, rampant teenage fucking, and substance ingestion, where on different occasions both Nick and Teddy lost their virginity to cousins.

The beds with their faded Pierre Deux coverlets, in one of which he spent his chaste wedding night with Mira, both of them comatose from the wedding, Mira snoring adenoidally, which she afterwards denied.

The raspberry jungle that Nick set on fire one drunken September weekend during his freshman year, destroying the grass on their side of the cove and almost burning down the house.

The army of ceramic and wooden frogs brought to his mother by houseguests over the years, three of which, with no particular explanation, smiling, she threw in rapid succession at his father one night.

The wheelchair ramp his mother used during her last summers, that someone, probably Teddy, painted sky blue with large tadpoles that look like giant sperm.

All this and more will begin to disappear tomorrow, when the caretaker's wife comes to start packing up the house, which has been sold to a millionaire restaurant owner from Providence with twin boys and a pregnant second wife. The wife is good-looking and has taste. She will eliminate the seventies kitsch of the Reiver family and strip the house down to its essentials, then add extravagant extensions. Cedar decks, a cathedral-size kitchen with restaurant appliances.

Bring it on, thinks Nick.

For all the beauty of its setting, Froggy House has never been loved, never been a cult, as most Maine vacation houses are. His parents bought it from a Reiver cousin just after the death of Nick and Ted's golden oldest brother, Meade. And certainly that is why there is the fundamental coldness of the two remaining sons toward the place. Because the endless, resolutely idyllic summers of sailing and blueberries were built around the empty niche in the family, the space that neither of them is ever good enough to fill. In fact, in spite of all the memories, there is pleasure at its sale, a certain relief, an undisguised glee at the whopping price it brings. Maine waterfront and tradition, in the hottest real estate market ever seen.

When the market quiets down, he and Dhel intend to buy a vacation house in Quogue, near her sister's place. But at this moment, Nick doesn't own a square inch of land in the United States, and the thought gives him a curious feeling of freedom.

And now there's the video that no one will ever watch, but that had to be made. This final act of record, of official mourning for a house that was acquired as part of mourning. An act implicit in all his summers. Haunted by the phantom of his middle-aged self, graying blond hair swept back under a watch cap, cheeks slapped by the arctic spring wind, circling around with his camera.

Outside his parents' bedroom, he crunches into the frost-rimed blueberry patch to spend a minute filming Widowstown. China, across the cove.

1987 · REVELATION

One morning you wake up early and you see Mira with her back turned toward you as usual, her whole body shaking, not with sobs but just trembling like she's got Parkinson's or something, and you take her by the shoulders, lightly, because you haven't touched her deliberately for weeks, and you sense that your fingers could become iron hooks and crush her bones.

And you turn her around and inform her in a voice that does not admit other possibilities that now she is going to tell you the fucking truth. Because it's time.

A September morning, so early that Maddie is still asleep and there is no traffic noise, just a few clanks and shouts from the market vendors opening their stalls at the bottom of Via dei Serpenti.

Into Nick and Mira's room, across the gated blind alley where they once saw the thief, comes a strange incandescent glow that appears only during the clearest dawns in Rome, in the fall, when the tramontana wind from over the Appenines sweeps vapor from the sky. The light reflects in the wavering mirror of the nineteenth-century clothes press that stands at the foot of their bed. And shines on Mira, who sits on the tangled sheets, cross-legged like a storyteller, in her T-shirt and underpants, head bowed sullenly as, with a few melodramatic choked sobs, she steps onto the hard ugly road of revelation.

In a low voice she says all the usual things, which to the two people concerned seem as fresh and new as the words *I love you* once seemed, their particular meaning reviving the faded substance of the old clichés the way faith reilluminates the words of the scripture.

The old bitter message. I have betrayed you. I don't love you any more. I love someone else. Our life together is at an end. Nick sits there in bed, also illuminated by that strangely gorgeous reflected light. Listening to what he already knows. Dimly aware of a harsh, specific satisfaction in some frontier of his heart, the awful pleasure of certainty. And realizing also that the fucking bitch is enjoying this moment of confession, if only for the relief that comes from cutting off a mangled limb.

Around him he feels the city collapsing, like a slow-motion film of a bombardment or an earthquake. Not just Rome falling down, its ruins exploding into dust, but his personal city, the metropolis of certainties that sheltered him until now. When a bomb drops, when buildings topple, there is always a savage influx of sky. On the wall outside where he is staring, he can see the shadows of swallows sweeping cleanly through the sky in their huge bladed flocks, and remembers with some fragment of his brain that Roman seers sought signs of divine will in bird flight. A skill they learned from the ancient Umbrians.

The sound of traffic increases, and church bells. The morning smells drift in through the window: car exhaust, coffee, garbage, fresh bread from the bakery two doors down, hot chemical steam from the little dry cleaner. Furnishings of a small antique world, and Nick's world is now huge, huge and bright and cold. Later, in the gnawing hours of reflection, he will think that it feels as though a curtain has suddenly dissolved. As if he and Mira, joining their lives together, had knit a fabric, a screen, a safety net, that at this instant has dissolved into mist. Leaving him alone, naked, seared by the glare of the truth.

Later there will be time for bargaining, for many more words in the traditional liturgy. You whore. Can we try. I thought we were different. Come back. I'll kill him. Kill you. You stole the best days. Think of the child. Hate. Hate you. Come back. I still love you. Get out.

But now it's Mira's turn, and with each word she speaks, with each of her craven self-serving gusts of tears, he mentally sends her farther away from him, to an ice floe caught in a swift current, spinning into the polar noon. He doesn't want to kill her, he just wants her to disappear, to leave him to get used to the light.

TREE

My name is Mariateresa Rosales and I come from the city of Davao, Mindanao Island, Republic of the Philippines, and I came to Italy through Austria, hiding under the seat of a bus.

I worked for Signor Nick and Signora Mira for four years total, from the time Maddie was eighteen months old until Signor left Italy and the baby went to kindergarten. First in the big apartment near Via Nazionale and then, after they separated, going back and forth with my little Maddie between Via Nazionale and Signora's new place on the Aventino.

They were my second employers in Italy. The first, an eye doctor and his wife who lived on the Flaminia, I left because they made me sleep on the dining-room floor and refused to put my documents in order with the *questura,* and paid me half the proper union salary because they said I was slow to understand Italian. So it was a relief to come to work for Signor and Signora where I could speak English, which I know because of the air force base in Mindanao. They said so many *please*s when they told me how to keep their house that it was like they were scared of me. Until they understood that it is not the custom, they tried to get me to sit down at meals with them.

A kindness that frightened me, not for myself but for the two of them, with their long legs and their big American teeth, like the soldiers from the base, and their round eyes like kittens that saw so little. If I had been a different girl and had no faith, I could have taken advantage like so many girls do with their employers. They never asked to see the shopping receipts. It was always "Take the afternoon off, Tree" and "Here's a present for your daughter, Tree." When I told Signora about the problem with my husband and the drug and how I had to leave my children for my sister to raise, she offered money to send them to school with the Ursuline sisters.

Maddie became my secret baby, my passion, as happens with all the Filipina girls who have hearts hungry for children far off in the hot soft air of home, and she was more lovely than any other baby. I used to dress her up in ruffles and take her to San Paolo, which is our Filipino church in the Prati neighborhood, and my friends taught her the word *maganda*—beautiful.

But it was Signor and Signora I felt I was protecting. They were also like my children. I was twenty-three and they were nearly thirty, yet I felt they had no idea of how the world always has terrible traps waiting. Italians know about it. Italians have cold hearts, cold as the old stone statues that lie around Rome, and the traps are part of how they live their life.

Signora Mira was the one who got caught. I noticed nothing until one day my cousin Dolo told me she had seen Signora getting out of a cab with a strange man in a neighborhood up near Villa Ada, where Dolo works. She was certain it was Signora, all dressed up and looking sexy like a stewardess or a fashion model. Then I began to remember all the times that the phone would ring in the middle of the morning, and Signora, who had been typing in her study or playing with the baby, wearing jeans and with her hair all over her head, would put down the receiver and say she had an appointment for lunch. Then she'd drop everything and wash her hair and put on lipstick and dress up and look so pretty it hurt your eyes. She had a closet full of the most wonderful clothes that she hardly ever wore with her husband. I'd say, Signora, you should dress like that for Signor Nick, and she'd laugh and say he loved her the way she was, without trimmings. And all the time there would be a fever-glow about her that made me recall, though I tried not to, my husband when he was on the drug. Then she would hug and kiss the baby a dozen times so that it was impossible to settle her down afterward, and run out the door.

Until Dolo told me, I never thought of another man, because Signor Nick was *maganda*. You'd have to see him, going off every morning in his suits which I kept in perfect condition, never a grease stain or wrinkle. And he loved her. It began to seem to me, after I understood what was going on, that he was always in a way on his knees in front of her, which was not right. It was like someone saying a Hail Mary in front of a statue of the Mother of God and finding out that it was Mary Magdalene you were praying to.

Though anger and hatred are sins, I must say I began to hate Signora a bit.

Then she began to travel a lot for her work writing for magazines, and one night I found Signor Nick at the table with a bottle of vodka and he looked at me in a way that reminded me once again of my husband when he was on the drug—his eyes bloodred around the blue—and said that the bitch was leaving him, that she loved somebody else.

And I said that he musn't speak about Signora that way, and that sometimes women get these ideas and why didn't he talk to her—thinking why didn't he give her a good smack—and surely she would change her mind.

And he looked at me with those eyes glowing like embers, like a demon's eyes, and said something that I've always remembered, that seemed like both the truth and the worst news that anyone could hope to hear. They both said some awful things later, things that made me never again want to lay eyes on either of them, those children who had everything in the world and threw it away on a whim. But I understood this thing that he said, because I was, the same as they were, a foreigner in this stone-hearted land.

It's just too late, he said. She's lost her country now.

27

ZENIN

2005 · BURQA

A woman veiled in black from head to toe is walking the streets of Zenin's city. *I bambini si spaventano e gli automobilisti si bloccano per vedere quella strana apparizione,* reports *Il Gazzettino.* Children are terrified, traffic stops at the sight of the strange apparition.

Faceless, as dark as the thought of death, moving across the cobblestones of the center and along the roadside of the periphery, sometimes clutching plastic shopping bags and at other times accompanying a little girl to school.

Oh, for heaven's sake, to be shocked by a woman in a burqa, says Zenin's girlfriend, Mariella. Sometimes I don't know what is worse, Muslim fundamentalism or provincial small minds. The priests don't help, those scoundrels, and did you read what the assistant mayor— Gentili, that Fascist *leghista,* he went to school with my cousin—said? He claims he'll have any woman in a burqa arrested because going around in public with your face covered is a security violation. Well, I ask you. Can it be that no one has figured out that we're part of the rest of the world now? Women in veils show up in Italy every day. What I want to know is why nobody's figured out who that woman is and whether she wants to be covered up like that, poor thing.

Zenin glances nervously at Mariella, who is driving them up a steep mountain road near Val Noana in her Range Rover, managing to smoke, shift gears, and gesture indignantly as she talks. She looks pretty in smart olive tweed and a man's loden cap, but when she gets excited and polemical—about women, about Tibet, about rainbow peace banners—her eyes bulge and her voice grows shrill in a way extremely distasteful to Zenin, reminiscent of his sisters and many past girlfriends.

He looks out over the huge amphitheater of rust-colored autumn foliage sweeping down from Croce d'Aune to the glinting thread of the Cismon River, the higher gnarled peaks of the true Dolomites, already powdered with October snow, standing guard in the distance over the bell towers and huddled stone houses of impossibly remote Alpine hamlets. He knows this region because it was part of the route he took when he sold encyclopedias, rattling up vertical half-paved roads in the faithful old Giulietta. It's a desolate area, where no one goes to ski, and he has allowed himself to be dragged up here by Mariella, who as usual wants him to buy something. In this case it is an entire medieval village restored and transformed by an architect friend of hers into a deluxe time-share condominium complete with helipad, private ski lift, solar panels, high-speed Internet access, and a standing contract for organic cheeses and produce from local peasants. Zenin thinks it's a piece of flimflam, like most of Mariella's projects, and he suspects also that she is fooling around with the twenty-five-year-old architect behind his back.

But it's mushroom season, and there's a place famous for *canederli* in the village up ahead, and he doesn't mind spending a day alone with Mariella once in a while. She travels easily with him, but doesn't whine when he leaves her behind. After years of high-strung beauties, he has found a companion who never makes scenes, who amuses him by the depth of her stratagems to marry him.

And why the hell not, asks Zenin's mother, in dialect. You need somebody to take care of you, and even Padre Giacomo isn't against civil remarriage anymore. Even pederasts can marry now. You can't run around with sluts in that plane and that ridiculous boat forever. Look at your gray hair—you're not a *ragazzino* anymore. You wouldn't marry Tere, so take Mariella. Another nice sensible girl from a respectable family. A girl from here, who speaks your language. You know what they say: *Moglie e buoi dei paesi tuoi*. Wife and cattle should be from your own village.

Zenin ignores her, knowing that what she says may well be true for a poorer man, but that he himself will never be abandoned with rotting diabetic feet and hairy nostrils in an old-folks residence. Doesn't he still have his ex-wife and various ex-girlfriends and poor neurotic Tere, and his resentful clinging daughters, not to mention his surviving sisters? One, or several, of them will be around to care for him in his cottage. And Mariella, like all Italian fiancées, is capable of hanging on for a good twenty years.

A few days after his trip to the mountains, Zenin himself catches sight of the veiled woman. Late on a November afternoon on an ugly stretch of the state road toward Belluno, where the cornfields have been invaded by a French hypermarket and scruffy lanes of small factories and public housing apartments. Burqa rippling in the wind, she is picking her way along the side of the road, pulling a small collapsible shopping trolley stuffed with bags. And Zenin, driving by in one of the small cheap cars he replaces like Kleenex to befuddle kidnappers, is stunned to find her very beautiful. Tall and slender and fearsome in her fluttering black disguise, a walking secret, an envoy from the land of shadows. The woman without a face, symbol of foreign strangeness in his home town. The opposite of the women he knows and can't stand. It's as if he invented her himself, and he knows one night she will walk into his dreams.

Later, Mariella finds the woman's name in the newspaper and tells Zenin. She is Roushana, from Bangladesh. Married to a construction worker who also emigrated from her country. And she wears the veil willingly, she tells the reporter, *per amore di Dio e di mio marito*. For the love of God and her husband.

1987 · WHEN TO PAY

Casually, over a glass of wine, Zenin learns from a lawyer friend that, as he has guessed already, he has no formal responsibility. In the case of an American girl running off from her husband. Impulsive, as are so many foreign girls. It's natural that, like so many of her sex, she has a weakness for Zenin. Who has, it is true, often spoken of marriage, but fortunately without actually proposing.

Zenin is often amazed but rarely rattled by the talent of women for avalanches of emotion and general chaos. Over the years he has seen more hysterics than Mira could ever imagine, and learned to negotiate them with detached practicality and surprising good humor. He is actually in love with Mira, as much as he can be, and wants more of her, though he would have been content to leave her assigned to a husband and family. The end of her marriage is not an apocalypse but an ordinary annoyance. And once he has ascertained that neither Nick nor any male relative of Mira's is going to try to shoot him, he makes a few rapid calculations and then, as always, steps back to observe.

The mess. Mira moving out of her house into a residential hotel on the Aventino. Glimpses of barbaric American divorce practice, in which it seems children can be shared between mother and father. The desperate phone calls, tear-drenched lovemaking, melancholy lunches and dinners from which Mira no longer has to hurry home.

It becomes clear to Zenin that Mira, unlike an Italian girl, will not demand that he marry her.

He lets this run through his mind as he sits in the Madrid stadium with his small son on his knee, both of them bouncing up and down and screaming themselves hoarse as the Juventus Dream Team pummels Real. His son in a miniature black-and-white-striped Juventus shirt, and his son's mother, Tere, in tight jeans and a Juventus scarf, also screaming. One of the best things about Tere is that she's as rabid a Juve fan as Zenin is, and she is raising their son in the same noble tradition. From time to time, he wonders whether he should let the two of them come live with him. But then Tere will have won a complete victory over him, and he'll lose Mira.

Although at this point Mira is tiresome and often, when he sees her, looks unattractively red-eyed.

This runs through his mind amid the despairing groans of the Spanish fans, through the singing and chants and waving of banners. He is slightly distracted but not worried, because he knows he can afford as many lives as he wants. He is just waiting as he always does, to see which direction the wind will blow.

Zenin knows you always have to pay for things. But his great talent, which has made his fortune, is knowing when to pay, and paying less than anyone else.

ROUSHANA

No one is like me here. The women go around with their faces bare to men, and their skin gets hard and cracked like clay in the sun. At first boys threw stones and soda cans at me, but now they let me pass. This is a rich place. No children die and they all go to school. Outside the city there are flat fields full of water in ditches and rivers like in my country, and the big shops are temples full of music and light and food and furniture. The hypermarket is like paradise, and they give plastic bags for free. We will try to stay in this country forever, and I am learning the language. *Buongiorno. Grazie. Per amore di Dio.*

28

MIRA

2005 · JUST SAY IT

How many times have I told you that you have to say you're sorry, says Mira's friend Foy. You have to call him or write him a letter. How many years has it been?

Almost fifteen, I guess. You're crazy, Foy. He won't read it. He hates me and you can't blame him. And what's the point anyway? Do not, re- peat, do not say the word *closure* or I will be forced to smack you.

Closure. Now just try smacking me. Foy gives Mira a dangerous grin. She's from Bend, Oregon, a six-foot-tall artist with platinum hair and bronze skin who a few years ago strode up to Mira at a Castello di Rivoli opening and said, So you're the other colored girl in town.

The two friends, in tank suits and regulation nylon caps, are in the whirlpool at the gym, stretching after their Sunday morning fifty laps. Swimmers churn through the lanes beside them, awash in chlorine- scented anonymity, while through the steam on the glass wall along- side the pool, sunlight glistens on late snow that still dots the Turin hills.

You still have to settle things, insists Foy, who is childless, a hard- core romantic happily married to a misanthropic Turin architect half her size.

Settle things in what way, for fuck's sake? Mira raises her voice so that the two older Italian women sitting across from them in the whirlpool pause in their quiet discussion of how to cook lamb's brains. We've been divorced for a million years. Yes, I screwed around and left him, and it was awful. Awful, awful. But we've moved on.

But have you? Did you say you're sorry?

Of course I did. I'm sure I did. I think.

You probably said some hysterical guilty things in the heat of the moment, but you need to say it again. Calmly, like a grown-up. I just feel it in my guts, Mira. You could have taken him aside at Maddie's high school graduation.

He hardly spoke to me. He came bearing gifts, he sat through the ceremony, he hugged Maddie, he took off.

That proves it, girl. He's still wound up in the past, and so are you, and indirectly so is everyone who touches you both. You know me—I'm instinctive and I believe in karma, and I just know that you'll all have better luck and better lives, better hearts, if you say you're sorry. You're a writer, Mira, so write him a letter.

Letters are magical, adds Foy, sinking down in the warm water. I saw this installation in Paris where the artist glued all his old love letters together and made a tent. You can't imagine how powerful it was.

Mira looks at her, thinking about how it is that girlfriends get under your skin when you live overseas. You go away from your home and family, and then reconstruct the intimacy, the pressure, the invasiveness.

The two women wrap up and head into the changing room, a sea of naked women whose chatter is overlaid by the usual world-music tape.

Wait, I know this tune, says Mira, stripping off her bathing suit. It's "Greensleeves."

The two friends fall silent, scrub their bodies, peer into the mirror for signs of damage and age, check out other women's breasts and asses. Listening to the music and the eternal web of conversation, the same in Italian as in English, as universal as birdsong. About weight and chiropractors and boyfriends and what another man likes for dinner and somebody else who can't move out and live her own life because of the children.

Would an e-mail do? asks Mira suddenly.

A letter, darling. Foy pauses, combing oil through her hair. No, on second thought, any words will do.

1987 · A PREVIOUS LECTURE

The only thing Zenin can give you is money, says Madame S. Don't be a little fool and don't whine about dignity. You gave all that up, first when you started running around with him, and second when you managed things so stupidly as to leave that poor boy, your husband.

Madame S. refuses to read the tarot for Mira this afternoon.

The two women sit at her dining table under the chipped Capodimonte chandelier, and Madame S. wears her normal indoor attire, a slightly grubby peacock-colored zipped dressing gown. Her pink-and-white face glistens with homemade beauty cream, and her belladonna eyes are neither visionary nor languishing, but fixed pitilessly on Mira. Who is crying.

Non piagnucolare. Non sei più una bambina. Don't snivel. You're not a little girl. I don't know why I have to talk to you like this. It seems to me it should be your mother helping you to see things clearly. But you don't seem to have a mother, at least not the proper kind, otherwise you wouldn't be in this disorder. So you must listen to me.

First, I think Zenin cares about you. Not love, because a vampire like that is incapable of love for a woman. But there is something about you he values. Also, because he's a Veneto peasant—she spits the words—he feels guilt about breaking up a family. If it weren't for those two things, he would have thrown you away. You have no idea, my girl, how a man that rich can scare you into letting him alone. It can be terrible!

Second, because he is a peasant, he worships his son. A male child means his country, his past, his future. And that gives the other woman, the mother of that child, power over him, and it means he won't marry you, or even let you live with him. At least not now. If you are smart and patient, it might happen in the future. So what you must do now is settle down calmly and request a proper *sistemazione*. Any Italian girl would do the same thing, and I am sure that that son of a whore is expecting it from you. He should buy you a house and set aside money for you to live properly. After all, you have a child yourself, and you can't live decorously just by writing little stories.

Mira mops her eyes and starts to say something, but Madame S. forestalls her, raising one slender arthritic hand. No, I don't want to hear anything about love. You don't love Zenin—it's a kind of possession. You broke a sacrament, and now you have to pick up the pieces, and those pieces are called money and safety. Or—the older woman glances around the room with its splintered rugless floors, the outlines of vanished pictures on the bare walls, the jungle of plants on the terrace, the two lit bulbs in the chandelier above—*forse ti piacerebbe finire come me?* Perhaps you'd like to end up like me?

FOY

She has to do it.

MADAME S.

She has to do it.

29

NICK

2005 · INCENSE

Go ahead, take one, says his old friend Poppy, holding out two lit sticks of incense.

Nick takes a stick and pushes it into the sand of a blue-and-white vase so that the strand of smoke drifts up toward a portrait of some of Poppy's grandancestors, stiff in Qing Dynasty brocades, as flat and anonymous and ornate as Elizabethan portraits. Then, with a certain contained pride, Nick kowtows.

Not bad for a white boy, says Poppy, but I'll beat you, *gweilo,* even in Manolos. It's genetic.

She places the incense carefully, and with amazing grace in three-inch purple stilettos almost brushes the ground with her forehead. Demonstrating what he first noticed almost thirty years ago when they were classmates at St. George's, that Poppy is one of the few Chinese girls he knows with a great ass. Twice married, Poppy is running the vast family textile business out of Hong Kong and she still looks gorgeous. Probably for that reason, Nick's wife, Dhel, is unenthusiastic about her, though when Dhel's in Hong Kong they go to dinner together and hit the designer handbag outlets in Shenzhen. Mira, who met her once or twice when Poppy was at Yale, disliked her too. That old morale boost, a female friend your wife can't stand.

Nick plays squash with her at the Mandarin when he's in town, and occasionally calls her if he needs a number—every big shot in southeast China seems to be her uncle.

Your ass is still up there with the great ones, says Nick.

Thanks. Ballroom and Pilates, and a trainer four times a week, or else it would be dragging on the ground. Dhel should know—she's seen me buck-naked at the gym. Poppy winks and gives the rowdy one-of-the-boys laugh that was her trademark as an investment banker in New York.

She and Nick met up this morning in Soochow, where Poppy showed Nick a spinning factory in one of the new special industrial zones that might interest a client of his. Now she's brought him to see her family's ancestral hall in the historic garden area of the city, a house the clan bought from the government and is now restoring.

So, salute great-grandfather Chen Li-Xiang, says Poppy, gesturing at the painting. He was the one who won the title for the family by defending a group of imperial messengers during the Boxer Rebellion. And built the house. Through here is the apartment of wife number one, and through here is the lion-stone garden. Roomy, isn't it? They say eighteen families were living here at the time of the Cultural Revolution.

She takes him through a maze of graceful white-walled rooms lined with dark wood, a set of nesting boxes, chambers within chambers, giving onto big and little courtyards filled with the tawny contorted stone from Lake Tai that is a specialty of Soochow gardens. Except for the shrine, the rooms are empty and smell of fresh paint.

It's magnificent, says Nick. Are you moving in?

Poppy grins. Of course not. We're working to make it into a semi-museum, on the Soochow garden and canal tour. I'd never leave Hong Kong, except for maybe Shanghai or New York. Or maybe Hanoi—we have some interesting work going on there, and you can buy a whole colonial block for the price of a room on the Peak. The thing is that this is our family house, our city, our land. My father dreamed of buying it back his whole life. It was in the back of his mind when he had to flee through Shanghai to Hong Kong with just the clothes on his back. And it was always his motivation when he was a trader in Kowloon working fifteen hours a day. In May we're having a family reunion here—two hundred Chens from four continents.

It makes me feel guilty for a whole four seconds that we sold our family place in Maine.

The Froggy House, says Poppy. Where we from St. Geo's had a few historical stoned weekends. I thought you were crazy when I heard. Didn't anybody in your family care?

We're all scattered, and nobody had the time to look after it. So I guess nobody cared.

Poppy looks at him, standing in the humid sunlight, with his expensive suit, his London City pallor, and his graying blond hair limp over the blue eyes that to her always seem just a bit too wide open.

Uncharacteristically, she persists. But don't you feel like you need something—fixed? A reference point?

Fixed? he jokes. But nothing's broken, Poppy. We have the place in London. I think I am just turning out to be that not very unusual thing, a lifetime expat. Dhel's the same way. Anyway, we may be coming this way next. To Shanghai.

Never thought I'd see you turn into an old China hand.

I'm not an old China hand, says Nick in Mandarin.

That's true—your accent's still terrible. And you certainly didn't become a bloody Brit.

My theory, says Nick, is that the more foreign places you live in, the less you absorb. There's only one time, the first time, when your pores are open.

That was the U.S. for me, Italy for you, wasn't it? says Poppy softly. Yep.

Both of them are silent for a minute, wondering why it is that in all the years they've known each other, they've never slept together. Then Poppy adds, Anyway, you should think about your daughters. They need a piece of America.

They have to find their own way. If they want to buy back Froggy House, they're welcome to it.

Poppy is profoundly shocked, but smart enough to turn it into a joke. That is exactly why I didn't stick around Goldman Sachs and marry one of my preppie swains. You white boys have no respect for roots. She links her arm in his. Come on, F. Scott. We just have time for a bowl of noodles before we hit the airport.

1987 · WHAT YOU DO

Hey Romeo
What are ya gonna do?
Hey Romeo
Now that she's leaving you.

Well. Night after night you go running. Trying to shake the slimy black rag of shame and rage and despair twisting like a serpent tighter and tighter around your guts until you think you might suffocate or explode. Down the Corso at three A.M., speeding across Piazza Venezia where the all-night *porchetta* vendors call out, *A fanatico!* Footsteps echoing alongside the Forum, the Colosseum, the temples and public buildings that in the streetlit darkness look like heaps of dirty Styrofoam. Through the pine scent of the Aventino, uphill past the junkies and Moroccan dealers outside the sleek walls of the Food and Agriculture Organization. Running in the middle of the road, imagining truck brakes screeching, being tossed like a crash dummy across the Styx. Getting as far as the Appia Antica, turning off onto gravel, into the smell of gardens. The Nigerian whores and Brazilian transvestites standing beside their oddly cozy fires, which they feed with crumpled tissues and used condoms so that they're surrounded by the stink of burned latex. Some in cars, flashing headlights so that you feel like some kind of sicko celebrity, calling out, *Dai, bellissimo,* come on, *biondino,* Blondie, I'll do you for free.

And you lie on the telephone to family and friends in the States. Both you and Mira are still lying, so that your marriage still exists in a different time zone, just like daylight does when it's night in Europe.

Like any other cuckolded businessman, you work, harder and better than ever before. Though you don't know it, all three of you, Zenin and Mira included, throughout your constellation, have always worked with miraculous concentration.

You watch cartoons with your small daughter: *Thundercats, Mystic Knights, Scooby-Doo, Masters of the Universe.* And then you play elaborate games of pretend with Maddie, based on composites of these characters, creating whole imaginary countries and civilizations, filled with your characters like the high plains were once filled with bison. Worlds with unique languages and complex destinies that can take over your attention for hours. There aren't many princesses or queens in the worlds you create, and in fact, to your secret satisfaction, Maddie chooses to be a prince with a magic longbow. When Mira comments on this, you tell her it's none of her fucking business.

You start to go to parties on your own, and such is the lightning speed of expatriate gossip in Rome that you quickly rediscover something: women. Beautiful, sympathetic, and infinitely available. Women, and the intense toxic pleasure, forgotten since high school and college breakups, of fucking your brains out with people you don't even need to pretend to like.

You get drunk, you get high, with friends, without friends. Italian wine and grappa don't do it anymore. Stoli, nose candy, a little Tunisian kif, Dr. Tedward's sovereign remedy, as your little brother calls it: drunk and skunk.

You don't talk about the bitch, and what she has done. Not yet. She hasn't even become "the bitch" yet.

You just look at the spaces in the closet, the half-used creams and boxes of tampons in the bathroom cabinet that she says she is going to pick up once she gets settled in the residence hotel. She says this in a pleasant, considerate voice, as a roommate in a student apartment might say to another roommate when she moves out. The same tone, give or take a bit of tender maternal brightness, in which she talks about friendly separation, and in telling Maddie that Mommy and Daddy will have two houses now but will always be her loving family. The exquisite thoughtful courtesy that sluts use once they've been found out.

And the sleaziness of all this stiffens your spine, gives you the power to look at her as she moves, damn her, around what used to be her home, with a martyred St. Cecilia smile that seems to hint that she is suffering as much as you are. As she makes arrangements, actual plans for a mysterious future separate from yours. You can look at her through a sort of lens, colder than the ice on Mercury, harder than a diamond. To see the face that once meant all riches, the Indias of spice and mine, and realize that it is quite an ordinary face—prettier than some, less pretty than a lot of others.

Last but not least, you watch Italian men on the street, in airports, and think with a racing heart and a kind of blankness, Is this him? Rich businessmen with tans and silk suits, getting out of armored cars, trailing their jackets on their shoulders the way only Italians can. Is this what the fucker looks like? Without realizing that Zenin can never have a real face for you because he is too powerful an image, a presence, a fear. Zenin is money, age, foreignness, as enormous and potent an enigma in your life as in Mira's. He has been there in the background since the beginning of your time in Europe, like Old Testament God on the mountaintop. You would never dream of protesting, of trying to fight for your wife the way you might with some ordinary jerk. And it will never dawn on you, not even years later, that Zenin is in some ways the most ordinary jerk of all.

BRIDGET

Nick Reiver? Oh yes, definitely a hottie. I met him at around the second party I ever went to in Rome. It was given by these two gay guys who are friends of the art teacher at Marymount, which is where I'm a preschool intern. Anyway, it was in this incredible penthouse apartment right smack overlooking Piazza Navona where tourists were milling in this human carpet down below and the fountain was, oh my God, your basic private backyard Bernini. So I'm drinking caipirinhas and feeling very Roman Holiday when everybody starts teasing me about my twin brother, and it turned out to be Nick, who does look a lot like me, and who managed to say something not too lame about incest. And it turned out that one of his freshman roommates at Harvard married a girl who went to Portsmouth Abbey with my roommate from Georgetown. So we got together. What you do—went out for pizza and Giolitti's ice cream, drove up to Castelgandolfo. But he was going through a divorce and was kind of—um—bitter, though I've got to admit he didn't obsess about his ex the way some guys do. The thing is, though, that if you come to Rome, you don't want to end up with an American guy. If you're blond, Roman men make you feel like a goddess just for walking down the street. So now I have adorable Enzo, love of my life, and I'm taking intensive language lessons. And Nick the cutie got snapped up by that group of Spanish and Italian girls from USIS, the ones I call Europussy Central. Well, it's appropriate, because he's blond after all, and they'll definitely help him heal his broken heart.

30

ZENIN

2005 · OUT OF THE BLUE

Zenin's second youngest sister beckons to him from across the cathedral but Zenin doesn't move, packed as he is in a sea of industrialists and lawyers who all seem to be wearing the same loden coat, and whose cologne seems to blend with the incense in a single lugubrious perfume. If a bomb went off in this corner, he calculates, at least nine companies would be left without chairmen.

The city has turned out to mourn the deaths of five of its own. Two young women and a young man in their early twenties, friends of Zenin's son and nephews. The parents of the young man, a famous newspaper editor and his wife, a center-left politician. It was planned as a dream trip, a celebration of harmony between generations—the kids celebrating their new university degrees, and the married couple, their thirty-year anniversary. They'd been traveling together across the stark beauty of the trackless desert of Mali when their small plane fell out of the sky with an impact that so thoroughly pulverized everything that, the whisper fills the church, there is hardly more than a handful of sand in each coffin.

A gray late-fall morning and Zenin has raced over from his office so fast that he lost two points on his license.

The rustle of packed humanity rising up to the seventeenth-century apotheosis of saints and apostles in tender faded colors framed by gilt and Verona marble on the famous Duomo ceiling. The unexpected feeling of being part of a popular movement, like a demonstration. The small social pockets in the congregation: the sobbing university students in the front, where Zenin can just see his son's cropped head among his cousins'; the journalists from all over Italy; the politicians who will be photographed later coming out of the church.

The voice of Cardinal Pnin, who speaks of the mysterious significance of tragedy. The good lives taken, and the need to look beyond the taking.

Zenin thinks that it could have been himself and his son. He and Daniele have talked for years about a trip together to some remote place, perhaps with Zenin's girlfriend, perhaps with a group of his and Daniele's friends. Daniele is an avid mountaineer and has gone trekking in the Andes and in Nepal. They've talked about riding motorcycles through the desert in Libya. Daniele likes harsh climates, challenges, things that Zenin privately admits that he is too old and lazy to undertake.

Still, he muses, not a bad way to go—in good health and happiness, in a minute's fall. The worst thing would be to know that your child, your future, was falling too. There is, he thinks, a legend about that, isn't there.

So many ways to lose a son: to war, to a freak accident, to a drunken skid on the road returning from a country disco late at night. To heroin, scourge of rich Italian kids. So many ways, also, to lose one's own life: from a heart attack to cancer to the slow rot that is called healthy old age. Zenin stares again at the kids in the front of the congregation and feels a shudder of possessive love and desolate apprehension that he has never felt for anyone else. And his son will never know how he has mastered his father's heart.

Meanwhile, the five coffins are carried out of the church, and as they make their last journey something like a swell of unanimity passes through the crowd, something far stronger than the response evoked by the cardinal. The mood, the shared certainty beyond grief that for a moment unites the people at the funeral is this: the superstitious emotion of a small city, rooted in time and place, toward those who dreamed, as everyone in the provinces does, of leaving and going to the remotest corners of the world; and how it was the foreignness of the place, more than chance or destiny or divine whim, that cast them out of the sky. It was the strangeness that destroyed them.

1987 · SNAPSHOTS

Mira is spending the weekend at Zenin's house, and she and Zenin are about to drive to Venice for a lunch of crab—the famous Adriatic *moeche,* in season just now—at the tiny nameless restaurant on the island of San Pietro in Volta.

And Zenin catches a flash of a photograph as Mira closes her handbag. He takes the bag from her, opens it, and finds two snapshots of his son that he keeps in his bureau drawer. Daniele on miniature skis, screaming with delight; on the beach at Porto Cervo, staring solemnly into the camera.

A mixture of rage and fear sweeps through Zenin. What are you doing? he demands. What is this?

Mira wilts. I just wanted to look at him. Your son. He's darling, beautiful. I wanted to take a good look, calmly. I was going to put them back. She says this in a warm insincere voice that she has never used with Zenin before.

Zenin takes the snapshots away from her and puts them back in his drawer without saying anything else. He is infuriated with Mira for prying—a feminine failing he thought an American writer would be too sophisticated and intellectual to possess. Most of all, though, he is surprised at his own new vision of her as a menace. As if she might have stolen the snapshots for purposes of kidnapping or black magic.

It reminds him of that terrifying American movie he saw a year or two back, *Attrazione fatale,* with that sexy blond actress who turns into a monster, confirming all of Zenin's fears.

There's no doubt that Mira is now a problem. She is good-looking enough—seems to have gotten better-looking through all the fuss of the last six months since she left her fool of a husband. Though these days she overdresses, he thinks irritably, always in designer skirts and dresses, not understanding the way an Italian girl can wear jeans on a weekend and look elegant.

As they leave the car in the parking garage in Piazzale Roma, as they take the water taxi out to the bare anchorite's rock that is San Pietro, as they sit eating at one of the five tables lit by the pewter sheen of the cloudy Adriatic sky, men look at her. Porters, waiters, fishermen, tourists, yachtsmen he knows who are out for a Saturday afternoon jaunt with their girlfriends.

She is still desirable, then, still an asset, and fucks better than any girl he's ever come across. But there is the matter of the power shift that occurs when mistresses run off and leave their husbands.

The snapshot episode is just the latest step in a farcical situation evolving in Zenin's house. Where Mira arrives from Rome on weekends and Tere comes to visit with his son during the week, and where the two women have embarked on a clandestine war of espionage, each interrogating the household staff and poking in closets. Moreover, gossip is flashing through the city about his affair with an American gold digger.

Though Zenin realizes he created the situation, he vaguely blames Mira for it.

Because it's mystifying, this bizarre American ease in transferring a life to another country, in unmarrying oneself, which, in light of the lingering fuss over his own divorce, seems to him almost indecent.

Cautious as usual, Zenin would not be surprised to be confronted with a pair of American gangster brothers or a crazed father, brandishing a hillbilly shotgun to defend Mira's honor. Or to find out that the husband has been playing a deep game of lying low to make his vendetta more of a surprise. It has crossed his mind that perhaps some sort of legal or financial scam is in the works.

Yet apparently it isn't. How can a husband just step back and let his wife go?

The whole thing is eerily convenient for Zenin, who finds himself nonetheless wondering whether Mira can be a respectable girl if there is no one to fight for her. And she hasn't come to ask him for money, though he has already mentally sketched out an appropriate settlement.

The moment is arriving, he thinks, when things will have to be put in order.

After their crabs and pasta with razor clams, they eat vanilla ice cream with black coffee poured over it. And look at each other.

Mira says that she borrowed the pictures of his son because she wants to know more about Zenin's life. And, because she adds slowly, as Zenin knows, her daughter, Maddie, is the same age. And she misses the little girl dreadfully during the days the child spends with Nick.

Ma quanto hai sacrificato per me, says Zenin, squeezing her hand across the table. You've sacrificed so much for me. He tries to say it playfully, affectionately, to lighten the atmosphere as they sit in the dingy little restaurant looking out over the afternoon expanse of sea toward Croatia.

È vero, says Mira, her face unreadable. It's true.

Zenin, waiting for the check, looking forward to an afternoon in bed with her, feels oddly grateful to Mira for saying it so quietly. An Italian girl would have sobbed it or screamed it.

LIBERA

I've been *guardarobiera*—laundress and person in charge of linens and wardrobe—for *dottore Zenin* for close to fifteen years, and I've seen a lot of women come and go, but never anything like this. What goes on in this house nowadays is like an Alberto Sordi movie or one of those old five-lire dancing and singing shows that used to travel around the Triveneto after the war. With the wife and the lover in and out of the closets, over and under the bed, chasing, chasing, until everybody goes crazy. But here, who can tell who should be the wife and who's the lover? Make up the pink room for Signora Tere and the Signorino, then clear the room, change the towels for Signora Mira, divide up the clothes that both women left to be laundered. And both of them, La Tere and L'Americana, come to me with big tips and try to find out what is going on, something the *dottore* tells us strictly not to say. Jobs aren't so easy to come by these days, not with all the Romanians and Peruvians stealing the work. So I keep quiet and watch the show. The little boy's a darling innocent, and the two women are both decent girls, just both a little crazy about the *dottore*. It's his fault, of course. Like all rich men he thinks the sun shines out of his ass.

31

MIRA

~~

Mira writes in her journal:

Rome, this weekend, the first time in so many years. An official family trip, Vanni and the boys in tow. It's all prompted by the shameful fact that Stefano and Zoo, at nine and seven, have visited Beijing and Nairobi and Orlando and New York, but never the grand capital of half of their ancestors, the birthplace of their sister Maddie. We've come through the airport countless times, on our way home to Turin from somewhere else. We've heard the Roman accents, and glimpsed as we landed the insinuating faded colors of the Lazio countryside. And once I flew in to interview a Roman leftist filmmaker who has one of those beautiful sixties apostolic faces, and who spoke, as all leftists do, with nostalgia for his comfortable middle-class childhood. After the interview, I ate a chocolate tartufo at Tre Scalini like a tourist, and then fled in a taxi. Rejecting the spell of Rome like an offered garment.

But yesterday I stood giggling with Stefano and Zoo in a line full of Japanese and American tourists whose digital cameras flashed like heat lightning in the gloomy loggia of Santa Maria in Cosmedin, as each person went up and put his hand in the ice-cold stone slot that is the Bocca della Verità. The mouth of Truth.

*A mask of Hercules so degraded by time that it resembles, as Ste-
fano remarked, nothing so much as a great big leering pizza. So
great big overwrought heroic ideas are worn down over time into
popular fare. The other tourists were determinedly grinning and
posing for photos as if they might need proof of truthfulness for
some document. Everybody but the boys and me. We hadn't even
brought a camera. We just laughed and stuck our hands for fun
into that big unwelcoming mouth that not even the touch of a
thousand palms can warm. And I wondered at the strange vulgar
indifference of that great stone face, as my two skinny sons with
their ruddy cheeks clowned around in front of it. I thought, Should
I be scared for them?*

*Vanni, scorning the plebeian line, waited in the rental car.
With his* Corriere della Sera *propped in front of his handsome
face with its heavy saturnine lines, he projected as always a sense
of composure, maturity, a benign Mediterranean darkness. Though
he comes from Turin, he has his own past in Rome, where he lived
as a child and then as a university student. So he bored us by taking us through mustard-colored bourgeois neighborhoods, showing
us the neighborhood bar where his buddies met on their motor-
bikes, the old school whose Fascist architecture is now covered
with graffiti, the aristocratic gardens filled with generations of cats,
the Belle Epoque apartment where he'd sneak in through the window of a girl named Matilda. . . . It made me happy to underline
what I already knew, that my past in Rome is one of as many as
there are pores in a coral reef.*

*Z and S raced their father around the side of the Colosseum.
Father and sons had a real test of their agility in making their way
among the mountebanks, the fake Roman soldiers in their plastic
armor, the Indian souvenir vendors, the school groups, the lovers,
the massed Polish and Chinese tour groups. Seeing the three of
them disappearing and reappearing in the crowd ahead gave me a
sense of security.*

*I walked behind, my feet fitting themselves to the familiar ir-
regularity of the old stones. I noticed—as I never did when I was
younger and more easily awed, and this scene was part of my daily*

*landscape—that the color of the ruins is weathered into a soft or-
ganic hue that runs from living gray, to a tawny lion color, to deep
ocher red. And the decayed edges of the monuments looked like
wounds. Huge extravagant wounds. On this trip I have to admit
that something happened: for the first time I looked on Rome with
a certain compassion and fellowship, as a city maimed by time.*

1987 · UNFORESEEN

Nick is the first one to realize that Mira is pregnant. Not even she
knows it yet.

One Sunday morning they are standing watching their daughter in
the play garden of Villa Borghese. Not too close beside each other, with
the searing awareness of physical frontiers that only separated couples
have. In the deep pine shade near the Promenade of Poets where Mira
used to run at dawn, a stone's throw from the Casino Valadier where
she used to meet Zenin, not far from the underground gym where Nick
demolishes other young businessmen at squash.

Almost a year has passed since Mira moved out.

This morning they mingle with the handsome bourgeois families of
the Parioli neighborhood who are out for their ritual stroll after Mass
and before Sunday lunch. Sleek mothers and fathers smoking compla-
cently as they watch their children, overdressed in Shetland sweaters
and big embroidered collars, riding the merry-go-round and swarming
around the balloon seller.

Maddie runs among the other kids, wearing a pleated red wool
smock, curls flying, brandishing a balloon in the shape of a dolphin.
Turning from time to time, her eyes searching out the parents who
have stopped shouting at each other and now live in different houses,
each of which has a room that is Maddie's. The parents who talk about
still being a family though they live apart. The parents who meet on occasional Sundays like this one to take Maddie on the bumper cars and
miniature train and perhaps to eat a quick pizza at Da Romolo.

Still a couple in the eyes of the Roman crowd, a pair of young
Americans dressed with weekend sloppiness among all the elegant

Italians—running shoes, jeans, Mira in an old sheepskin jacket Nick recognizes from college. Nick, who knows now that she dresses up like a high-class hooker for that rich bastard, feels she is condescending to him.

They can't exactly see each other, can't exactly use their eyes. Instead, with another sense, they view the reality: two spectral silhouettes in a burning wasteland.

They chat sporadically, toss husks of private jokes and observations about Maddie. Sometimes without realizing it they fall into their old wisecracking shorthand speech.

That guy looks like a fish.

So did Lenin's girlfriend. She had a disease.

There's a fish-face disease?

More of a syndrome.

They give a simultaneous snort of laughter and then stop short. Looking off into the distance as if someone is arriving.

And Mira at one of these forgetful moments, yawns, rubs her eyes, complains that she isn't feeling good, nothing special, a flu perhaps.

Maybe you're pregnant, says Nick.

This just pops out in what he intends to be a dry quizzical voice, the tone of a friendly but dispassionate observer. But both of them hear the spasm in his throat. And as he says it, they both know it is true. He seems to know her face, her pallor, the chemistry of her body better than she does, and recalls with instinctive precision the exact smell of her when she was expecting Maddie.

A flush like a sudden bruise comes over Mira's face, and she shakes her head and walks away. Leaving the words to drift after her: Not possible.

After a minute she recovers herself, changes the subject, and calls to Maddie to come and see, that the marionette show is starting.

Parents, grandparents, children, and dogs flock to the recorded fanfare that blares from the little stage near the belvedere. They hand ticket money to the woman with the tired Gypsy face and the bowler hat. Nick, Mira, and Maddie with them. They sit in the heart of the crowd as little Pulcinella in his papal-white robes and highwayman's mask, with his screechy eunuch's voice, sings out his loves and fears, rights his wrongs with a big stick. Whack, whack, whack. The children scream with delight. Even the grown-ups laugh without faking, as if they hadn't seen it all a hundred times before. And Nick and Mira, too, forget their woes long enough to laugh, only from time to time letting their eyes drift toward the shadow of the pines beyond the stage.

PULCINELLA

Adesso vi dico, bambini, che questo mio nemico e molto molto furbo e cattivo. Now, I'm going to tell you children, that my enemy is very wicked and clever. So I need your help. I'm going to hide in this big pot, and when you see the devil come in and try to kiss my Colombina, shout, There he is! And what will I do? I'll jump out with my cudgel and go Bam! Bam! Bam!

So let's rehearse what you have to say.

Children: There he is!

Pulcinella: Louder!!

Children: *There he is!*

Pulcinella: And now what do I do?

Children: Bam! Bam! Bam!

32

NICK

Dad, asks his youngest daughter, Eliza. Is it true that I'm a little bit black?

It's a couple of hours after sunset on Halloween, and Nick, who is walking her through the gusty leaf-scented darkness of Cadogan Square to a party at Garden House School, gives a start as if some yobbo in an orc mask had jumped out of the bushes. No, you're not, he says. Where'd you get that idea?

Eliza, eight, is dressed as Wednesday, the daughter from *The Addams Family,* and in the street light the resemblance is unnerving—the tightly parted hair, the Victorian orphan's dress, the ghoulish, knowing pale face. She glances up at him as the wind rattles her trick-or-treat bag.

From Maddie, she says. When she was here this summer, she told me and Juju she was part black. And Maddie's our sister.

Your half sister. Nick raps out the correction with such sharpness that he feels he has done a violence to two tender creatures. To sweet spindly Eliza, and to Maddie, sleeping like a nymph in her dormitory across the Atlantic. Bad dad, he thinks. Down, boy. He's just flown in from Brussels and he's worn out, and besides he hates Halloween in England—a tame self-conscious expat kind of thing compared to the anarchic masked gangs of kids skidding up and down driveways, screaming, gorging, that he remembers from Little Compton long ago. It would be nice, he thought, if Dhel and some of the other mothers from the group of schools sponsoring the party would ditch the Morgan le Fay robes and dress up as Catwoman. His own minimalist persona is indicated by a ketchup-smeared T-shirt and a toy stethoscope and the title Dr. Death, from a fifth-season *X-Files* episode.

Half sister, Eliza repeats. That means—

We've been through this a million times, Lize. Maddie is your half sister because I am her dad, but she has a different mother.

Because you were married a long time ago to somebody who wasn't Mommy. And she was Maddie's mom, and she was the one who made Maddie part African American. The way Mommy made us part Vietnamese. When Eliza gets hold of an idea she reminds him of a terrier worrying a rat. We are a mixed-up family, aren't we, Dad?

Yep. We are. It seems to Nick that Dhel and the girls do nothing but discuss the subject—the Notting Hill flat is filled with enough books on multiculturalism to supply a Save the Children conference, with videos of family reunions in Rhode Island, Quogue, Zurich, Saigon.

They've crossed the lamplit street and are walking by the leafy billows of Cadogan Square Gardens, where later in the depths near the swings and the Wendy House there will be refreshments and a Thai fire show for the kids who've made it through the haunted house and a carefully selected trick-or-treat route among the lamplit terraces of Belgravia. Nick has seen a pub closed down for a private celebration with a lot of little kids in costumes, but otherwise no other signs of Halloween. Do you think they'll have the blood-and-guts tunnel this year? he asks.

Yes. Boiled pasta and grapes. Boring. Eliza holds her lace collar from blowing in her face. So Dad, am I even a little bit Italian?

No. Why would you think that?

Because Maddie has Italian brothers.

Thank God, thinks Nick, there are only two blocks left. Eliza, he says. Sweetie pie. What is it with you tonight? It seems to me that Mom and I have explained this to you girls enough times to get it right. Listen, you are my daughter. Maddie is my daughter. I was married to Maddie's mom a long time ago, and then we got divorced. I fell in love with your mom and we got married, and Maddie's mom married an Italian man. Maddie now has two half brothers and two half sisters.

So those Italian boys aren't even a tiny bit related to me?

No. Look—there's the school. What's that, jack-o'-lanterns in all the windows?

Can I meet them?

What?

I said I want to meet those boys. Maddie's brothers. Juju does too. When can we?

It would be easy enough, as he realizes later, to murmur something equivocal about someday. The next trip to Italy. When Maddie graduates from college; when Maddie gets married. But they hurry toward the school, and the word springs off his lips and then turns to stone in the air as if frozen by a Harry Potter spell: Never.

Da-ad! How come? Eliza squeals, but then they are at the school, its ample Victorian brick spaces transformed into a ghastly labyrinth for the night and a Gandalf clone handing out flash tubes under a phosphorescent spiderweb at the door. Here, mercifully, Eliza is swept up by her giggling friends and borne inside on a tide of monsters and heroes of her own generation.

Leaving Dr. Death to look around in vain for Catwoman, mentally declining the verb *to haunt*.

1987 · AN OFFER

Of course one can get to him if one wants to. *Uno può trovarlo, se uno vuole.* All these small-town rich men are paranoid and yet completely unprotected. They're tightwads and they only pay their bodyguards part-time. They invest in armored cars—in fact the damned Socialists are handing them out as perks nowadays—but then they get sick of them and take the Ferrari to show off to their girlfriends or the Cherokee to go to lunch at their mother's. Careless. Rossi got kidnapped right in front of his house in the country. Not that you intend kidnapping or indeed anything illegal. Just a token reminder to a son of a whore who took what didn't belong to him.

Nick sits staring at the sheep-faced blond man in the polo shirt and Timberlands who is squeezed at a tiny aluminium bar table beside Nick's friend, the well-connected lawyer Lorenzo. The man saying this stuff, not with the cinematically appropriate Sicilian hiss or sadistic Teutonic aspirates, but in the comfortable fussy tone of an Emilia-Romagnan discussing his personal preferences in baked pasta.

Of course this encounter is all a dream, at least it should be. But it has the straightforward outrageousness of real life. In fact, it is real, the fruit of the sympathetic machinations of Lorenzo, also known as Lorenzaccio, who since Nick and Mira's separation has been offering, with the pressing warmth of a midwestern neighbor at a funeral, to "help out." The proffered help at first took the form of evenings with comely Russian exchange students or ambitious RAI starlets, which lasted until Lorenzo—with the kind of private manly relief one might feel for a backward teenage son—learned through his foreign gossip contacts that Nick in his recovering grief seemed to be boning half the female staff of the American embassy. It only remained for Lorenzo to drag his young friend to this dubious appointment at a tubular metal café in one of the palmy Blade Runner suburbs off the Cassia. Where the three of them sit over drinks—the sheep-faced man takes only an iced tea—under the awning of a small grim terrace that overlooks a sun-broiled supermarket parking plaza filled with housewives loading cars with bags of groceries. Nearby is a *tabaccheria,* a newsstand, and a tanning salon called Neri per Sempre—Black Forever.

Nick hardly knows why he's there, but the real reason is that he's curious. The small part of him that is most himself, that is untouched by hurt, that will recover again and again from profound losses in his life, as it did from that early loss of his brother, wants to know what it looks and sounds and tastes like to plot a vendetta.

A half-remembered line comes into his head; he thinks it's from Hemingway: more or less it says that all that's necessary for survival is an interest in life, good, bad, or peculiar.

In this moment, though he'll never know it, he is closest to what Mira felt when she took her first steps toward Zenin.

And this is what it's like: The syrupy taste of the vermouth he ordered, which is rumored to have powdered Egyptian mummy as one of its secret ingredients. The early summer heat, the Cassia traffic fumes, through which arrives the tiny finger of sea breeze that Romans call the *ponentino.* A billboard over the supermarket showing three bikini-clad models smiling on a generic Mediterranean beach, all gorgeous but with strangely simian foreheads. Across from Nick, the broken capillaries on one side of the blond man's nose as the man pauses in his vague shop talk and addresses Nick in a fawning interrogative as *dottore,* as if urging his honorable assent before proceeding to specifics of ways and means. And Nick sees that he is a *ragioniere,* a small-time bureacrat, not a thug, not a thug's agent, but a thug's agent's agent. And what is he going to prescribe in the mild case of Nick's honor? Jumping out from behind a palm tree with a Darth Vader mask? Beating his rival lightly with a lead pipe? Sending Zenin's mother a nasty note?

A plaintive song is playing on Roma 105 FM, which Nick recognizes as one of the *canzone d'autore* anthems for Italians who grew up in the seventies. It's called *"In questo mondo di ladri"*—in this world of thieves.

He finishes his vermouth and says, *Riflettendo, credo che non mi conviene.*

Out of polite respect for Lorenzaccio, who set the whole thing up, he tries to give concise utterance to his feeling that once half the stars have been sucked out of the sky, there's no fucking point in revenge. That payback means nothing. Isn't that right? And it's more satisfying not being a shit. Didn't Hemingway write that too?

Non mi conviene, he repeats. It's not worth it to me.

The five-o'clock sun beats on the asphalt. A friar from a suburban convent shuffles by in bulky sandals, sweating, clutching a supermarket bag. And for a minute before they recover themselves, the two men, Lorenzo and the blond stranger, sit looking at Nick as if he were an extraterrestrial.

ELIZA

I love it when I get Daddy all to myself without that show-off Julia hogging the attention. Halloween isn't really scary but anyway nothing bad can happen in the dark when I'm walking with my hand swallowed up in his great big hand. Daddy works very hard and travels a lot and always brings us back hotel chocolates and chopsticks for my collection. He's teaching Juju and me about war games, except Juju's too dumb to understand strategy, and sometimes when we're on the motorway he puts on the Clash and we sing and drum on the seats until Mom tells us to shut up. I think he's the coolest of all my friends' dads, almost as handsome as David Beckham. But he doesn't know everything. And I think those Italian boys are related to us no matter what he says. I'll ask Maddie about it. Maddie looks like a model in a magazine, and she can do henna tattoos. She tells us about her Italian brothers in Turin and how one whines worse than Juju and how they built a maze for lizards they caught. Juju and I already swore we're going to run away and visit them. They're our sister's brothers, and that makes them part of us. I think families are like spiderwebs: they stretch all over the place where you don't expect them.

33

ZENIN

Che rottura di palle. What a pain in the ass, thinks Zenin, seated at a very elegant kitchen table in the neighborhood that is the Upper West Side, the Left Bank, of Rome—the Via Margutta zone. He hates eating out unless it is with family or old friends, with whom he can drink and joke around, or clients, when there is a clear goal in sight, or, rarely these days, in an expensive place to impress a pretty woman.

But this is another one of Mariella's social projects. First cocktails at an antique dealer in Via Giulia, who is showing off a remarkable School of Caravaggio painting recently acquired for a song from an impoverished Calabrian prince. Zenin had flown down willingly from Rovigo, hoping to see some decent-looking girls, but the vernissage looked like a convention for aristocratic senior citizens, too many old trout with yellow teeth and fur scarves framing wrinkles. Including three of Zenin's ex-lovers, bleached, tanned, tits and faces lifted, looking like fossils cleaned up for display.

Now he's stuck at a fake informal dinner in a penthouse kitchen with walls studded with Morandis and Vedovas—he tries mentally to add up the cost—with a vegetarian second course of zucchini blossoms, which he loathes, stuffed with ricotta from someone's country estate. Just six of them at a table laid with earthenware dishes, but displaying heavy old silverware with a family crest: Zenin; Mariella; Smeralda, the hostess, a lissome, blue-eyed countess famous for her column in *L'Espresso*; Paolo, a leftist editor, friend of Einaudi and Primo Levi, who writes cryptic books with kabbalah images on their covers; Melina, a blond war correspondent; and the Old Man, who is no richer than Zenin but, having for years headed up the country's largest publishing empire, is as much a monument to Italians as the Colosseum.

All the women are dressed in designer black, with jewelry that is either North African or elaborately crafted family gold.

Everyone is chummy, asking about children, grandchildren, and vacation plans at their country places down in the Maremma.

Zenin is nervous about his table manners.

It looks as if things might be amusing when before dinner the Old Man starts pawing Melina and asking her to pull up her shirt so he can see if she has love handles.

But then the conversation shifts into English, which everyone else speaks better than Zenin. They dissect current events, crack jokes quote bons mots and outrageous excuses made by journalists and political mandarins on the Anglo-Saxon side of the world. From time to time in a way Zenin finds humiliating, they thoughtfully translate terms they think might be too complex for him.

Then they talk about books. About Philip Roth and Anna Maria Ortese and Fleur Jaeggy, and an array of Indian authors with incomprehensible names.

Zenin sits there with his big speckled hands on the table. Thinking how much more fun Rome used to be a long time ago when he used to fly down to fuck Mira and eat platefuls of fried fish.

When discussing their children, the Old Man says that, as everyone knows, his own son is a worthless dimwit who is blowing his inheritance in bad investments. He's just gone off to India to stay with Sai Baba. But what does it matter, says the Old Man. I'll be dead, and the little turd will be poor, with expensive tastes. It's the way of the world. Has a fortune ever lasted longer than three generations? Think of it—Bardi, Krupp, Rothschild, Morgan; what do they mean now compared to the Asians, the Russians? It's like waves washing up over the sand. The world is littered with the rubble of big fortunes. What do you say, Zenin? How long will it take your *ragazzi* to piss it away?

Holding the crested dessert fork in his hand, Zenin makes an acceptable joke that makes Mariella flash him a smile. He who rarely allows himself to get angry thinks how much he loathes these people with their sneering assumption of privilege, their arrogant careless nihilism possible only for brats who were born with forks like this. Joking about his dearest, most secret kernel of a dream, when his son, Daniele, is enthroned, extending the empire he has founded. With proper table manners and perfect English.

Non ti sei divertito, tesoro? croons Mariella, when they are back at the hotel. Didn't you have a good time? Zenin, already on the bed in his underpants, channel changer in his hand, does not even bother to tell her to shove the whole evening up her ass.

He should have bought the School of Caravaggio painting in front of all those *figli di puttane,* he thinks. Just thrown down a check and carried it away under his arm.

1987 · WHAT ZENIN DOESN'T SEE

He doesn't see that the limousine, of average length, seems blacker than other town cars, blacker and glossier than piano keys or black caviar or a black alligator purse. That it blends in its blackness with Mira's coat, a soft sheath of cashmere that Zenin bought her on an earlier, happier New York trip by walking into a Madison Avenue shop and paying with his usual wad of dollars. That as she sits slumped groggily on the soft leather of the seat opposite him, she looks out of the window at the lines of taxis gleaming through the evening rush on Park Avenue and knows that she has been swallowed at last by the beast that has been sniffing around her for years. What beast? Huge and gorgeous, dark and deadly, studying her for so long with its wolfish golden eyes. Mira's awake yet dreaming. Free of pain. They call it twilight sleep.

Stretched out in the opposite corner, his sharp features and lank hair barely outlined in the moving city lights through the tinted glass, Zenin looks like the personification of the word *silence*. He tries not to breathe in the slight medicinal smell emanating from her, not to think of anything that is wounded, spoiled, bleeding. In his relief, he is farther away in spirit than the invisible third person in the car, the Sri Lankan driver who did not seem surprised to have to help a stumbling, apparently drunken girl, not out of a fashionable restaurant or a club, but from a darkened doctor's office in the East Sixties.

We'll take care of it in New York, Zenin told Mira, three days earlier, when the test twice comes out positive. There is nothing to discuss. The words, the decision, emerge stamped on a tablet of stone. It is the first time Zenin has let Mira see him unveiled, in the full, austere power of his money and the cold implacable will that made the money. And he sees that in the middle of her confusion and distress, the tiny part of her that is eternally curious is gratified. To see someone in extremis, forced to use his full strength to defend himself, is, for a moment, to have complete intimacy. And Zenin is in extremis. Suddenly ferociously aware of the threat of being manipulated as he was by Tere, of the threat to his son, Daniele, who is now the center of his world. From the moment Mira tells him she thinks she is pregnant, he keeps looking at her, shaking his head and giving a slight knife-edged smile. A look that also has an edge of wary admiration in it, as if for a worthy opponent.

Swiftly, it's all programmed like clockwork. Zenin's jet to London, Concorde to New York, a suite on a high floor at the Plaza—a hotel where Zenin does not usually stay—overlooking the carpet of autumn color that is Central Park. And a doctor, a famous obstetrician recommended, unbeknown to Mira, by an Italian hotel concierge who is used to resolving such intimate problems for his top clients.

The obstetrician, Dr. C., as his patients and television fans call him, is German, redheaded, gay, and adores women. He is very nice to Mira, whom he finds time to examine, though his waiting room is overflowing with beautiful South American and European mothers-to-be, and he tells her that her IUD failed and that she is about six weeks into a healthy pregnancy. If she doesn't want to continue the pregnancy, he adds in a quiet voice, she should come back that evening.

And that of course is the plan until Zenin goes out for a walk in the late afternoon, leaving Mira to rest in the hotel. He hasn't left her alone for several days. But now that everything seems under control, he strolls up Fifth Avenue, glancing into shop windows, looking benignly over the hordes of fat midwestern tourists in sweat suits, as foreign in Manhattan as in Italy, at Puerto Ricans and blacks and Orthodox Jews and strange robotic businesswomen in pinstripes and running shoes. Idly wondering what life he would have conquered had he gone off to live in America like Macaco's Zio Giorgio.

When he comes back, Mira is looking out at the darkening expanse of the park under a glassy, perfectly clear, early-evening New York October sky. At Olmsted's dream of an American Arcadia.

She turns around and says, We could do this differently. *Potremmo fare questo in modo diverso.*

Zenin curses himself for going out and letting her get ideas in her head. *Potremmo, potremmo,* he says. We could, we could. Here's your coat. The car is downstairs.

He hears an odd dry tenderness in his own voice. It's true, he does feel tender toward her. What he doesn't know is that Mira is looking, really looking, at him for the first time in many months, and that to her he looks old, older than she has ever seen him. Gray in his hair, his skin pale and mottled, eyes sunken, the hawk nose sharper.

We could do things differently, Mira persists. We could keep this child.

Zenin gives a bark of laughter so sharp, so flagrantly amazed at what she is proposing, so insulting and dismissive that it is like a magic word that throws Mira from one dimension to another. Someone more perceptive than Zenin might have seen in her eyes what has happened. A pantomime backdrop of conventional marvels has collapsed and for a minute shown her the true view: the monotonous extent of dry mountain ranges and gullies that make up her folly. For an instant she sees herself as she actually is: pregnant, divorced, alone, crazy, the slave of Rome and the rest of the Old World in her own country, in the city where she once basked in love and freedom.

I'm going out, she says to Zenin. You can't rush me into this. I want to think about what to do. I don't want to see you right now.

You're not going anywhere except downstairs and into the car.

She tries to walk past him and he grabs her arm. Her arm through a silk blouse feels as small as a child's to him, as brittle and cold as an icy twig. And he lets himself scream at her. It is a curiously terrifying griping wail that, as much as the hold he has on her, stops her dead.

Sei come tutte le altre puttane, vuoi prendermi in giro, incastrarmi. You're like all the other whores, trying to catch me. To squeeze money out of me. Do you think that just because I fucked you once or twice that you have a hold on me?

And in a quiet voice he adds that if she doesn't come with him that second, he'll make sure that things are worse for her.

That is all it takes, Zenin is relieved to see. There is no need for anything else to make her come to her senses. Mira is not brave at that moment in the suite at the Plaza. It's as if she has been turned into stone or a store mannequin. Only a few tears leak down her cheeks, and she doesn't wipe them away. Silently she allows him to put on her soft black coat as if she were a child. Tame as she is, he takes no chances, and returns his grip to her arm as they go down the elevator filled with people dressed for dinner and the theater. And does not let her go until she is safely in the car. All next week she'll see five finger-shaped bruises fading from purple to yellow.

DR. C.

To me a woman's body is the most amazing thing: a blossom and a labyrinth made out of flesh and blood; infinitely precious; predictable, yet always surprising. I adore babies too; I help make them. But in this work you get to despise men. Straight men, the sperm givers, the moneymakers. The models and the little prep school girls come in with their rich, sleazy older boyfriends to get the evidence scraped away; the millionaire bully husbands come in to talk about their wives like brood mares.

When the mixed-blood girl came back for an after-hours procedure, I said what I always say to the ones who look like they're being forced. Her po-faced Italian boyfriend was tucked away in the husbands' parlor, so I asked before we prepped her if she was sure she wanted to go through with it. I can just pretend to operate, you know, I said. Or, there's a back door here. It wouldn't be the first time.

And she gazed at me as they always do, and said I was an angel. And thanked me and said that it was too late to help. And a minute later, when she was already on the table and drifting under, she murmured, Where would I go? I'm from Italy.

And that was an odd thing because this girl was most definitely American.

34

MIRA

2005 · SECURITY

Ma'am, could you step this way?

The Boston airport. A local flight from Boston to Philadelphia. The man without a face—erased, excised, or is it just that she can't look at him?—the animated uniform in the airport security line, holds Mira's passport and boarding pass and those of her older son, Stefano, and makes the request that is not a request, in a southwestern military twang that makes her think of dust and barracks and linoleum corridors awash in disinfectant and olive-drab filing cabinets with an infinity of manila envelopes.

A tenebrous fantasy of Fascist bureaucracy always grips Mira at the slightest nod from authority. And transforms her into an illegal immigrant from Honduras, vainly proffering badly printed false documents; or a timid Colombian mule, nauseated from the drug-filled condoms she has swallowed; or a trembling suicide bomber, forgetting the sweetness of revenge, the promised paradise of the faithful, only aware of the sweetness of the body that is about to be smashed to atoms.

You always look so damn guilty, Vanni tells her. *C'hai l'aria colpevole.* You're a sitting duck. Why the hell do you look so guilty? You own the world, bourgeois American wench. Just strut on through. Look at me. Nobody ever bothers me, not even the customs people.

And in fact, nobody ever stops Vanni because he looks exactly like who he is: one of the lords of the earth. Rather a short lord—a wily Mediterranean trickster rather than a tall blond ruler like Nick Reiver, who also never gets stopped—but unmistakably one of the men who run things. The men who are never suspect, even in the long fearful wake of 9/11.

Step this way. And your son too, Ma'am.

Is there a problem? asks Mira, knowing in some feral victim's way that you should never question them.

Problem? No. No problem, he says, in the tone Hollywood FBI agents use to talk down the psychopath with the Uzi.

Mira's heart begins to knock against her ribs. A small uniformed woman with dry peach-colored lipstick defining where her thin lips would be if she had a face has materialized and is hurrying them through a crowd of travelers that parts asunder in Old Testament fashion, with faces turning to gaze at them like a field of sunflowers. As two other uniforms unroll a crowd divider of red tape that leads to a separate set of metal detectors apart from the crowd.

Stefano cocks his cropped head and looks up knowingly at her with long dark eyes that his father and brother teasingly call ferret eyes. He's wearing a Gap sweatshirt that Maddie gave him two days ago when they visited her at Harvard, with a tiny silver pin that he got at the Peabody Museum. Hey Mom, he hisses. Look, they're cutting us ahead of everybody. Cool. What is this, some kind of upgrade?

No. No, sweetie. It's an extra security check. It happens sometimes. Just hurry up and follow the lady.

Step along, please. Now please put your hand luggage, shoes, and jackets on the belt and step through.

They have to go through the metal detector twice and then both of them are patted down and searched from head to toe with a handheld device. They have to bend over and simultaneously stick out their hands, then kick each leg out behind. Then they have to open their carry-on luggage and watch as the woman and two other men go through everything. Mira's copy of *Framley Parsonage*, her dark Peyrano chocolate, Stefano's Lego Bionicle and *Calvin and Hobbes*.

The man patting down Stefano chats purposefully with him. So, dude, you live in Italy. Do you really speak Italian?

I *am* Italian, says Stefano firmly. I'm American and Italian. His naïve excitement has faded. He has traveled all over the world and been through all sorts of security, but he sees his mother's anger and fear, and knows that this is different. Mira feels a heavy resentment build in her as she sees his small face grow pale and his eyes grow large with her own apprehension. Who do they think we *are?* he whispers to her.

You've got to learn to take it in stride, Mira's friends have said over and over to her. It's your passport with all the back and forth on it, all the foreign visas, the fact that you have residence outside the States. It looks suspicious these days. Then, it's the way you look. That swarthy mixed-race thing. You used to be just colored. But now you could be from any terrorist nation on the planet. We're at war, a war based on idiocy, but a war. Deal with it. Don't take it personally.

But she does take it personally. Is this something I chose, to be treated like a criminal in the place I was born, to have my son puzzled and scared and mortified by people staring at him? Is it my destiny, because, no matter how elegantly I dress, I look like a Cuban or North African and acquire a refugee bloom of guilt that shines like a spotlight whenever I pass a checkpoint?

She wants to scream at the faceless woman with the lipstick, who has a thick Boston accent, that she, Mira, has more generations of American ancestors than all of the woman's white-trash family put together. But instead she grabs Stefano's hand and tells him not to worry, forces a smile, tells him that this is something that has to be done to keep the airlines safe. Together they gather up their scattered possessions on the belt and repack their luggage.

Passengers in the normal security lines are still staring at them.

You can proceed, Ma'am, says one of the uniforms, without adding thank you or goodbye.

The military ma'am, thinks Mira. Also used for the queen of England. But when Mira hears it, she always thinks for some reason of the scene when Tom Sawyer is disguised as a girl, and then unmasked when he claps his legs together. And from there, she thinks, it's just a skip and a jump to Huck Finn and Nigger Jim. Fugitives on the river, strangers in their own land.

1987 · MIRA'S RUN

Mira is running away through Venice. Actually not running but walking quickly in the low-heeled shoes she put on this morning as if she knew she'd need to move fast today. Usually she wears high heels with Zenin, but these shoes are like dance slippers, supple black leather embroidered with black silk flowers by some Third World couture slave. They carry her swiftly and surely along the *calles* and alleyways, slippery with April rain, that lead away from the pullulating tourist fields of San Marco across the Accademia bridge and on a circuitous route through the Sunday-afternoon quiet of Dorsoduro and San Polo. Away from Zenin, who sits waiting for her to return to the table in Harry's Bar.

She attracts glances as she passes by in her handsome tweed suit, her skirt short and her hair long and loose, as a woman wears it when she is dressing for a man. A fur coat rolled up under her arm like a bundle of newspapers. Not running but moving with a furious discretion, as if she knows where she is going and is determined to get there unseen. Near San Pantaleon, she stops at a cash machine and takes out a hundred and fifty thousand lire and then hurries on. Occasionally she stops and asks directions and when she comes back onto the Grand Canal at the Rialto, she climbs onto a *vaporetto* headed for the train station at Santa Lucia.

On the *vaporetto* she stands on the outside platform, feeling the mild drizzle on her face and refusing to have any tears join it. She will not be caught crying on a *vaporetto* on the Grand Canal. This is not a movie, and the only way to keep the moment for herself is to make immediate practical plans and lock her tears away for a time when she can howl in a place without history or atmosphere. And so she rides the next few stops to the station, only noting, as everyone in Venice does, that the colors of the water and the buildings in any weather are so many and so changeable that they are nameless, and that beauty so unremitting is hardly beauty at all but something more like pain.

When she gets to the station, she goes into a shop and buys a pair of jeans and changes out of the tweed skirt, which she stuffs into the shopping bag along with the fur coat. Then she buys a bottle of water and a paperback in English and a ticket to Rome and runs to catch a train that is just pulling out. Then for four and a half hours she sits staring out the window at the changing terrain of Italy, occasionally glancing down at the novel. At the newsstand there had been a choice among only Agatha Christie, Wilbur Smith, and a budget edition of *Middlemarch* in almost invisible print. She chose *Middlemarch,* which has brittle yellow pages as if it's been sitting neglected a long time in the sea air, and her eyes run absently over the fates of Lydgate and Dorothea, which she knows almost by heart.

She walked out on Zenin because it had become suddenly enough, in the abrupt way that comes to strong people who for one reason or another have made themselves weak.

It began as an ordinary Sunday, as ordinary as possible for Mira and Zenin, who were just beginning to have habits outside of the rituals of secrecy. An early spring weekend around Venice; driving up from Verona under a colorless drizzling sky; stopping to poke around in a junk shop owned by a feral-looking mad marchese; pausing in Mestre to eat thumbnail-size raw shrimp at Da Angelina; a night at the Gritti Palace.

Five months have passed since she came back from New York, a shadow of herself, and with efficient blankness took up her work, the care of Maddie, her life that now revolves around Zenin.

Then Sunday lunch in Harry's Bar, adrift between gray sky and restless lagoon and overflowing with glossy Americans with loud vacation voices and Italian families intent on their food, where Zenin and Mira are greeted by Cipriani with the usual jokes in dialect and a downstairs window table. Where, as they are waiting for dessert, Zenin, in the most relaxed way possible, tells Mira that he plans to go away for Easter week with Daniele and Tere. Probably to Fiji or the Maldives.

And once again, as at that moment in the Plaza in New York, the scales fall from Mira's eyes; but this time she is not as vulnerable and the vision lasts. She looks at him, really looks, as you do at your first sight of someone. His tall figure, his eyes as flat and black as those of the Great Inca. She sees that he is not as offhand about telling her this as he sounds, and she sees the depths of shame and fear that underlie everything he does. And she sees also an icy immeasurable solitude running through him that stretches deeper than the roots of mountains.

Are you going to marry Tere? Strangely, she is able to talk. She is in a state of complete clarity where it becomes important to say things, to gain information.

Zenin gives a sour smile. No, I'd never marry her, he says. But you have to realize that the two of them are part of me. I have to look after them.

And what about me? It sounds better in Italian, thinks Mira. *E io?* A wail—mourning, martyred, out of the ancient days—of black-veiled women who have sacrificed everything, left behind on the shore like Medea on Naxos.

You have to be patient. I'm not breaking it off with you. You know I love you. But we need to work out an agreement. A *sistemazione*. You know I'm already arranging things for you. Money, a house. You'll take it, I suppose.

I'm not honorable or stupid enough to refuse.

And so you have to be patient. I'll send for you the week after next. We can go to Malta or perhaps Essaouira. Then Zenin makes a sign to the waiter with his big hand and orders dessert for both of them. Chocolate cake, with coffee to follow. Then he looks across the table at Mira with a kind of complacent affection. As if they have finally called a truce and begun to understand each other.

And Mira sits for a minute and lets him run his hand down her knee. She calls back the waiter and asks a question about the cake. Then with wily naturalness, she excuses herself to go to the bathroom, gathering up her bag and flashing Zenin a sulky half smile like a girlfriend who has taken offense but is beginning to give in.

Men stare at her as she picks her way through the crowded restaurant, and she knows they see the masklike face and desirable body of the young beauty owned by the older rich man. But she sees as never before the peculiar haunting charm of Harry's Bar. How it has survived authors and movie stars and manages to be both American and ineffably Italian, both provincial and sophisticated. Meretricious and somehow innocent. Perhaps the only place that she and Zenin were meant to occupy. Afloat in the foggy afternoon, a small vessel freighted with money, a place she'll never see in quite the same way again.

She doesn't know what she intends to do, but as she heads down the short hall toward the bathroom, she sees, as if she had created it herself, that there is a back door, and it is open. Framing dripping walls and paving stones and a damp gray light.

At first Mira tells herself that she intends just to get a breath of fresh air, but the black shoes carry her out and over a bridge and then she just keeps going. No one at Harry's sees her exit, except for a young waiter or dishwasher, a teenager with acne and curly fair hair, who gives her a wink and puts his finger to his lips as if to say he won't tell. Probably she isn't the first girl he's seen leave like that.

CHICCO

We laughed our asses off in the kitchen at the poor son of a bitch sitting there with his two plates of chocolate cake. And just for a minute I felt like a richer man than old Zenin, because I knew what happened and he didn't.

35

ZENIN

2005 · WALKS WITH KINGS

But, *dottore,* if you'll pardon the presumption, you are far too modest about your own achievements.

The ghostwriter, a tall dandified young man with a thick Piedmontese accent, a rosy prematurely balding head, and a pair of stylish heavy-rimmed glasses, reaches over to make a minute adjustment to his tape recorder, brushes a speck of lint off his monogrammed shirt cuff, and then regards Zenin with the eager eyes of a sycophant. They are in Zenin's plane, flying from Milan to Venice, strapped in facing each other like prisoners.

This dickhead wants a job or a handout or both, thinks Zenin. After about fifteen minutes of impertinent, fawning Bocconi University questions on labor paradigms and modular economic approaches and ancient government-union disputes, Zenin realizes that this bullshit idea of his writing an autobiography, dreamed up by his son-in-law and Gilardi of the press office, is just that: bullshit. Another way to try to edge out the old man. Write yourself an epitaph, he thinks, and you'll be underground in the blink of an eye.

The ghostwriter has already proposed an ass-kissing title: *Camminare con i re—Walk with Kings*—which he informs Zenin is taken from a famous poem: "Se" by the English poet Kipling.

Zenin has always shunned publicity. He's been turning down offers from Rizzoli and Mondadori for years. In the early period because of a superstitious belief that his new prosperity would be snatched away if he flaunted it; later because he feared his rivals would be infuriated and screw him doubly; still later in the Years of Lead because he feared the Red Brigades; and finally, when he fell in love with his son, Daniele, because he was terrified of kidnappers.

He agreed to the book in a weak moment after certain private disturbances this past summer and fall. Nothing really wrong, yet nothing right. A gentle indifference when it comes to food or women or his friends, or even soccer. Little pleasure even in adoring Daniele, who he can't avoid observing has grown up to be a sweet-natured, decent, but entirely ordinary young man.

In Yugoslavia on the boat this summer, Zenin's old friend Macaco dubbed him Il Premio Nobel, the Nobel Prize Winner, because he never looked up from studying his copy of *Panorama* or *Il Gazzettino,* even when his pretty niece arrived with a group of girlfriends from Padua University, who sunbathed in nothing but tangas and tattoos.

The same thing happened at his shooting lodge in Scotland, and at his place in Cortina. And when the company continues buoyant even in the stagnant European economy, when it escapes even the shadow of the Parmalat scandal that brings down his old fox of a traditional rival, Gualtieri, he feels none of the glee that should attend a lifetime victory. He feels it as something far-off, something that happened a long time ago.

Then there are the dreams that wake him in a sweat. Dreams of familiar people and places, all behaving in shadowy alarming ways. The worst is that the river outside his bedroom is flowing closer to the walls, is actually trickling through, and is filled with dead and dying voices, the voice of his father, that of his sister, ebbing away there in the clinic in Switzerland.

His tireless girlfriend, Mariella, offers for the hundredth time to move in with him, saying that he is understandably becoming a pack of nerves rattling around in that big house. And when Zenin refuses, she smiles, knowing that before long she'll be there.

Privately he worries that this is the beginning of senile dementia, and so makes arrangements to see a priest and a doctor. The priest, an aristocratic Jesuit and former missionary from an old Venetian family, receives him with the warm welcome and light-handed man-of-the-world chiding due to a divorced reprobate tycoon, a local prodigal son who hasn't taken Communion since he was twenty-seven. He speaks of spiritual adolescence, of the mysteries of the Sacred Heart, and elicits, to his own surprise, a grant for an entirely new elementary school and maternity clinic in Burkina Faso.

The doctor, a director of Umanitas Clinic, is a sanguine Pugliese who shuttles back and forth between Milan, where he has a wife and family, and Monte Carlo, where he has a beautiful Ukrainian mistress. He's used to examining troubled rich friends and tells a couple of good jokes as he inspects Zenin's body cavities and oversees his entrance and exit, like a loaf of bread, into and out of the MRI machine. He tells Zenin that his prostate is that of a man in his forties, that except for a benign cyst on one kidney and a bit of high blood pressure, he is enviably healthy, and that if he wants to take care of the bags under his eyes, there are superb plastic surgeons right here at Umanitas.

And of course he waves the little packet of blue pills in Zenin's face. The gift of the Magi, *mio caro,* as if you didn't already know about it. That apathetic feeling just means you need Saint Viagra in your life. That and a few Russian blondes should take care of everything.

And about the same time, Zenin says yes to the book idea, and now he's stuck with this baby-faced fool following him around and double-checking everything, though it is clear that the kid wouldn't know truth if it ran up and bit him on the ass.

Zenin tilts his seat, and closes his eyes rudely in the face of the ghostwriter, and wonders what would happen if he really told the truth. About how you have to screw people before they screw you, whether the screwing takes the form of impressing them or fucking them, or making them want to buy something, or grinding them into dust. How knowing how to make money is not something contained in some innovative idea or bullshit philosophy, but something he knows the way a bird knows how to fly and a leopard knows how to track down and tear apart. How that instinct carries its own shadow: not fear, exactly, but a growing detachment from the world, just when you are busiest heaping up the world's prizes. Detachment that makes you not give a shit about young Russian blondes or buying sainthood from some swindler of a Jesuit. That makes you just want to fall asleep in the river that flows through your bed.

He opens his eyes sharply and catches the writer staring at him in bemusement, and realizes that he must have dozed off. And abruptly decides to cancel the book.

The plane bucks slightly in the tramontane wind blowing south from the Dolomites. Near Verona the cloud cover breaks, and as they circle for landing, the brown-and-green expanse of the Veneto unrolls beneath them, in air so limpid they can see the factories of Mestre and the archipelago of Venice, and behind them in a faint smear of civilization, Zenin's town and the other cities of the plain.

Guarda. Casa, says Zenin, almost automatically, feeling an unreasonable surge of pleasure, in spite of his woes. Look. Home.

1988 · ANOTHER PHONE CALL

Zenin is thinking about the widow on the train to Brussels. The woman he met decades earlier on one of his first sales trips outside Italy. Zenin, twenty-seven, married a year, full of himself and his big black snap-over display case. And like a traveling salesman in a joke, he meets this Belgian widow—hardly more than a blond teenager, with huge calves in black cotton stockings and pale red-rimmed Flemish eyes—traveling home to some peasant village after her Italian husband dropped dead during the rice harvest in Vercelli. And near the French border Zenin takes her to a railway hotel and fucks her all day. Fucks her in ways that he never dreamed you could to a decent woman—in her ass, in her mouth—as she shudders with pleasure and weeps and moans that she is going to hell. And when the girl falls asleep, hair plastered, skin slippery with grief and sex, her clumsy black coat and dress thrown over a chair, he pulls his clothes on, slips out, and jumps onto a night train. He remembers washing his cock over and over in the tin basin in the train's washroom as the train rocked through the dark beet fields, thinking with nervous satisfaction that at least he left her with money for the hotel, a good dinner, and first-class fare back to her village.

The memory, for some reason, floats into his mind when he gets a call on his private line from an unknown old woman. Mira's friend Madame S.

His first response is cold fury. How dare the bitch give out his number, after walking out on him in Venice like that?

Then he becomes wary and concentrates on understanding what this old woman knows, what she really wants, and how it can work to his advantage.

She didn't want me to get involved, but I insisted, says Madame S.

From her voice he can picture her exactly: the kind of old battle-ax who goes around bossing parochial projects and feeding armies of stray cats. Sister in spirit to the Princess Caetanae, his own mother, his aunts and sisters, and even his dour oldest daughter. The phalanx of respectable women who form the ultimate barrier—the shaping force that substitutes morality—to the behavior of men like Zenin.

There is a tinge of ingrained cynicism to the voice with the Bolognese accent, of a crafty awareness that Zenin will doubt everything she says. And Zenin respects this, and by extension respects Mira herself for having made such a friend.

He's increasingly impressed as the conversation continues. I need to have this old biddy running the press office, he thinks, instead of that brainless Gilardi. In one minute, Madame S. manages to sound conversational, compliment him believably and extravagantly, and then, with brutal frankness, come to the point.

And of course, *Cavaliere,* I realize that a man of your extraordinary resources would be all the more aware of the precarious position of a young woman in a foreign country without official protection in the world. She needs a *sistemazione.* A secure position.

She wants nothing more to do with me, says Zenin. She walked out, and she won't even speak to me on the phone.

And she also left her husband because of you, comes the relentless voice. She was a respectable wife and mother, not a tart. She fell in love, though it was madness. And beyond that, though I don't like to go into it. . . .

The old witch knows everything, thinks Zenin. Hastily he assures her that he is aware of his responsibility to Mira, that she will have a house, investments for a proper income, whatever she needs to live—

Per vivere in modo dignitoso. To live in a dignified manner. Madame S. actually says these words, with the gravity of a judge.

And because she is truly a woman of the old school, who understands instinctively Zenin's way of thinking, she names a figure.

And Zenin, not the least bit surprised or insulted, names a lower figure. This language he understands, and his respect is growing for the tough old bird who speaks it. This is exactly the kind of conversation he had with Tere's family before his son was born.

The haggling is inconclusive, but they both know it represents a promise on Zenin's part.

And he knows as well that Mira would never have been practical enough to put her up to this.

She's lucky to have a friend like you, he says, and Madame S. actually gives a flirtatious chuckle.

We both understand that there is nothing in this for me. I just hate to see injustice. If it weren't for me, the child would be in the middle of nowhere. She has no sense of reality. She refuses to say anything to her family at home. And a foreign girl doesn't know how to make rascals like you behave.

Zenin laughs too. Relieved to have things made clear. Translated.

Ah well, Signora, he says. What can one do? Adding in a humorous tone, *Americanate.* An expression that can mean simply, American ways, or American nonsense.

And they take leave of each other with great courtesy.

And later, when Zenin has spoken to the *commercialista* who handles his private transactions, he thinks with satisfaction that this is all for the best. Things should, he thinks, be organized. The security he will bestow on Mira will allow him to own her until he, Zenin, decides that it is over. And still later he again thinks of the Belgian widow who, in her grotesque garbled Italian, moaned on about her husband, even as he pulled her about on the sagging hotel bed, repeating, *Amour dopo mort.* Love after death.

THE GHOSTWRITER

I was born twenty-eight years ago in Torre Grimalda, a *frazione* of Cuneo, I have my degree in Italian language and literature from Bologna, and of course I write novels. Existential spy and adventure thrillers, set in exotic places like the Solomon Islands and New England, and also the backwater villages of Liguria, where I grew up; a bit of Maurois mixed with Salgari mixed with Pavese, if you know what I mean. Nothing published yet, so to keep the polenta boiling, as my grandfather says, I'm doing the line of *Our Great Business Minds* for Rizzoli. And everybody wants to know what it's like to travel around with Zenin.

Com è? What is it like? What was it like for Dante to visit the dead? The weightless, the eternally famished dead? He sits across from me like a sad clown in his jet or in his office or on that boat of his, and I feel like nothing, I feel how he despises me, that bastard, and yet I feel that to be despised by him is good fortune. I feel happy about my cheap suits from UPIM, my Fiat Panda, my Club Avventura vacations, and my not-so-gorgeous girlfriend Rinalda.

Because he is the most joyless individual it has ever been my bad luck to come across. Most rich men got where they are by being bastards, and Zenin is no exception, but the other shits have more fun. This one, with all his money, owns exactly nothing. And if I were to write a true story of his life, it would be called *The Emperor's New Clothes.*

36

NICK

2005 · AN ENCOUNTER

Amy hated Warsaw, says Nick's old friend Friel, squeezing his wife's
shoulder. Spoiled wench. Bitched every minute about the cold and the
shit food and coal dust in her hair.

I'm so not a trooper! giggles Amy, who is Chinese American and met
Friel back at Princeton.

Who wants to be? says Nick's wife, Dhel. I'm PTBHM—proud to
be high maintenance. Nick hates it but he reaps the benefits, don't
you, darling?

The two couples are eating dinner at the China Club in Hong
Kong, celebrating Amy's forty-first birthday. Nick is in town on business, and this time he's brought Dhel and the girls.

It's a great evening. Nick, having returned that afternoon from a
chilly two days among the scrolled hills and appalling hotels of Hunan,
relishes the lowlit opulence of the club, its ironic retro take on colonial Shanghai. He loves looking at the rich Chinese families eating
around him, the tycoons settled so comfortably into their wealth as if
it were silk cushions. He enjoys his old friends, who talk his language
with the raucous intimacy of longtime expatriates. They get Amy drunk
on wildly overpriced Château Margaux and make her go over the legendary tale of her roommate, the ounce of skunk, and the Princeton
wrestling team. And Friel, who works in Singapore and is both a fiscal

ultraconservative and an old-style freethinking Democrat, has them pissing with laughter at tales of his forays among the Republican toadies of Malaysia.

When they get up to go, Friel spots a friend in the corner. The friend is an Italian named Giorgio, a Milanese who heads up an economic-research project funded by the political party La Margherita and based in Beijing. He is seated with a beautiful Chinese woman, who seems to be his girlfriend, and another two Italian men who are very young, almost students. One of them strikes Nick as being especially good-looking, with an eager white smile that Nick imagines would be attractive to women.

Nick drags out his rusty Italian. *Si, ho vissuto a Roma, tanti anni fa.*

In the Pedder Building elevator, Friel says, High-class babysitting is what Giorgio's doing. Do you know who those two kids are? His new interns? One is Teodoro Agnelli, and the other is the son of Zenin. You know, the annoying cartoon toys.

Friel isn't a close enough friend to know the connection between Zenin and Nick, but does notice the quality of silence that falls, the microscopic glance that passes between husband and wife. What? he says. You know him?

Nothing, says Nick. I might have met him once.

And afterward on the ferry going back to Kowloon Side, Dhel—who in a feminine way has annexed her husband's first marriage by becoming an amateur historian conversant with its minutest facts and implications—goes on about the long arm of coincidence, and what a darling face that boy had, and how this confirms her theory that there are really only fifty people in the world, all doomed to keep crossing paths. And how that very pretty boy is about Maddie's age, and how ironic it would be if they met and fell in love. She sees Nick's face and shuts up for a minute, leans back against the sticky painted bench, and stares out at the lights of Central behind them.

Then:

Darling, is it portentous? she asks.

No.

Does it mean anything?

No.

Does it make you sad and thoughtful?

Nope.

Do you love me?

More than anyone in the world.

At that she leans over and bites his left ear, and they sit sweating and contented like any other tourists in the sticky late-night heat of the Star Ferry.

But before dawn Nick wakes in their bed at the Peninsula, with the face of the boy in his head. So handsome. So unaware. The mask of youth, mysterious in its conventional innocence, its lack of scars. Like a newly minted coin. Like his daughter's faces, or those photos of Keith Richards in the sixties or Joe Strummer in the seventies, when they look too gormless to be walking around without a nanny.

Like his and Mira's faces in their wedding photos.

And this kid had barely noticed Nick, had met his eye for a second and murmured a greeting like any well-bred European child. Never guessing that the middle-aged American before him had wept, cursed, contemplated murder, wanted to die through long nights invoking his father's name.

The child of my enemy. And what does the little bugger mean to me?

Softly he gets up from the bed and takes a piss in the bathroom, then walks to the living room of the suite and opens the curtains to look out at Kowloon Bay. The yellowish leaden sky of a dawn in ty-phoon weather over the incomparable spectacle of the expanse of steely water dotted with container convoys and passenger boats and junks, tugs, and ferries. And beyond, the lunar cityscape of Central, the tops of the Bank of China building, and the Peak shrouded in mist, the hills rolling back toward Stanley, the old earth dragons slumbering in a broil of black cloud.

He peers left down the murky coast toward Sha Tin, where there is a huge Buddhist temple complex that is modern but an exact replica of a Tang Dynasty structure, down to the bamboo nails that hold thou-sands of cedar shingles in place. Why build an exact replica of some-thing old? his daughter Julia asked when they visited. Why not make something modern? Because we need to see history, dumbhead, her sister told her.

And now his own drama suddenly seems like history, like something artificial and didactic on display. Those two very young people and their Italy. A sort of Williamsburg of the heart.

When did he stop hating Mira? He thinks now of the last time he saw her, at Maddie's high school graduation, still good-looking, though with her careful slimness and expensively sleek clothes and hair, she looked generically foreign, a woman who belongs more to her age and social class and painstaking elegance than to a particular race or country.

He recalls her expiatory chumminess to him, as they sat under big white umbrellas in the International School courtyard in a well-heeled group of international parents just like them. Her wifely asides in Italian to her husband, Vanni, who is a genuine good guy, though Nick is pleased to hear hints from Maddie that he leads quite a life. Mira the betrayer has achieved a husband with a wandering eye.

What does this woman have to do with the skinny sand-colored girl who enchanted him and married him and then wrenched out his heart?

The answer is: precisely nothing.

Forcing hate is just as impossible as forcing lust or hunger or faith. Either you've got it or you don't.

What he feels for her now—besides irritation at her disorganized approach to tuition payments—is a kind of distant, rather condescending camaraderie. Perhaps it's friendly pity, the devastating phrase Joyce uses in "The Dead," which was the single short story assigned in the poetry class where he met Mira.

Does this mean forgiveness? No. Nick has traveled a long way beyond the point where one forgives. Beyond bitterness. But he's just realized it now. He awakes to it so suddenly that he feels that he had something amputated, like an arm or a leg.

All the weight of his anger must have been gone for some time. And he feels free and also doomed, because along with the anger he has also lost the last pretense that he's still young. Only once could he feel such complicated pain, all linked by the glorious egotistical certainty of living a betrayal unique in the world.

And he has become aware of this in China, in a part of the world that makes Europe, and even America, seem like stuffy old relatives left behind somewhere. The place where Friel and Amy live exactly as Nick and his family do in London, in a cloister of international schools and clubs and the expatriate's wary deepening consciousness of the culture outside the walls.

But only once, thinks Nick, could he settle in a foreign country, and have that country colonize him.

Nick yawns and sits down at the desk by the window and opens the computer, fixing the earphones in his ears as his playlist kicks in with Kasabian's "LSF." A title that strikes him as unnervingly appropriate when he remembers it stands for Lost Souls Forever.

There are a couple dozen e-mails, including one from Maddie. He glances up once at the seacape in front of him and remains transfixed by an odd effect of sunrise passing between the heavy typhoon cloud cover and the wall of skyscrapers below it, giving the clouds, for a few seconds, a strange tender color like flesh. And Nick realizes suddenly that he is trembling.

This is nothing to get fucking nervous about, he thinks. It's just called living happily ever after.

1989 · . . . ALL STATES, ALL PRINCES . . .

Two years after Mira walks out on Zenin in Venice, Mira and Nick meet up at the American embassy in Rome. Nick has been promoted and is moving to the London office. Mira will stay in Rome with Maddie, who has begun kindergarten at the American school on the Cassia. They're here to sign custody papers and both are dressed up. Nick because it's a working day and Mira from vanity and the feeling that it's a ceremonial occasion.

She looks at Nick in his familar, slightly spotty gray suit and remembers how her throat used to catch in a spasm of tenderness when she saw him coming out of the office with his Italian colleagues, a mob of business apprentices surging onto Piazza Colonna with the touching wiseass air of schoolboys who run the world.

Nick looks at Mira with the armored heart of a man who has redis-

covered the pleasures of being a bachelor in a world of rustling crino-
lines. He encounters her once or twice a week because of Maddie, but
this sighting seems definitive. He notes with grim satisfaction that her
expensive suit with its gleaming buttons and tight short skirt is too
smart for a daytime errand at the embassy, and that in comparison with
some of the spectacular women he's been seeing, she looks ordinary.

They sign the papers, and Nick annoys Mira by horsing around
with the assistant consul, who's a friend of his. The assistant consul, a
baby-faced black preppie named Whittaker who wears suspenders and
ridiculous horn-rims, is on his first overseas assignment and clearly
wants to look dignified in front of the crowd waiting in the consular
section, not be loudly reminded of a recent mojito-fueled Trastevere
evening.

What an insensitive jerk, Mira thinks, scribbling her name, as Nick
goes on joking.

They leave the embassy and have coffee standing at a Via Veneto
bar that they have seen so many times in *La dolce vita* that the place
seems as though it should be scintillating black-and-white. Instead it's
a bland touristy cavern with trilingual menus and plastic chairs.

And after they've talked for the twentieth time about Nick's apartment full of Bollinger boxes, and his temporary quarters near the City,
and how Maddie will react to visiting London, Mira asks in a hostessy
tone what Nick is going to miss most about Italy. Besides us, of course,
she adds, with an awkward laugh.

Not specifying, Nick thinks nastily, whether *us* means herself and
Maddie; herself and the vast jolly throng of Italians and expatriates;
herself described in the royal plural; or herself and Nick as they once
were.

I'll miss the smell of bread, he says. Mira looks at him as if he's gone
mad.

Bread? she repeats blankly.

Yeah, when you walk down the street in the early morning, and
every other shop smells like a *panetteria,* like fresh bread. It doesn't
matter if it's Rome or some tiny village. I'll miss the bread smell, and
I'll miss how kind everyone is.

Kind? Italians? Are you kidding? Now she is really looking at him as if he's crazy.

No, I'm not kidding. It takes a while to understand it, of course, he adds. Nick looks at her steadily for a minute, and with a twinge of malice sees her struggling, wondering if there is something in him she missed all these years. Whether the white boy is subtle after all.

Then her expression changes to the speculative glitter that belongs only to Mira.

Yes, I guess everyone here is kind, she says thoughtfully. But in a terrible, awful way.

And both Nick and Mira give a snort of laughter, catch themselves up short in annoyance, and flash a look at each other that is full of deep knowledge, the instinctive affinity one has for one's own country, one's own people. They look at each other with anger, with contempt, and yet with the automatic relief and anticipation that a traveler feels upon catching the first glimpse of the coastline of his native land from the deck of an ocean liner. They look at each other with hate and love, the twin lenses that add perspective. With friendly pity, the way grown-ups do. With terrible kindness like all Romans.

I have to go, says Nick, setting down his coffee cup.

Me too.

On Via Veneto, Mira turns downhill toward Piazza Barberini, and Nick continues on toward his office. Before separating, they kiss goodbye, on both cheeks in a civilized European way. Then they turn away, immediately separated by a long line of sightseeing Ursuline novices in navy blue, and are then so quickly lost in the lunchtime crowd of office workers and travelers that it is impossible to say if either one of them turns to look back.

And there we will leave them.

WHITTAKER

First thing, I'm not the Agency's in-house man in Rome.

But I do like to think of myself as one of those low-key guys who no one would suspect has lived a long and intrigue-ridden career circling the globe as an undercover action hero. That is, mild mannered and naïve on the outside, with a hint of . . . well, profundity. It's not been a bad persona for a black mama's boy from Wheeling, West Virginia, making his way through the wilds of Deerfield and Dartmouth, not to mention the D.C. corridors of power.

After briefly slumming it at the bottom of the ladder in Lisbon, I got kicked upstairs to assistant consul in Rome, and oh Lord, it took no effort to act naïve, because I was staggered by my own sudden greatness and at the shadow of the ancient world. Power in my grasp, and Rome spread between my colossal bestriding legs—you get the idea. Augustus, Constantine were nothing compared to me. Head Nigger in Charge, still wet behind the ears, you may say, and I freely admit it, because it's only been ten months since I left D.C. Even the endless opera woven from the tales of woe of my fellow countrymen—stolen passports, knockout gas in train compartments, denied U.S. visas for pizza chefs—is still exotic music to my ears. Like everybody else, I always dreamed of Italy.

When I saw Nick Reiver and his ex-wife in the office and took care of their little custody amendment, the tragic strain in the music got a little louder. How, I wondered, could two people live together and have a child in this gorgeous city, and not be madly in love? I knew Nick, from more than one evening dash with the Anglo-American Barhoppers Guild, and he was an all-right guy, though, right then, being a bit of an asshole, with all that white-boy phat rap that I got fed up with at prep school. But it was the first time I had met the woman in the case, and she was quite hot, dressed up, and looking like my cousin Martine. I'd heard the story, like everybody else—that they'd come a few years ago, the perfect marriage, and then she'd gone off with some dago playboy, to put it in politically correct terms. When I heard she was staying on in Rome, it even crossed my mind to ask her out, though I'm into white girls and specifically Italians now.

Well, they signed and for a second I felt weirdly like a preacher presiding over their unmarriage, though the unmarrying part happened a while ago. Then they took off, and the rest of the afternoon was a sea of stolen passports belonging to Marymount girls with beefy legs and visa requests from little old Pugliese men with long-lost brothers in Pittsburgh. So that I completely forgot about the melancholy sight of the pair of them, and in fact, I filed them in my mental category of failures: Americans who are somehow on their way out.

I did see Mira a few times at parties over the next year, but hardly spoke to her because I am very involved elsewhere. In fact, if you have time for a coffee, I can tell you something about the ins and outs. It started with Marianina, the USIS events coordinator who is from Prato and has only one arm, but a face prettier than any of the Puerto Rican beauties at Dartmouth. And then there is my Italian tutor, Ombretta, a university instructor who's separated but still living with her husband, who is Pugliese and very jealous, and—shit, it's complicated, life here. Anyway, I've been studying Italian assiduously and I'm getting quite fluent.

E così, as Ombretta likes to say, *finisce una storia e ne comincia un'altra.* It's one of the first phrases she taught me. Here one story ends and another one gets started.

ACKNOWLEDGMENTS

My thanks to my wonderful agent, Amanda Urban; to my
Random House editors, Jennifer Hershey and Laura Ford;
to the great Helen Garner for inspiration; and, of course, to
my beloved family—especially Ruggero, who corrected the
spelling of all the Italian swearwords, and Alexandra and
Charles, who remind me constantly how many things are
more interesting than writing. My gratitude above all goes
to Elinor Schiele, a dear and generous friend who took time
off from her mosaics to bring order to my life, get my knick-
ers out of their twist, and enable me to finish this book.

ABOUT THE AUTHOR

ANDREA LEE was born in Philadelphia and received her bachelor's and master's degrees from Harvard University. She is a former staff writer for *The New Yorker,* and her fiction and nonfiction writing have also appeared in *The New York Times Magazine* and *The New York Times Book Review.* She is the author of *Russian Journal,* the novel *Sarah Phillips,* and the short story collection *Interesting Women.* She lives with her husband and two children in Turin, Italy.

ABOUT THE TYPE

This book was set in Fairfield, the first typeface from the hand of the distinguished American artist and engraver Rudolph Ruzicka (1883–1978). Ruzicka was born in Bohemia and came to America in 1894. He set up his own shop, devoted to wood engraving and printing, in New York in 1913 after a varied career working as a wood engraver, in photoengraving and banknote printing plants, and as an art director and freelance artist. He designed and illustrated many books and was the creator of a considerable list of individual prints—wood engravings, line engravings on copper, and aquatints.